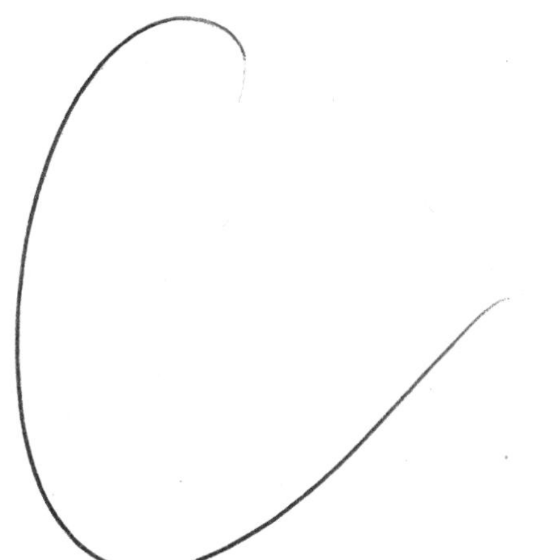

SEASONS OF LOVE

Recent Titles by Anna Jacobs

HIGH STREET
JESSIE
LIKE NO OTHER
OUR LIZZIE
SPINNER'S LAKE

SEASONS OF LOVE

Anna Jacobs

This first world edition published in Great Britain 2000 by
SEVERN HOUSE PUBLISHERS LTD of
9–15 High Street, Sutton, Surrey SM1 1DF.
This first world edition published in the USA 2001 by
SEVERN HOUSE PUBLISHERS INC of
595 Madison Avenue, New York, N.Y. 10022.

British Library Cataloguing in Publication Data

Jacobs, Anna
Seasons of love
1. Love stories
I. Title
823 [F]

ISBN 0-7278-5643-X

All situations in this publication are fictitious and
any resemblance to living persons is purely coincidental.

Typeset by Palimpsest Book Production Ltd.,
Polmont, Stirlingshire, Scotland.
Printed and bound in Great Britain by
MPG Books Ltd., Bodmin, Cornwall.

One

1835

"Mr Wintermaine is coming to tea tomorrow."

Helen smothered a sigh and said nothing. Even to think of Mr Wintermaine made her feel depressed. For some unknown reason, the new curate in the next parish had fallen in love with her as quickly as she had taken an aversion to him. And the more she got to know him, the more she disliked him, particularly his damp, thick-fingered hands and his cowlike eyes that lingered on her breasts when no one was around.

Her mother looked quickly sideways at her, assessing her reaction. "He's a very good catch for a girl like you."

"But I don't even like him!" Helen protested, desperation giving her the courage to speak out. "Can't you ask Father to – to tell him I'm not interested?"

"You aren't even trying to like him!" Mrs Merling told her daughter severely. "And you'll be mad if you whistle down the wind the best chance you are ever likely to get of establishing yourself." She saw mutiny on her daughter's face and added severely, "What's more, if your father hears you talking like that, he will be *most* displeased. I do not wish to hear any more talk of that nature, thank you very much."

So Helen made no more protests, but neither did she change her mind. She could not, she would not, encourage the man who made her flesh crawl, and as for marrying him, she would rather die.

The following day, Mr Wintermaine came to tea, as arranged, and when Helen's father sent her to walk round the garden with him, he tried to kiss her – making her feel sick with disgust.

She pushed him away, pretending to be shocked and he stopped trying to kiss her, thank goodness. She was very curt with him for the rest of their stroll – rude, in fact – but he didn't seem to notice. And he looked even more smug than usual as he chatted to her father at the front door before leaving. From the way their eyes turned towards her, Helen knew they were discussing plans to marry her off to the lecherous Wintermaine.

She went to bed quite sunk in despair.

The following week Mary, the maid-of-all-work, turned her ankle when she was fetching in some wood. The ankle swelled to enormous proportions, thus rendering Mary incapable of walking into Stowby for her mistress, as she did every market day.

"What your Father will say, I don't know," Mrs Merling complained to her daughter. "He has a book of sermons waiting to be picked up from the post office in Stowby. He will be *most* upset if someone doesn't fetch it for him." The only thing that ever roused Mrs Merling out of her mild apathy towards whatever life brought her was the thought of something disturbing her husband.

That worried Helen, too, for everyone in the house suffered when Father was in a bad mood. And she knew how much he needed this new book of sermons, because she had heard her parents talking. The Squire had sent word down to the parsonage that he was tired of hearing the same old thing year in, year out, and wanted something more cheerful than sin and damnation to whet his appetite for his Sunday dinner. Unfortunately, Parson Merling's mind did not have a cheerful turn, and he had striven in vain to compose something more to his patron's liking. Hence the new book.

A wonderful solution occurred to her. "Could I not go and fetch it, Mother?"

Mrs Merling stared at her daughter. Too pretty by far. She would rather the girl did not go into Stowby alone. "Your father would not approve of that. He hasn't forgotten the last time you went to market for me."

Helen hung her head. Once, she had lingered far too long and had not arrived home until after dark. Her father had scolded her severely and sent her to bed supperless, but, nevertheless, she had been thankful that he hadn't beaten her. "I'd promise to come straight back this time. I was only trying to help."

Mrs Merling hesitated. She, too, needed some things from Stowby, things which could not be bought in the tiny village shop. Only the draper's in Stowby sold the right colour thread for mending the church's fraying hassocks. And only in Stowby could one purchase fresh fish, to which her husband was very partial and which cost less than meat. "Well, perhaps we'll give you another chance to show us you can behave properly." Frivolous the girl might be, but her strong young body would make nothing of the three-and-a-half-mile walk, whereas Mrs Merling, with her bunions and her tendency towards breathlessness, would find it a severe trial.

Helen listened meekly to her mother's instructions and admonitions, then escaped into the sunshine. Even when she was caught in a shower, Helen didn't mind. She just sheltered under a tree until it had passed and enjoyed the sound of the rain pattering through the leaves. What was a little summer rain, after all? Not even enough to dampen her straw bonnet. She grimaced as she straightened it. The bonnet had been her mother's for several years and had been refurbished for Helen last year with a narrow brown ribbon to match her everyday dress. It looked old and tired, as did the dress.

Sometimes she imagined herself wearing pretty muslin or rosy pinks, instead of these dark, uninteresting colours. She dreamed of gowns made in fashionable styles, like the dresses the Squire's daughters wore. They were so pretty. She realised she was dawdling and daydreaming, which she had promised faithfully not to do, so she walked on more quickly, determined to earn her parents' trust for once.

When she got back home, her mother was delighted with her purchases. That evening, since Mrs Merling found herself sixpence better off than usual, she broached the idea to her husband of making the marketing a regular task for the girl. "I think the exercise did her good, Septimus. Perhaps we forget that young people need exercise. She's been very quiet and well behaved ever since her walk."

Helen, who was crouching quite shamelessly outside the study window – since the only way she ever found anything out was by eavesdropping – held her breath and crossed her fingers while waiting for her father's response. As neither of her parents knew about the glorious half-hour she had spent in the woods on the way back, paddling in the stream and just lying there, lazily "wasting the Lord's valuable time" they decided in favour of a trial period.

* * *

For the rest of the summer, Helen made the most of her freedom, for she knew it would not continue – good things never did. One day, one terrible day, Mr Wintermaine would stop courting her and actually ask for her hand in marriage, then she would have to refuse him, because she absolutely could not bear the thought of spending the rest of her life with him. She did not know precisely what was involved in marriage, but if she didn't like him to touch her now, it stood to reason that it would be even worse if she were to live with him.

In addition to being a man of the cloth, the curate apparently possessed a small private income and had influential friends who might one day do something to get him a good living of his own. Helen's father had no influential friends, which was why he had remained at Dendleford and why he wanted her to marry Wintermaine.

Only . . . if she did not accept the curate's proposal, her father would be more angry than he had ever been before and would undoubtedly beat her. If she'd had anywhere else to go she'd have run away rather than disobey him openly.

"The girl must have a new dress," her father said one day, studying her with disapproval. "That one is far too tight. It is unseemly. *More* expense, Mrs Merling!" From the way he spoke, the new fullness of his daughter's breasts was something shameful.

Helen hid her delight. A new dress was a very rare treat.

"Something dark and serviceable," he added.

Helen stared down to hide her disappointment.

The next week, her mother accompanied her to market, which meant they had to walk very slowly. They came home with a length of material in such a dark shade of blue that it almost verged on black. "It'll be very suitable for a clergyman's wife," Mrs Merling said – happily patting the heavy parcel which lay on top of the basket her daughter was holding – when they paused on the way home for her to get her breath back.

Helen, who had protested in the shop, said nothing, and just scowled at it. "May I cut it out and make it up myself?" she asked, not very hopefully. "You know I'm good with my needle."

"Certainly not. You would make it in a frivolous style. Your father and I have already discussed the matter. We do not approve of these huge sleeves which are in fashion nowadays. They waste a lot of material. Nor do we approve of clothing which emphasises the figure."

Helen did not say a word for the rest of the walk. What was the point?

The following day, there was talk at the dinner table of seventeen being a very good age for a young woman to marry.

"It allows her husband to form her character to his taste," Mr Merling pronounced, dissecting his pork chop with his usual precision. "You are far too capricious, Helen. But a husband will know how to chastise you until you mend your ways."

So Mr Wintermaine continued to visit. They went for sedate strolls round the village together, and he brought her gifts of posies and verses from the Bible, copied out for her in a florid script.

"Too mean to spend his money, that one is," Mary said one day in an incautious moment.

Helen absolutely agreed with the maid, but refrained from saying so in case her mother overheard.

"Your father and I think Mr Wintermaine should propose to you on your birthday," her mother remarked the following morning. "You can marry soon afterwards. In October, perhaps."

Helen tried to tell herself that her parents could not actually force her to marry Mr Wintermaine. But in the cold, clear light of morning, as she heard her father's voice booming from her parents' bedroom, she was not at all sure of that.

Two months after her first outing to the market, Helen heard talk in the village that a party of travelling players was to come to Stowby for three months to give a series of performances at the Assembly Rooms. They were fresh from triumphs in Cheltenham, and were to put on several plays, ranging from classical drama to comedies.

She knew better than to hope that her father would even take them to a performance of *Julius Caesar*, which was surely classical and very respectable. He had never been inside a theatre and had said many times that he hoped he never would. She decided not to mention the players to him. It would only put him in a bad mood.

She lingered beside the handbills in the draper's shop window and then grew breathless with excitement when she had the good fortune to catch a glimpse of the players in person. Magnificent creatures, dressed in the latest fashions, peacocks to the dowdy country fowls around them. As they strolled along, they laughed and chatted as if they had not a care in the world. How beautiful they were! How bright and fashionable! And the lady players had such wonderful sleeves, such full skirts.

With tears in her eyes, she stared down at her brown everyday dress, very tight around the chest now, with its narrow sleeves and frayed hem. How she longed for clothes more like theirs!

But when she got home, she found that someone had already told her father about the players. Over the evening meal, he mentioned it to his wife. "I'm disgusted to think of such a – a contagion coming so close to Dendleford. Actors are all thieves," he lowered his voice meaningfully, but he needn't have bothered, for Helen did not understand the implications, "and the women are worse."

"Yes, indeed, Septimus," murmured Mrs Merling. "Very shocking."

Her mother would have spoken in the same tone of voice whatever the situation – even if the bread had failed to rise, Helen thought mutinously. And why were players so shocking? Why were certain subjects not to be mentioned? One day she would find out more about life, she promised herself. Realising her father was speaking to and glaring at her, she jerked to attention.

"I tell you plainly, I would not willingly have an actor step inside the door of my church, not even one foot."

"Certainly not, Septimus."

There was a long discussion between Mr and Mrs Merling that night, after their daughter was in bed, about the wisdom of allowing her to continue her market trips.

Helen listened carefully, for they had no idea how sound carried in the small house, since no one else dared make much noise. She clenched her hands at her flannel-covered bosom and waited in terror for their final decision. If they stopped her going, how would she bear it? How could she bear anything if she didn't have her Thursday outings?

"I do think she is growing more sensible. She is nearly seventeen now, after all, and we've brought her up most carefully," Mrs Merling pleaded, thinking of the cheaper purchases Helen always seemed to make at the market. She had been so grateful for the savings that they permitted. "And she is very innocent. She is not at all like your mother."

"A young woman should be innocent. It is for her husband to educate her as he sees fit."

"Yes, Septimus."

"I shall ponder upon it and pray for guidance," he decreed.

As a result, Helen prayed more fervently in church that Sunday than she ever had done before and prayed again later, quite voluntarily, to thank the Lord when her mother informed her that she was allowed to continue her weekly excursions, but must not, under any circumstances, dillydally in Stowby or go near the players.

The following Thursday, on her way home from market, Helen was again tempted to linger in the woods by the long spell of hot dry weather. Dreamily splashing her feet in the cool water of the stream and watching the sunlight sparkle on the droplets that were thrown up, she didn't hear anyone approaching until a voice behind her laughingly declaimed, "A dryad! A nymph of the woods!"

She was horrified at being caught with her bare limbs exposed, and jumped to her feet in a panic.

"Please don't go!" begged the owner of the voice.

Helen caught her breath at the sight of him, for he was surely the most handsome man she had ever seen in her life! Not tall, but . . . a face like the statue of a young Greek god in one of her father's books. And he had a smile which would have melted anyone's heart – except her father's. He swept her a bow, which made her heart thump in her chest. Oh, he was all perfection, from his gleaming golden hair and smiling blue eyes to his neatly shod feet!

She twitched her skirt down over her bare legs and stood still in blushing confusion. Her hair had escaped from its knot and was spread over her shoulders, which further added to her embarrassment.

"My name is Robert Perriman." He executed a perfect bow.

"Oh. Well, my name is Helen – Helen Merling."

She received another bow. "A perfect name for a beautiful wood nymph."

He told her later that she had resembled a Madonna, with the sun shining down upon her rosy face and youthful figure. He told her many things over the next few weeks, and paid her compliments, which filled her starved soul with joy.

"Oh, sir! Please don't tell anyone you saw me here!" she begged that first time.

"My lips are sealed," he promised gravely. "But won't you tell me why you're so worried about being seen? Are you trespassing? Will the keeper lock you up if he catches you here?"

It took Helen a moment to realise he was teasing her. "Oh!" She laughed at him. "Oh, if that were the only problem, I should not mind that at all, for I know all the Squire's keepers."

"Then what is your problem? Pray linger for a moment, nymph, and enlighten me!"

No one had ever addressed her as nymph before, let alone bowed to her like that. She was tempted, hesitated – lost.

"The problem is my parents, sir. My father is the parson of St Matthew's, in Dendleford. And he – he would not like me to be out alone in the woods. Nor would he like me to speak to a stranger." As she spoke, she began to pin her hair up in frantic haste, realising she had been away from home far too long today.

"Ah, leave it down for a moment, longer," he begged. "You have the most beautiful hair I've ever seen in my life!"

She blushed even more violently, but shook her head and continued to subdue the hair. "I dare not. I must be on my way or I shall be late."

But the thought that someone considered her hair beautiful filled her with wonder, for her father seemed to hate the bright chestnut colour and unruly curls. He often told her to "tie that disgusting messy hair back", for it would pull out of its pins when she was doing the housework.

"May I walk with you for a while, then, fair maiden?"

Most of Robert Perriman's flowery speeches were culled from popular theatrical farces, but Helen had no idea that she was being seduced by second-hand words.

"Oh, no! Someone might see us." The hair was now up, but she glanced down at her legs, wondering how she was to put on her stockings again.

"Shall I turn my back while you complete your toilette?" he asked gravely.

"Thank you, sir." She was grateful to him for understanding her predicament. What a kind person he was! A true gentleman. So very unlike Mr Wintermaine. Keeping one eye on him, she hastened to complete her toilette, but he didn't even attempt to peep.

"I – I'm ready now." Hair pinned up, bonnet in place, basket in hand, yet she still hesitated to leave. "I always get home before four when I go into Stowby market."

At the road, he swept her a bow which had taken him weeks to perfect when he first left his father's butcher's shop and ran away to join a theatrical touring company as boy actor and general dogsbody. "Perhaps we shall meet again," he murmured in his softest voice, his eyes warm and his expression openly admiring.

"Oh, I do hope so!"

Helen walked home with stars in her eyes, but she was not so lost to reality as to forget to stop outside the village and check once again that her clothes bore no traces of the woods. Nor did she mention to her parents the encounter with a man who must, she realised when she thought about it in bed, be one of the travelling actors.

Robert walked home grinning. He had not found many willing maidens in Stowby, but this one was not only beautiful, she was stupidly naïve. Just made for a man like him. She should be grateful, really, that he was taking an interest in her. She would probably dream about him for the rest of her life.

"What have you been doing, Robert?" Roxanne asked that evening, as they were waiting to go on stage. "You're looking particularly smug."

"Never you mind, dear."

"I hope you're not pursuing the milkmaids again."

He didn't deign to reply. Milkmaids or fine ladies, they were all much alike in bed. Made to serve a man's needs.

He was waiting for her in the woods the following week, and for several weeks thereafter. He called her his water nymph and he made her laugh. She lived for those meetings. Suddenly there was something beautiful in her life.

The afternoon Robert first kissed Helen, she was upset about something, and he was trying to comfort her. When the kiss led on to other intimacies, she did not at first understand what he was trying to do and it was a moment before she realised that he had bared her breasts.

"Oh, Robert, you mustn't!" she protested, then gasped as his hands caressed her. And those hands were so delicately sensitive to her needs that before she knew what was happening, she was clinging to him, gasping and writhing in ecstasy. She had not believed such exquisite pleasure existed. Surely, surely something so marvellous could not be wrong?

And as he continued to murmur endearments and assure her that this was the way all men and women showed their love to one another, that he loved her so much, so very much, she somehow could not protest again. No one had ever used the word "love" to her before. No one had ever held her, cuddled her, whispered such sweet things to her.

Afterwards, when it was over, he kissed her again and begged her pardon. "I should not have taken advantage of you, my little love."

But she did not, could not regret anything. If Robert loved her, then they would no doubt get married one day soon.

She had at last found a way to escape Mr Wintermaine!

She floated home on a cloud of ecstasy.

Robert was thoughtful as he tramped back into Stowby. It got actors a bad name to seduce young virgins, and she had been so willing that he had not expected her to be untouched. If what he had done became known, the company might not be invited back here – or anywhere else – again.

No! Surely it could not matter that much. Her father was only a country parson. He would have no power to do anything to harm the company. And the chit was damned pretty – in spite of that dreadful brown rag she always wore – as well as very accommodating. Besides, the damage was done now, so he didn't see why he should stop enjoying himself. He grinned as he walked along. She was a responsive young woman, for all her inexperience. She had enjoyed it, too.

When he got back to his lodgings, the feeling of pleasure faded and he began to frown. He was not looking forward to the evening's performance. He had had several quarrels lately with his leading lady. Roxanne didn't like anyone else to get applause and she had even dared to criticise his acting skills. Since she had joined the company, having bought a half share in it, things had been rather awkward at times. Maybe he should look for another position. But not yet. He intended to enjoy the rest of this season in Stowby very much indeed.

The weather conspired to allow the two lovers to meet several times more, for every Thursday but one was fine and the woods deserted of all but them. Each time they met, Robert made love to Helen – though it was the kisses and cuddles she craved most. No one, not even her mother or father, had ever cuddled her before and she found herself dreaming of the way Robert held her close, waking with a warm feeling in her belly, absolutely longing for their next meeting.

And he loved her. He said it so often. Mr Wintermaine had never even hinted at feeling any affection for her. She was so glad she was going to marry Robert instead.

When Helen returned home from market one day in early September, the bubble of joy burst – abruptly. The maid was waiting for her on the kitchen doorstep. "You're late. And your father wishes to see you. Immediately. In his study. You're in trouble again, miss."

Mary's words shocked Helen rigid. It had been a long time since she had received a formal summons like this. "What have I done?" she whispered, desperately trying to think.

"Don't you know?" When the girl did not move, Mary clicked her tongue in annoyance and gave her a push towards the study. The maid didn't want to get in trouble with the master for not delivering messages quickly enough. He was in a foul mood today and taking it out on everyone else, as usual. He had made the mistress cry twice in the past hour. That poor lass was for it.

Helen tiptoed along the corridor and raised one trembling hand to knock on the door of her father's sanctum, a room she only visited for the purpose of dusting it – or when she was in serious trouble.

She was so desperately afraid that she nearly turned and ran away then, for suddenly she guessed what had happened. They must have found out about Robert. It could only be that. They would be infuriated. But she couldn't marry Mr Wintermaine now. Robert had brought her the only happiness she had ever known and she would not allow it to be taken from her. She would not.

She took a deep breath and knocked.

Two

When Helen entered the study, both her parents were waiting for her, standing together at the other side of her father's desk. It was unprecedented for her mother to be there as well. Helen's heart began to thump and pound in her chest.

She went to stand before them, eyes lowered, hands clasped, fear paralysing her throat muscles. She was always afraid when she was summoned into the study. It had been the scene of so many scoldings, not to mention beatings, that she couldn't even enter it to dust the bookshelves without becoming nervous.

Septimus Merling was finding it no easier to speak. His narrow face was as cold as that of a marble statue and his lips were tightly compressed to keep the rage in. As he looked at his daughter, he knew such bitterness of failure that bile rose in his throat. For Helen was as like his mother in character as she was in looks, in spite of the careful way he had brought her up.

He remembered his mother quite clearly, though he had been scarcely ten when she caused a scandal by leaving his father and running away with another man. And it was the legacy of this scandal which had prevented him from getting on in the church, he was sure. She, too, had had rich chestnut hair curling naturally around an oval face. She, too, had had that creamy complexion and those hazel eyes which sparkled with intelligence and mischief. Why could Helen not have resembled his wife, who was the most modest and virtuous of women? Beauty was of no value to the daughter of an impoverished country clergyman. And it was a snare for any woman.

As the silence continued, Helen could bear it no longer and raised her eyes inquiringly.

To Septimus, her face seemed suddenly more beautiful, more sensual, more "knowing of evil" than ever before, as he later declared to his wife. He set his hands on the desk, leaned forward and glared at her. The inquiring look faded from Helen's face and was replaced by fear.

"Who is the man?"

"Papa? I – I don't understand." But she did understand. This summons was definitely about Robert. How could they possibly have found out about her meetings with him?

"Don't lie to me, wretched girl! Who is the man? Who is it who has got you with child?"

Chalk-white now, she gulped for air but could find none and, as the room turned black and whirled around her, she slid to the floor in a faint.

For a moment, neither of her parents moved, then Mrs Merling looked at her husband.

"Leave her!" he ordered. "He that toucheth pitch shall be defiled therewith!"

So she stayed where she was, obeying her husband without question as she always had, feeling no sympathy for the girl whose faults he always blamed on her, but which came, Bertha believed, from his mother's side of the family. Like her daughter, she was afraid of him, unlike her daughter, though, she accepted that fear as normal.

After a few minutes, Helen struggled back to consciousness, to find herself lying on the floor, her head aching where she had bumped it on a chair. She looked round, wondering for a moment what had happened, then, as she saw her parents watching her, she remembered and terror filled her again. She closed her eyes, but the silence continued, so she opened them again and tried to sit up.

Neither of them made any attempt to help her up, and her father stood looking down at her with that cold disgusted expression which she so often saw on his face. Only it was worse this time. She pulled herself to her feet, but the room was still lurching around her and she had to sit down abruptly on the nearest chair or fall over again.

She didn't cry. When had weeping ever softened his heart? Instead, she tried to come to terms with the idea that she might be expecting a child. How did one get with child? Was it, could it be – the loving? What a wonderful way to beget a child!

When she looked as if she might be able to answer sensibly, Mr Merling repeated his questions.

"Who is the man? Who has got you with child?"

Helen was jerked out of a brief rosy dream of a son who looked exactly like Robert. She shook her head numbly. Her father would be so furious when he found out she had been meeting an actor. She had hoped that Robert would come with her to tell her family they wanted to marry. It would have been safer for her. She had been going to ask him about it the following week, for the company would soon be leaving Stowby and she wanted to go with them.

Slowly Septimus Merling unfastened his belt. This was a time for the sternest possible measures. She must pay for her sin and repent of it. As his mother had never done. He strode round his desk, caught his daughter by the shoulder and pulled her to her knees in front of him.

Helen did not plead or protest, for she knew what was coming. As she braced herself for the pain, the belt descended upon her back. At first she held in her cries, then she began to gasp and moan, for he had never hit her so hard before.

"Father, don't!" she begged. "Let me—" Another blow stopped her short and she whimpered in pain.

Again the image of his mother rose before Septimus's eyes, and for the first time since he was a boy, he lost control of himself. "You shall scream before I'm done," he muttered. "Scream out the name of your seducer. I shall cleanse you of this evil, whatever it takes to do so. You shall not follow in *her* footsteps."

Helen struggled to get away, but he was a strong man and he had no trouble holding her down. She could not help screaming each time the belt descended.

Eventually, Bertha Merling came round the desk and took her husband's arm. "She cannot bear any more, Septimus."

He breathed deeply and closed his eyes for a moment, then shook his daughter hard. "Confess your sins, you whore of Babylon. *Who – is – the – man?*"

Helen was in such a haze of pain that she could hardly think straight. "Robert. Robert Perriman."

"I know of no such person. You're lying." He hit her again.

Desperate, she shrieked, "I'm not. He's an actor. I met him in Stowby."

For a moment, Septimus let her go, holding on to the edge of the desk as shock made him suddenly weak. Then black anger filled him and he seized Helen again. His daughter was even worse than his mother, who had at least run away with a gentleman. "Dear God! The shame of it! An actor!"

Even Bertha did not dare try to stop him. But she could not bear to watch and left the room, holding a handkerchief to her eyes.

Only when his daughter lost consciousness did he stop and push her away from him with his foot. He threw the blood-stained belt down and sank into his chair, still trembling with rage. As he came to his senses and realised what he had done, he was not only furious with her for sinning, but angry with himself for losing his temper, for demeaning himself like that.

In the end, he walked out to seek refuge in his church. As he passed his wife in the hall, he said curtly, "You may tend her now, then lock her in her bedroom."

As he knelt before the altar, he felt no pity for his daughter. Like his mother, she had placed herself beyond forgiveness. Now, she and her shame must be sent away from Dendleford for ever.

When Helen regained her senses, she was lying on her bed face down, with the maid, Mary, bathing her back. "Lie still, miss. I'll try not to hurt you, but we have to get the pieces of your shift out of the wounds or they'll fester."

Mary bent down to proceed with her work, disgust filling her, and anger too. This decided it. She had been wondering whether to give notice at quarter day. Now she would definitely do so. The man was a monster. He had always been a nasty piece of work, for all his show of piety, but he had gone quite mad today. And the mistress never said him nay, not even today when her daughter was being beaten senseless.

Mary had peeped through the kitchen door and seen Mrs Merling standing in the hall, wincing as she listened to the screams. She was a poor kind of mother, Mrs Merling was, and a poor broken reed of a woman. But Mary did not have to stay here and put up with such things. She had a little money saved and could leave the village for good, move somewhere a bit livelier. And she wouldn't keep her mouth shut about what had happened today, either. She definitely wouldn't.

The pain was so bad that Helen groaned and writhed, soon fainting again. Which was a good thing, because Mary managed to get her back clean before the poor girl came to her senses again. It was no wonder that she had got pregnant, they had kept her so ignorant of life. And in spite of their mean, carping ways, she had been a nice child, always polite and grateful for any bit of attention, and had grown into a young woman bursting to love something. Not like her brother, that was for sure, for he had resembled his father even at the age of five, and he grew more like him every day.

When she had finished, Mary covered the poor girl as best she could and left her to sleep. Then she went into the village, ostensibly to buy some sugar – but actually to spread the tale.

For days Helen lay there in a haze of agony, tended only by the maid. The wonder was, as Mary told her cronies, that the poor lass didn't lose the baby. Cruel hard, he was, the master. Treating his own daughter like that. Miss Helen would be scarred for life where the buckle had bit in. As if girls weren't always getting themselves pregnant – for nature would out – and where was the harm, as long as the fellows married them?

The villagers lost no time in spreading the news more widely afield. For all his piety, the parson was not liked in Dendleford.

For most of the days that followed, Helen was alone, locked in the attic, too weak even to sit up. She had no idea what was to happen to her.

Time passed very slowly. She listened to the sounds below her of the household going about its daily tasks and she escaped from time to time into her memories. Neither of her parents made any attempt to see her.

And although Mary felt a certain sympathy for the girl, she knew better than to express it or to deviate again from the very explicit instructions she had received – that she was not to speak a single word to Miss Helen. She wasn't giving them any excuse to withhold her wages at quarter day.

As she grew better, Helen tried to make plans to escape. She had to let Robert know what had happened. Mary was the only one who could help her, the only one who could get a message to him. The next time the maid came to tend her back, she whispered, "Can you take a message to Stowby for me?"

Mary shook her head immediately and glanced over her shoulder. "I daren't, Miss Helen."

"But you're my only hope. If we don't tell Robert, he won't be able to rescue me."

Her father's voice boomed up the stairs. "Mary! I hope you are not talking to that sinner."

"Indeed not, sir. She was just moaning as I dressed her back."

There were footsteps on the stairs and a shadow fell across the bed. Helen didn't even try to see who it was. She knew those footsteps.

When Mary had gone back downstairs and the key had grated in the lock, Helen wept, silently, into her pillow. That night she reached the blackest moment in her whole life and afterwards she lost hope, refusing to eat, for what was the point?

Life continued as it always had done for the other members of the household, following the rigid pattern set by the master. As she listened to the noises coming from below, Helen thought it was as if she had ceased to exist. Downstairs the mornings still began with prayers in the parlour. Her father's voice had a peculiarly penetrating nasal quality and, twice a day, she heard him praying for the Lord's continued blessings upon his family and household.

Helen's mind wandered from one idea to the next. Why he should think them blessed by the Lord was something she had never been able to understand. She knew that, unlike her brother, she had always been a great disappointment to her father – the cross he had to bear – for he had never hesitated to tell her so. Her older brother had been a placid child, a model son, who had recently followed his father into the church and gained his first position as a curate. Edward was as poor as any villager, they all were, but he was just as proud as his father. And he disapproved of his sister almost as much as his parents did.

"Why?" she moaned to herself as she tried to find a more comfortable position in the stuffy little room. "Why do they all hate me so? And why are we so very poor?" A village as small as Dendleford could not provide lavishly for its clergyman, but Helen knew that the Merlings were connections of Lord Northby on her paternal grandmother's side. Yet they were never invited to dine at Northby Castle, which lay just west of Stowby, the largest town in the district, nor had His Lordship made any attempt to help his relative to a more substantial living.

Perhaps when she was better she could run away and obtain employment as a companion to an old lady? Or even get a position as a maidservant? Anything would be preferable to staying here.

Or best of all, she thought, as she lay there half delirious with pain, Robert would come and rescue her and carry her far, far away from Dendleford. Only he didn't know she needed rescuing, or he would surely have come for her by now. If she could find some other way to escape, they could run away together and get married. For if she stayed, if she did have her child in Dendleford, her father would make its life as miserable as hers had been.

Then her thoughts came to an abrupt halt. The idea that there was a baby to consider seemed incredible and also terrifying. A child would stop her from finding work. You had to stay home and look after babies. She smiled in spite of her pain. She loved little babies. They were so warm and adorable, and they smelled so sweet if you looked after them properly. She had held babies many a time when she and her mother were making parish visits. They always smiled at her.

Then she frowned as something else occurred to her. How did one have the baby, anyway? Was it – was it like the cat having kittens? Helen fingered her stomach and desperately wished that she were not so ignorant. She had asked her mother once about such things, and received such a tongue lashing for her immodesty that she had never asked again.

Oh, if only Robert would come for her! Why did he not come? She didn't know how many days had passed since their last meeting, but surely he would be wondering what had happened to her? Surely he would make inquiries?

When Helen had recovered somewhat, Septimus Merling rode over to Stowby to take counsel of Lord Northby, who was a Justice of the Peace, as well as a relative. When he got to the Castle, he asked one of the servants to hand Northby the terse note he had already prepared, saying there was trouble in the family.

His Lordship stared at the scrap of paper and made a disgusted noise. "Damn fellow! I suppose you'd better show him in, Barns." He could not refuse to see Merling, but his valet had already told him about the beating, which had become quite a scandal in the district. And because no one had seen Miss Merling since, there were even folk who said the father had beaten her to death.

Basil Northby thought badly of a man who would treat his own daughter so harshly. He had always despised Septimus Merling, and the man's father had been as bad. He had wondered at the time how his cousin Rosamund could ever have married John Merling, for the fellow had nothing but looks to recommend him. And it might be reprehensible but, after she'd run away, Lord Northby had always nursed a secret hope that sin might have made her happier than virtue and prayers had.

Septimus was shown into the room and made his usual fuss, bowing and scraping.

"Get on with it, man!" snapped his Lordship. "You said there was trouble in the family."

Septimus sighed. "I fear so, My Lord." He explained the horrifying situation, then bent his head to await judgement.

Lord Northby nodded slowly. "Hmm. She'll have to be married off, then. Is there some local fellow who might take her or do you want her to wed the actor?" Was this the only reason for the beating? What did the fellow think young girls were? Saints?

Septimus reared back, affronted. "I don't want her living anywhere near Dendleford. All I wish is to ensure that she marries the rogue, for the sake of the child. After that, I'll have nothing more to do with her."

Typical! thought his noble relative, pinching his nose and giving the matter some thought. "Very well, then," he said at last. "I'll go and see this scoundrel myself, then."

"We'll be extremely grateful for your help, My Lord. Extremely. We—"

"I'll find out what his intentions are and let you know." He got up to signify the interview was at an end. As he said to his wife later, the poor girl would probably be better off married and away from that canting hypocrite, with his penchant for beating helpless women.

The interview with Robert Perriman was conducted in the best parlour of the Angel Inn, to which the actor had been summoned peremptorily by a message from His Lordship.

"What's that about?" demanded Rugely, the ageing actor-manager, who was there when the summons came. "Is there some trouble, Perriman?"

Robert shrugged. "I have no idea." But he did have an idea. The girl had stopped coming to the woods, and she had not been at the market, either, last week, for Robert had made careful inquiries. The parents must have found out, then. Pity. There were still a few weeks to go in the town. But good things never lasted.

And he'd have had to leave her behind, anyway, at the end of the month. So perhaps it had saved him the trouble and tears of a parting. For he had no intention of getting married and had been secretly amused when she just assumed that they would wed. He'd never met anyone as naïve as Helen Merling, poor little bitch. Hardly knew what colour the sky was, that one. And hadn't asked for presents, just a show of affection.

"See you don't offend him, then," Rugely warned Robert. "I can soon replace you, you know. But Northby owns half the county – and has connections in London, too."

At the inn, His Lordship eyed the raffish young man with extreme disfavour and did not ask him to sit down. "Hear you've got a young girl in trouble."

Robert blinked. In trouble? Oh, hell, the bitch was whelping! "Me, My Lord?"

"Yes, you, damn your eyes! She's a connection of mine, so I take this matter very seriously."

Robert stiffened. Damnation! If she was related to this stiff-necked Lord, there would be trouble. Rugely would have a fit. So would Roxanne. "She's with child?" he asked cautiously, admitting nothing until he saw exactly how the land lay.

"Didn't I just say that?"

"And she claims it's mine?"

His Lordship thumped the table. "Aye, she does. Are you going to deny it? Because if so, I'll call you a liar to your face."

After one look at His Lordship's empurpled countenance, Robert abandoned that idea. "Alas, what can I say? I was tempted and succumbed. She is very beautiful. And was very willing. I did not force her."

Lord Northby leaned forward. "And also – very innocent."

Feeling somewhat afraid of this crusty old nobleman, Robert

tried to think of something to say that would sweeten him a bit, make him see reason, but he was not given the chance.

"Well, the matter's quite easy to settle. You've had your fun, and now you'll have to pay. She's already paid very heavily, I might add, because her father's beaten her senseless. Her back's in a mess, apparently. Hit her with his belt."

Robert felt slightly sick at the picture this painted. He felt even more sick at the thought that the damned father might come after him next.

Lord Northby thumped the table and his voice became even louder. "If you don't do the right thing by her, Perriman, and marry the poor girl, not only will you never act in Stowby again, but neither will your company. And what's more," he leaned forward and shot the words out like bullets, "I have enough connections in the theatrical world to ensure that your name will be blackened beyond redemption – even in London."

Robert stared at him open-mouthed. Impossible not to believe this threat.

Another pause. "Do I make myself plain? Hey? Answer me, you dolt! Do I make myself plain?"

"Yes, My Lord. Very plain." Robert was sick to his soul at being trapped like this, when he had successfully avoided marriage until his thirtieth year. He contemplated, and just as quickly rejected, the idea of making a run for it. His face was his fortune and he could easily be recognised the minute he set foot on stage.

Another look at His Lordship's angry face and riding crop tapping furiously against a highly polished boot made Robert quail, and he decided there was nothing for it but to make the best of a bad case. After all, the wench did have connections. This thing might even work to his advantage. He drew himself up. "I have no intention of refusing to marry Helen. Had I known that she was with child, I would have gone to see her father at once."

"Hah!"

"Unfortunately, I have to confess that the takings in Stowby have been so bad that I do not even possess enough money for a special licence, let alone a ring." He sighed and tried a wistful look. "An actor's life is not without its problems, My Lord."

"I'll see to all that. You just be there." Lord Northby pondered on his coming engagements. He didn't want to miss a day's shooting. "Monday next. Noon. At Stowby parish church. And don't try to run for it in the meantime."

"I wouldn't dream of it, My Lord."

"I'll bring the girl and her belongings into town for the ceremony, then she'll be your responsibility. Her damned parents have disowned her." His voice became heavily sarcastic. "No doubt you can attend to such trifling details as finding lodgings for the two of you?"

"Indeed I can, sir." Robert was about to mouth some platitudes about love and being the happiest of men, but the old fellow just walked out on him.

He turned and thumped the table instead. "Damn!" Then he called for brandy and got royally drunk.

A pale bruised travesty of Robert's wood nymph was led into Stowby's parish church on the Monday by her father, who declined to take part in the ceremony, or even to give her away.

"I have come," said Septimus Merling coldly to Robert, folding his arms and taking up a position at the rear of the church, "only to ensure that justice is done and the baby is given a name. Albeit a disgraceful name."

Helen said nothing. She was white as a sheet and swaying on her feet. Even Robert Perriman felt shocked. What had they done to that poor child? The old fellow had said she'd been beaten, but this – this was vicious. He looked at the lank hair and dull eyes in dismay. Where was his glorious wood nymph?

Lord Northby poked Robert with his cane. "Go and wait at the front, you."

Blank-faced, Helen stumbled down the aisle on Lord Northby's arm. At the altar, Robert had to support her, or she would have fallen.

Neither of the two principals ever remembered the words they spoke at their wedding ceremony. Helen was conscious only of the pain in her back and the difficulty of standing upright. Robert was bitterly aware that he was now trapped in marriage.

When the ceremony was over, Septimus Merling left the church without speaking to his daughter.

Lord Northby waited for the newly-weds at the church door. "You should know, Perriman, that Helen brings with her a marriage portion of some forty pounds a year, a legacy from an old aunt."

Robert brightened visibly.

"It'll be paid to her quarterly. Here, this is the lawyer's address in London." He gave Perriman a folded piece of paper.

"And the capital?" Robert asked delicately.

Lord Northby snorted. "That's untouchable and is entailed upon Helen's eldest daughter." He turned to Helen. "Wish you luck, my dear. If you're ever in trouble, come to me for help."

He then turned and marched out, going across to the Three Feathers for a noggin of ale to take the bitter taste from his mouth. Merling had half killed that poor girl. This would be the last favour Lord Northby ever did for him. In fact, he'd tell his servants never to admit the fellow again.

Helen didn't hear what His Lordship had said. Even clinging to Robert, she could barely manage to stand upright.

Forty pounds every year! thought Robert, pleased – and for doing nothing. He hadn't expected Helen to have anything at all. Very conscious of the small group which had gathered outside, he helped his wife tenderly down the church steps, found a boy to carry the pitifully small pile of luggage which Merling had dumped in the porch, and took her back to the lodgings he had found for them both.

There, Helen collapsed on the bed and begged her husband to help her off with her dress. At the sight of his wife's back, Robert felt distinctly sick, but he gathered his wits together enough to race off to find Roxanne and beg her to help him. She might have her faults, she might criticise his acting ability, but the leading lady had a kind heart and a practical disposition. She would know what to do.

For the time being, Robert's concern for the trembling creature lying on the bed, the creature who had treated him like one of the heroes he played so often, overshadowed his anger at being forced into marriage. After all, she was the source of forty pounds a year for doing nothing.

Dammit, the thing might work out very well, he thought optimistically, as he left Roxanne to deal with Helen. A wife could be dashed useful – and not just in bed.

Three

It would be no exaggeration to say that Helen Perriman owed her life to the actress's nursing and support. Roxanne Marlborough, born a mere Janet Snape in the back streets of Manchester, took one horrified look at Helen's back and sent Robert hotfoot for the doctor.

"Who did this to you?" she asked Helen gently.

"My father."

She exchanged disgusted glances with Robert, but her voice was quite even as she replied, "Well, if that's an example of fatherly love, I'm glad mine died before he'd had time to show his for me!"

"My father hates me," Helen whispered. "He always has done. And I've never understood why." Tears of utter exhaustion were trickling down her pale cheeks.

"Who could ever understand men?" The look Roxanne threw at Robert included him in this general condemnation.

He scowled at her, but said nothing.

The doctor came bustling in, a fat man exuding self-importance. He was not overly pleased to be dealing with mere actors, as he disliked dealing with the poor, but he had also heard the gossip about "the whipping parson" and was not unhappy to be able to witness at first hand the brute's handiwork. He tutted over the back, approved Roxanne's treatment, then gave the patient a draught of laudanum.

"Sleep," he announced. "Nature's own nostrum." He found himself looking at the back of Robert's head. The new husband, who had got over his access of pity for his wife, was standing looking out of the window, yawning and scratching his armpit.

The doctor was unused to being ignored. He tapped Robert on the shoulder. "Did you hear me, sir?"

"Yes. Right. She needs to sleep."

"And I'd advise you to apply a lotion to the back, which I can supply at a modest cost, but to leave the injuries uncovered as much as possible."

"How much?" Robert demanded.

The doctor made a quick estimate of his client's means and regretfully reduced his intended fee. "A mere two shillings, sir." He remembered Lord Northby's involvement and added hastily, "For the lotion, that is."

Robert growled, but did not quite like to protest with Roxanne standing there looking at him so scornfully. "And how much for this visit?"

"The same, sir. The same."

"What? You're going to charge us four shillings, just to give us a bit of grease and to tell us to let her sleep! Four shillings!" Why, that amount of money would allow him to toss a few dice in the inn, or buy himself several drinks.

The doctor's face turned bright puce and he made a gobbling noise in his throat.

Roxanne nudged her fellow actor in the ribs. "Shut up, Robert!"

"But—"

"Shut – up! I'll lend you the money if you're short, but she needs help."

His expression brightened, but his words were still grudging. "Oh, very well!"

Roxanne breathed deeply and poked him in the chest. "And you needn't think you can get out of paying me back, either. I'm doing this for your poor little wife's sake, not for yours."

Given this lack of appreciation for his services, the doctor did not bother to return, which was probably fortunate for Helen. Roxanne showed Robert how to tend his poor young wife and stood over him to make sure that he carried out her instructions.

When they had finished, she decided it was no use appealing to his better nature, because she'd never seen any signs of one. "If you don't do it properly, you'll be paying out a lot more to the doctors than four shillings. It'll be more like four guineas."

He shuddered. "I heard what you said. I do understand English." And he did not intend to waste any more money on doctors, thank you very much.

"Then make sure you do it right, or that back'll not heal." She was satisfied that she had got through to him, but she decided to keep a close eye on things, nonetheless.

But Helen was so grateful for her husband's care and asked so little of him, seeming to regard him in the light of a young god who had saved her life, that even Robert Perriman's heart could not fail to be touched.

"You're so good to me," she whispered the following morning as he carefully washed her back.

He patted her arm, liking this new, benevolent image of himself. "Well, you are my wife now."

Her smile was glowing and it reminded him of how beautiful she was normally. If they did something about her clothes, she would be a credit to him once she had recovered. He made himself a bed on the floor and, since he had the happy knack of being able to sleep anywhere, slept like a log until a damned cockerel crowed its head off and woke him up.

In the days that followed, Helen wept softly over the baskets of fruit and other delicacies that were sent to their room by anonymous well-wishers. Robert wiped away her tears and coaxed her to eat by setting a shining example. He had always been partial to a piece of fruit, and with two people to feed from his slender share of the company's takings, the gifts were a godsend. Robert was, in fact, a hearty trencherman, given the chance, even to the extent that he was considered a greedy devil by those less besotted than his wife.

It was nearly two weeks before Helen was well enough to leave their room and take the air upon her husband's arm. Robert, knowing what a picture they presented – she so slight and pale, and he so handsome – made the most of it. He bent over her solicitously as they strolled down the main street of the busy market town.

There was considerable sympathy for her in the district, and he did not scruple to take advantage of it to boost the audience numbers at the company's performances, and especially to increase his own applause. Never had Robert been so dashing and gallant on stage. Never had audiences applauded so loudly. At his suggestion, Helen sat at the doorway and helped take the money, blushing at the attention she received.

Roxanne watched all this very cynically, but did not say

anything, since she owned a share in the small company and benefited even more than the Perrimans from the increased takings.

On the whole, during the first month or two of his marriage, Robert was inclined to think that matrimony was not nearly as bad as people made out. As she grew stronger, Helen was able to make him comfortable in dozens of little ways. She was a skilful laundress, which saved him the considerable expense of sending things out to be washed, and she could mend things in the most invisible way possible, which also helped a fellow who had to make his clothes last.

She was not demanding of his attention, either, and was pathetically grateful for any time he deigned to spend with her. And she had a very good sense of humour, as she grew more used to her new freedom. He thoroughly enjoyed telling her all his old jokes, for she had heard none of them before.

Best of all, she did not try to tell him what to do, as he had feared a wife would. She simply accepted whatever he said or did as right and proper. She was even able to correct his pronunciation and make suggestions about how a gentleman would react to certain situations in some of the plays. This had a positive effect on his performance, making it less of a caricature of nobility or gentility. It was very convenient, he thought complacently, to have a wife who was a lady born, even if she didn't have any useful connections in London. But she did have a small income and when the first quarter's payment became available, he took her out for a hearty meal in the nearest inn and patted the chinking coins in his pocket as he toasted her beautiful eyes.

Another pleasant surprise was that he had no need to buy her presents (something he had feared a wife would expect). He soon found out that what she treasured most were compliments and kind remarks, of which she had been starved, and those cost a fellow nothing at all.

Even a man as monumentally selfish as Robert could not help but realise how unhappy her previous life must have been. It was a good thing, he thought smugly, that he had rescued her.

Helen, helping her husband to learn his lines, laughing over an incident at the theatre or mending his clothes, thought herself in paradise.

* * *

As Helen regained her looks, both she and her husband began to worry about her clothes, she because her waist was growing thicker and her breasts fuller, he because he thought she did not do him credit, dressed so dowdily. So when a lucky game of cards left him more flush than usual one day, he tossed her some largesse and told her. "There you are! I dare say you can buy yourself a length or two of material with this and sew yourself some dresses."

"Oh, Robert!" Helen wept tears of gratitude all over his waistcoat.

"Here, I say! Stop that." But such a reaction made a fellow feel good all the same.

She was not yet confident enough to trust her own judgement, so turned to Roxanne for help, for the actress had been a good friend to her.

"How much did he give you, then?"

Helen displayed the ten precious guineas.

"Mean, I call that!"

"Mean! Ten whole guineas!"

"Yes, he always was stingy. You won't get much with that. And I know for a fact that he won fifty guineas. He's a far better gambler than he is an actor."

But Helen could not be brought to criticise her husband. In her eyes, he could do no wrong.

"I'll tell you what," said Roxanne, suddenly seeing a way to help her friend and herself at the same time. "If you don't object to making things over, I could let you have some of my old things. They're not worn out or anything, but I've put a bit of weight on lately. I was going to sell them, but I could let you have them cheaply instead. For your ten guineas, you'd then have half a dozen dresses."

Helen immediately tipped the guineas into Roxanne's lap.

"But you haven't even seen them yet!"

"Oh, I trust you, Roxanne. You've been so good to me."

"More fool you. Listen, love, don't ever trust anyone totally, not even your own husband."

But Helen only laughed. She had never enjoyed life so much. Every minute of the day was a joy to her, for there was no one to scold her and no fear of the morrow. Why, Robert was a thousand times better than Mr Wintermaine.

Six wonderful, if over-trimmed dresses were brought round to the lodgings for Helen's nimble fingers to transform. Roxanne, seeing the excellent job her little friend made of them, grew thoughtful. The girl had instinctive taste and flair. Delicately, Roxanne sounded out Robert on whether or not he would object to his wife earning a bit of money on the side, then laughed at herself for worrying. As if Robert Perriman would look a gift horse in the mouth.

"She's a good needlewoman, you know, Robert. She could do a few bits and pieces for me, and I'd pay her. I was never any hand at sewing. Maybe she could help the others, too. And then there are the costumes. Every now and then they need a bit of work doing on them. The company would pay her for that. She'd be able to make a few shillings from time to time." Her frugality made her add, "or we'd give her some of the things we didn't want to wear for herself."

Robert had no objections whatsoever. He was, in fact, delighted that his wife could contribute more towards her own keep and thus take some of the burden from him. That money of hers only came in once a quarter and the dashed dice hadn't been rolling his way lately.

Roxanne took Helen aside the next day and put the proposition to her. "Mind you," she warned, "I'll only arrange this if you promise to do it my way."

"What do you mean?"

"You must promise never to hand over more than half of what you earn to that husband of yours – let alone tell him what you earn."

Helen was horrified. "I couldn't do that!"

Roxanne steeled herself. "Then I won't give you any work."

"But, Roxanne . . ."

"No buts. You do it my way or you don't do it at all." She sighed and shook her head over Helen's naïveté, "I don't know why I'm bothering, I really don't. I must be getting soft in my old age. It's just that I can't bear to see you being so stupid about him! No man is worth it!"

"Robert's been very good to me," Helen insisted.

"Your precious Robert seduced you! It was *his* fault your father beat you and threw you out!"

"My father disliked me before I met Robert," Helen said

quietly, staring into some private internal hell. "And has been wanting to get rid of me for a while now."

There was silence, then Roxanne patted Helen's hand. Poor little bitch, she thought, you've had a rotten life, and I don't think Robert is going to make you happy for long. She searched for a way to explain. "Look, love, you must have realised by now that Robert is a gambler. I know the signs. He's been on a winning streak lately. But it won't last. It never does. He'll start to lose soon. And if he knows you've got any money of your own, he'll take it all and lose that too. And then how will you and the child eat?"

Helen shook her head in disbelief. "Robert's not like that. He wouldn't take all my money. He just wouldn't!"

Roxanne sighed. Never, in all her life, had she met anyone as naïve as Helen Perriman. She was dreading the inevitable disillusionment, not looking forward to seeing the glow fade from Helen's beautiful eyes, for one of her friend's charms was her ability to enjoy life, the small things as well as the large. But she knew Robert. He wouldn't be able to keep up this good behaviour for much longer. She was surprised he'd managed so far. Or perhaps he hadn't managed. Perhaps the harmony between the Perrimans was the result of Helen's sunny nature.

"Look," she tried again, "what have you lost if you do save some money? If he stops gambling and settles down, you'll be able to surprise him. If I'm right, and he doesn't stop gambling, you'll be glad to have some money tucked away."

Helen's eyes filled with tears. "How could you ask me to deceive him like that?"

Roxanne shrugged. "Well, do as you like. Only I'm not paying you good money for him to gamble away." Seeing Helen's tremulous mouth and pleading eyes, however, she tried one final tack. "Think of the baby. You'll need a lot of things for the baby. Men never consider such things."

"Well . . ." And the thought of the coming baby won the day, for Helen was longing to have her own child, someone to love and cuddle and care for in every possible way. She would lie in bed and dream about him when the show was over – she felt sure it was going to be a boy, a boy as handsome as Robert! "Oh, all right, Roxanne! I'll keep some money back. But I don't like it."

"You don't have to like it, just see that you keep your bargain."

The deception cost Helen hours of anguish over her duplicity. Only her promise to Roxanne prevented her from giving Robert all her first earnings. It was even harder to keep quiet when he tossed the shillings she offered him back into her lap.

"You earned them, my pet, you keep 'em!" Robert enjoyed making lordly gestures, even when he could least afford them. It was, he felt, the mark of a gentleman to do so. The cards had not, however, been favourable the previous night, so he did let Helen spend her money on a few tender chops and sat chatting as he watched her fry them for him over the fire in their room, which saved the cost of purchasing a dinner at the inn.

When the company moved on to another town, the cards were even less favourable, and, after a while, Robert was glad to let Helen purchase food for them from her earnings. There were even times when she had to pay the cost of their lodgings.

She hid her disappointment that Roxanne had been right and never uttered a word of criticism to her husband. It was she who had been foolish, she told herself, investing him with all the virtues. She had expected too much of him. He was only human, after all.

Robert, with no idea that his wife was a trifle disappointed in him, developed the habit of spending most of what he earned on gaming or on clothes, and leaving Helen to provide for their daily needs. He still did, however, remember to praise her regularly.

"You're a little wonder." He saw her joy and smirked at how easy it was.

Another night. "I don't know how I ever managed without you." Tears came into her eyes and she picked up his hand to press it to her cheek, which made him feel dashed silly.

"Yes, of course I love you." He even patted the bump of the unborn child as he spoke and refrained from yawning when she speculated about whether it would be a boy or a girl, and whom it would favour, and what they should call it.

So, for all their problems, Helen continued to live in a glow of happiness. And Roxanne continued to marvel at her friend's blindness.

* * *

In Cheltenham, however, Helen's happiness came to an abrupt end. The company played there regularly and Robert had his best following among the sentimental old ladies who yearned for the heroes of their youth, heroes who had probably been as much creatures of their imagination as Robert was.

When he came home from the theatre, flushed with success, he found that his wife had gone into labour. Helen had never looked as ugly. The landlady had sent for the local midwife, and the latter had come, inspected her patient and said it would take a while yet. After that, she had gone home to continue her night's sleep.

Helen bore the labour pains stoically, stifling her cries under the pillow during the night, for fear of waking Robert.

But as the process dragged on for two days, Robert thought it best to move out and share a room with one of the other actors, so that he would not lose sleep and appear haggard on stage.

Helen was left to the tender mercies of an indifferent midwife, who looked in from time to time and did not even think of giving her a drink or seeing that she had some food to eat. It was Roxanne who did that when she called upon her friend during the afternoon.

When it was all over, the midwife dumped a mewling bundle into her patient's arms and told her she had a son. "And you're a brave lass," she added, impressed by Helen's stoicism and in spite of her distrust of actors.

Helen wept tears of joy all over the baby's head and covered his little face with kisses. She had always known she would love her child, but hadn't realised how fiercely. Oh, you shall be happy, she promised the child silently, and you shall always be most dearly loved. And no one shall ever, ever whip you!

Roxanne came in again after the show and stayed the night with her, but Robert did not turn up at all.

Helen tried to hide the unhappiness this caused her, saying stoutly that he needed his sleep, was useless without it, and the show must go on. "He has some new lines to learn, has he not?"

Roxanne, who knew that Robert was out gambling – not learning lines at all – said nothing, but she went and confronted him the next day. "Have you been to see her yet?"

"Not yet. I've been busy." He flicked a speck of dust off his coat.

"Well, she needs you. You should have stayed with her."

"What use would I have been? I'd just have been in the way."

Roxanne held on to her temper with an effort. "She's your wife. And you haven't even been to see the baby. Your own son! My God, you're a rotten sod!"

Robert scowled. "I'm no hand with babies. I never did like the damned squalling things!" He was the eldest of seven. He knew exactly what babies were like.

"You should have thought of that before you seduced an innocent girl!"

He drew himself up. "It was love at first sight, not seduction." He still maintained this fiction, for it added, he thought, to his gallant air, and besides, it kept other women off his back. He had enough on his plate with Helen. He didn't want any more complications, oh, no. He was going to stick to the dice from now on. Dice didn't get pregnant on you.

Roxanne threw back her head and laughed. "You can save that sort of talk for the theatre and for those stupid enough to believe it, Robert! I certainly don't. Anyway, if you love your dear Helen so much, go and see her. Praise her a little. She's been very brave."

He looked at the clock on the theatre wall. "If you must know, I've arranged to meet a few chaps again after the show. I can't stop now. I'm on a winning streak." He put an arm round her and said coaxingly, "You stay with her for a day or two, Roxanne. You're her friend. You'll be much more use than I would. Please!" His hand wandered over her breasts and she slapped it away.

"Shame on you, with your wife lying there waiting for you!"

But he just grinned at her. "Will you, though, Roxanne?"

She sighed and shook her head. "I must be getting soft in my old age. I will – but on one condition. You go and see her quickly now, this very minute, before the show. Take her a bunch of flowers. And don't forget to admire the baby! It's a pretty little thing." She saw sheer disinterest in his face. "I mean it. If you don't go to see her, I won't help you."

He shrugged. "Oh, very well. But you'll have to lend me something to buy the flowers with. I've only got enough for my stake."

"I thought you were on a winning streak?"

"I am. It's just starting."

"I never met a gambler yet who came out a winner in the end." She slapped a coin into his hand. "I'm a fool, but here you are. A bunch of flowers."

He pocketed the money. "Oh, I don't do so badly with the old dice. It's just finding the stake sometimes – especially with a wife to support."

"Support! She's supporting herself, and well you know it." But he had gone.

Robert went immediately to visit his wife. Best get it over with. Pulling a face at the sour smell of the room, he bent over the crumpled red face of his son and studied it dutifully. "People always say they look like someone, but I'm damned if I can see any resemblance. Can you?"

"He looked a bit like you when he was first born, but now he just looks like himself. Aren't you pleased with him? Isn't he lovely?"

Robert tried to summon up his acting powers. "Yes, of course. A man likes to have a son, I suppose, but I don't know much about babies, my pet." He wasn't going to risk anyone involving him in the damned brat's care. "He's got all his fingers and toes, I suppose?"

"Of course he has! He's a beautiful baby!" She tried to blink away the tears that this ungracious speech had brought to her eyes.

Robert saw that he had upset her and apologised. He didn't want Roxanne withdrawing her help. "Sorry if I'm not saying the right sort of thing. Bit hard to get used to, being a father. What was it you wanted to call him? Damned if I can ever remember."

"Henry Robert – but we'll call him Harry."

"Why not call him Harry straight out, then? Why bother with Henry at all?"

Head on one side, Helen considered this. "Yes. Why not?"

"Why Harry anyway?"

"After Henry the Eighth."

He roared with laughter. "Henry the Eighth! What's so special about him? He's dead!"

"Because he had such a gusto for life. He enjoyed it. And because – because no one in my family is called Henry."

"Well, that makes a bit more sense than calling him after

Henry the Eighth. Wouldn't want a son of mine named for that mincy-mouthed brute of a father of yours. You've still got a couple of scars on your back, you know. Lovely back you've got." He ran his finger up her cheek, looking forward to having the use of her body again, and she nestled against him trustingly.

Before he left, he coaxed a few coins out of her to swell his stake, disarming her by a frank admission of his guilt at playing so deeply, but assuring her that he couldn't lose, that it was a game of skill they were playing tonight, not a game of chance.

He had brought no flowers, had even forgotten he was supposed to. It would not have made a difference if he had. Helen had seen how little he cared for their son – or for her. And she wept when he had gone.

Four

By the time the Marlborough Players were ready to move again, Helen had recovered her strength and Robert had discovered just how much he disliked living with a baby. Its crying set his teeth on edge, there were always cloths and little garments drying around the room, filling it with a steamy smell, and, worst of all, the baby regularly disturbed his sleep.

Moreover, Helen was no longer solely at his service, which he had rather enjoyed. She was now more often at the service of the red-faced, howling stranger, who had to be fed at the most inconvenient times. In fact, Robert decided indignantly, that damned baby always came first with her. Not that she didn't see to her husband's laundry as efficiently as ever, and feed him well enough but, dammit, a man liked his wife to sit with him and look pretty and *listen* to him! Nowadays, Helen always seemed to have one ear cocked, just in case Harry cried.

And Robert detested, totally and utterly detested, going out for walks with a woman carrying a baby, which looked more like a bundle of dirty washing to him than a son and heir. It was not, in his opinion, a good thing for an actor to be seen like this. He enjoyed having a pretty woman hanging on his arm and listening adoringly to everything he said, but he did not enjoy squiring one who cooed at a baby, pointing out the trees and flowers to a mindless and smelly little creature which could not even focus its eyes correctly, let alone understand what she was saying.

And so he told her.

Which made her weep softly into her handkerchief and made him feel like a brute.

But he wasn't going to change his mind about walking about town with a baby in public view. Definitely not!

So the gloss wore off the marriage and its brief flowering came to an end. Helen found it more and more difficult to manage on the money her husband gave her, if he gave her any, and Robert took to staying out as much as possible, to avoid the caterwauling, as he called it, of his son.

Some of the proprietors of the rooms they lodged in objected to the noise the baby inevitably made and other tenants objected, too, for Harry had a lusty pair of lungs.

Then there was the amount of washing a baby generated. As if a baby would notice whether its clothes were clean or not! But Helen would not give way on this point. She had dainty tastes and insisted on keeping herself, her baby and her husband immaculately clean, however many pails of water she had to lug up and down the narrow flights of steps to do so.

And since Robert was providing less and less money, she also had to spend every minute she could sewing to earn more, so that Harry should never, ever lack for anything.

"Oh, Roxanne," she sighed one day. "Does nothing beautiful ever last?"

"Not in my experience."

"What does last then?"

"Money."

The first time Helen dared to scold her husband was when he bought himself some new neckcloths with the housekeeping money. It was also the first time he was unable to bring her to a state of repentance afterwards for upsetting him before a performance. She forgave him, but he was in the wrong and she warned him never to do such a thing again.

When Roxanne asked her bluntly one day if she intended to have another child, Helen just gaped at her.

"Intend? I thought it just . . . happened." She blushed and didn't know where to look.

"It needn't happen if you don't want it to. How do you think I've managed all these years?"

"But you're not mar—" Helen broke off and blushed even more hotly.

Roxanne laughed. "Helen, my love, it's time you faced a few facts. The things your mother and father taught you – well, those sorts of morals are all very well for those with money and a position in the community, but if you're a woman and you've your way to make in the world, you can't afford to behave virtuously all the time. And you certainly can't afford to keep getting pregnant."

She put her arm round the younger woman. "I don't steal and cheat, but if a gentleman wants to pay me for the use of my body, well, I think it's a fair enough exchange, for I keep myself clean and I give them good value. Does that make you want to stop being friends with me?" As Roxanne waited for an answer, it occurred to her that she would be very upset to lose her companion's friendship.

Helen thought for a moment, then shook her head. "Of course not! Nothing could! You've been the best of friends to me." She gave Roxanne a hug, as if to prove it, and was surprised to be drawn into her friend's arms and given a long cuddle, which ended with a smacking kiss on the cheek.

After which, Roxanne laughed at herself for being so sentimental and wiped away her tears. "That's good, then. Friends we'll stay. But I do think you should know how to stop yourself having any more children. He'll leave you if you do. You do realise that don't you?"

There was a moment's silence, then Helen swallowed hard and whispered, "Yes."

She fiddled with the edge of her apron as Roxanne spoke, but she listened carefully, for all her embarrassment and, afterwards, she went to the apothecary and bought some sponges to use for birth control. And in this, at least, she had Robert's whole-hearted support. It even made things go more smoothly between them for a while, for he had been terrified of lumbering himself with another blasted baby.

So the first year of young Harry Perriman's life passed. In spite of all the difficulties of her new life, Helen was still far happier than she had been when living with her parents. She had written to inform them of the birth of her son, but had never received a reply. This hadn't surprised her, but it had made her very thoughtful and, after a while, she asked Robert's permission to write to Lord Northby and inform him also, since he was a cousin, albeit a distant one.

"Why d'you want to do that? He hasn't done anything much for us, has he?" Except poke his damned nose into Robert's affairs and saddle him with a wife and child he couldn't afford.

"Oh, just in case – well, just in case it's useful for Harry one day to prove who he is."

Robert nodded slowly. Perhaps there was some more money in the family. He nodded. "Can't hurt, I suppose. Do as you please, my dear."

Lord Northby sent her an impersonal little note in return, thanking her for the information and enclosing a silver christening spoon for the infant.

Robert was unimpressed by the spoon. "That won't fetch much. I call it paltry."

"We shall never know how much it will fetch," Helen said coldly. "It's Harry's and shall be kept safe for him." As she spoke Helen looked so fiercely at her husband that Robert put the idea of selling the spoon out of his head. He was beginning to find her intractable on some points, and had learned that she did have a temper, slow to rouse, but which could turn her into a raging fury if he did anything that might upset the boy.

Once or twice, when Robert's luck was right out, they became very short of money. Only Helen's tiny quarterly income saved her and the baby from going without the necessities of life and she had to fight to get a share of that, even. Now, Roxanne did not need to remind her to keep some of her money secret. She had a reserve of coins hidden in the lining of her sewing basket and the thought of them was a great comfort to her.

She began to dread a certain look on Robert's face and to wish that he would not gamble quite so often or stay out so late drinking with his cronies. She also wished that he were a more loving father and that she had a proper home of her own with a little garden. Nothing grand – she would have been content with a cottage.

But she did not voice these wishes. She had married an actor and must take the consequences. Just as long as no harm came to Harry. That she would not stand for. And to give Robert his due, he was not actively cruel to the child.

In Bath, Robert fell ill, so ill that he could not go on stage. This was a rare occurrence, because an actor was always expected to play his part, as the members of Robert's company said to encourage one another, "Go on, even if it kills you." They always laughed and added, "Besides, the audience will never notice."

The understudy was hurriedly coached for the part and Robert lay fretting and coughing in bed, delirious half the time, with a raging fever. He made a poor patient, complaining about everything Helen did for him, objecting most of all to the noise little Harry made.

And for all Helen's devoted nursing, Robert got worse, not better. The company was to move at the end of the week, but there could be no question of him going with them. Another handsome young actor was engaged and everyone packed their boxes.

Roxanne came to their lodgings to say goodbye in a whirl of silks and furs (she had a new admirer, who was showering presents on her). She hugged Helen to her and said huskily, "I shall miss you, love, miss you a lot. And this little fellow too." She tickled Harry, who had crawled over to tug at her bright-coloured skirts, and he crowed and gurgled up at her.

"Can't you . . . keep that brat . . . quiet?" gasped the invalid.

Helen picked up her son and cuddled him, grimacing at Roxanne.

"I don't envy you," whispered Roxanne, seeing that Robert had dozed off again. "Is he always so bad-tempered?"

Helen's eyes filled with tears at this expression of sympathy, and she could only nod and cuddle her son more tightly. "I shall miss you too," she managed, after a while. "Never mind, though, perhaps we shall be together again once Robert's better and we can rejoin the company."

Roxanne fiddled with the lace on her bodice. "Yes, well, that's what I came to tell you. I'm leaving the theatre. As I shall be selling my share of it to Miles Barker, the company will probably re-form after Bristol. And – well, you know he doesn't get on with Robert."

Helen swallowed her disappointment. "Oh? I – didn't know you'd saved enough money to retire."

"I haven't. But my gentleman friend has offered to set me up in a house of my own and settle some money on me. It's a generous offer and I'd be a fool not to take it." She smiled grimly, "At least, I'm going to take it if the lawyers can agree. I'm not doing anything till it's signed and sealed."

"Oh." Helen tried not to look disapproving.

Roxanne smiled wryly. "I knew you wouldn't like it, love, but I'm not getting any younger, am I? I do have something saved, but not enough to live on in comfort for the rest of my life if I stop working." She laughed. "I've not been a great success as an actress. Oh, I'm competent enough, but I'm past my prime and I know now that I'll never be famous."

"I think you're a wonderful actress," Helen said stoutly.

"Thanks, love," Roxanne's face softened as she looked at her young friend, "but you're as bad a judge of acting as you are of husbands. Anyway, my Jack's well-heeled. He'll look after me for a while and, when he's gone, well, I'll still have the house he's buying for me. So – I reckon you'd better tell Robert," she jerked her head towards the bed, "to find himself another company when he gets better." If he got better. She really didn't like the looks of him. And that cough sounded bad. She'd heard coughs like that before and knew what they presaged. But she didn't say anything about that to her young friend.

Helen couldn't hide her anxiety about their future.

Roxanne decided to look on the bright side. Why face trouble before you had to? "Robert will be all right, don't you worry. His looks'll last a good few years yet, but be sure you make other plans for later on. He's not got a great deal of talent, so when his looks fade, he'll be out of a job."

Helen nodded. After over a year in the theatrical world, she did not need to be told that. "Yes. I see."

"Is that all you can say?" Roxanne demanded. She had expected tears and pleas not to be left behind.

"I – don't know what to say." Helen picked up Harry, who had put his thumb in his mouth and stopped crawling around. She cuddled him and concentrated on not weeping all over her friend.

"Well, you could start by saying that you won't disown me, and that you'll come and see me when you're in London." Roxanne tried to smile, but looked more like a woman about to cry. "You know, love, you're like the daughter I never had."

Helen set the baby down in his cradle and flung her arms round the only friend she'd ever known. "Oh, as if I would! Of course I won't disown you! And I'd love to visit you when we're in London! You've been more like a mother to me than my own ever was. I hope you'll be *very* happy with your – with Jack."

Roxanne wept a little more, dashed away the tears and insisted on taking Helen out for a farewell meal. After paying the landlady's daughter to keep an eye on the invalid and the sleeping baby, she swept Helen off to the nearest chop house. Over a nice plate of steak pie and boiled potatoes, she loaded Helen with as much shrewd advice as she could think of, and left her with the name of Jack's lawyer in London. He would know where to contact her.

When Helen got back, the baby was howling and Robert had taken a turn for the worse. Bleakly, feeling very alone in the world, she tried to make her husband comfortable.

Somehow, during the next few weeks, Helen found the strength to cope with the baby and the needs of her husband, as well as the complaints of the landlady and the problems of making the money last. Red-eyed for lack of sleep, she struggled through an interminable series of days and nights which blurred into one another.

She was near collapse herself by the time Robert began to recover, but she dared not give in to her weariness, for fear Harry would suffer.

As Robert improved, he grew more querulous.

"That damned baby never stops crying." He scowled at Harry.

Helen picked the child up and shushed him, rocking him until he was asleep.

When she served Robert some oat gruel, he flicked her hand with one fingertip and grimaced at it. "Your hands are all red and cracked. You look like a kitchen maid."

When she brought him more gruel later in the day, he pushed the spoon away. "Why do you feed me this slop? I want some proper food."

At that her patience snapped and she turned on him. "Shut up!" she screamed. "Shut up, shut up, *shut up*!"

Someone thumped on the floor above them.

Helen spoke more quietly, but the tone of her voice was still anguished. "You're worse than a baby! Lying there complaining! If you want better food, then give me some money to buy it, for I can afford nothing else. You won't eat well till you go out and earn something. I've nothing left – nothing! – and you haven't even got a job to go on to! The company's changed hands." She gasped and clapped her hand to her mouth. She had intended to wait until he was nearly recovered before telling him this.

"Closed down! Why didn't you tell me before?"

"You were too ill. I thought – I thought you were going to die." She fumbled her way round the bed, collapsed upon it next to him and buried her head in the pillow. "And I can't take any more, I can't, I can't!"

He realised that matters were serious and tried to pull himself together. Her sobbing penetrated his awareness, so he patted her heaving shoulders and kept murmuring, "It'll be all right. We'll come about. You'll see. I'm getting better now."

Gradually her sobs stopped and her breathing deepened. Mercifully the baby had fallen asleep, too. Robert lay there and thought things over. So he'd been that ill, eh? Good thing he'd had her to look after him, then. He owed her something for that. He eased himself off the bed. Helen didn't wake, only rolled over and muttered in her sleep. There was little sign of beauty about her now. She was stick thin, and her eyes had dark circles round them. Even her hair looked dull and lifeless. That's what marriage did to people, he thought grimly – took all the fun out of life. Gave them responsibilities they didn't want. He scowled at the sleeping baby. Stupid thing!

On legs that felt nearly boneless, he staggered over to the fly-specked mirror above the fireplace and studied himself in it. He looked even worse than she did. Not much sign of his good looks now. And he wouldn't get another acting job till he looked right again. He knew that as well as anyone. He had few illusions about his own acting capacities.

Feeling a sort of greasy nausea after even that minor exertion, he tottered back to the bed and flopped down on it. Look at him, couldn't even walk across the room! He'd definitely be dead if it wasn't for her. At that moment, Robert became convinced that with Helen to look after him, he could survive anything. And this conviction would stay with him for the rest of his life. Helen was – dash it, she really was – a sort of lucky piece for him. She even had money. Forty pounds wasn't much, but it was steady.

The next day, Robert began a deliberate programme of self-help. He got up several times to walk round the room, and sat for a while in a chair by the window, where he could get a bit of sun on his face. He always felt better when the sun shone.

"Here," he said later. "You'd better go and pawn my signet ring." He always kept it as a last resort, and considered it another lucky piece, for he had never yet failed to win it back again. "And for heaven's sake, bring back some proper food for us all."

"But – I don't know how to pawn things."

"I'll tell you. It's not hard."

She looked across at Harry.

"I'm quite capable of keeping an eye on the brat while you're out."

So she went and pawned the ring, then wandered on to the market to haggle over a piece of fish. Helen no longer enjoyed going to market nor did she feel a triumph when she picked up a bargain. It was merely something you had to do if you were to afford food. Furtively she picked up from the ground some pieces of spoiled fruit – bruised apples which still had good bits in them. These could be stewed for Harry. She saw a woman watching her scornfully and tears came to her eyes, but she didn't stop picking up the fruit. Harry had to be fed.

In two weeks, Robert had recovered enough to insist on dressing himself in some of his best clothes and going out in the evening to meet up with a few kindred spirits and maybe take a hand of cards. "Only, I shall need some money for a stake."

How she dreaded hearing those words! She kept silent as he looked at her.

"I know you've still got a few coins hidden away, or you wouldn't have managed all these weeks. I've always known about your little hoards. Roxanne's idea? I thought so. You wouldn't have thought of it yourself. Well, I don't mind. Comes in useful sometimes to have a reserve."

Her voice was cold and she felt as though she were speaking to a stranger. "I can't spare anything for your gambling, Robert. We need it all for food. You've got some money left from the ring. Use that."

"Not enough. And if I don't make some money, we won't have enough to pay the fares to London, where I can find another job."

Obstinately she shook her head. The thought of him losing everything they owned in the world made her feel sick with horror.

"If you don't give it to me, I'll tear your things apart until I find it! Where do you keep it?" His voice was quiet, but there was a sharpness in his words and in the look he gave her. As she made no move, he shrugged and took a step forward.

She glanced towards her workbox, glad she'd stitched the coins into the lining.

He laughed aloud and went to pick it up. "The money's in here, isn't it?"

Desperately she tried to take the box off him, but he pushed her away and tipped the contents on to the floor. He fumbled round the lining till he felt the coins and laughed in her face as the silver christening spoon and her last three guineas fell out. She had held on to the spoon through thick and thin, for it was not hers to sell, it was Harry's.

"Clever girl! Just what I need!" Robert put the coins in his pocket, picked up the spoon and studied it, then saw the expression on her face. "No, I think we'll keep that for a real emergency." He tossed it on the floor at her feet. "Just in case."

Picking up his hat, he sauntered towards the door, feeling the luck start to throb within him. "Don't wait up for me!"

Dry-eyed, Helen picked up the spoon and cradled it to her breast. "You're not having this," she muttered. "Never." After a few minutes, she gathered up the threads and pins and bits of ribbon Robert had scattered over the floor and sewed back together the torn lining of her box. From time to time, her eyes turned to Harry. The mere sight of him was a comfort.

Only when she had finished and arranged all the sewing materials neatly inside the box again did she speak her thoughts aloud. "I've not been clever enough! Roxanne was right. I can only rely on money from now on. And myself."

When Harry awoke, she fed him – for he was now weaned and becoming very active – on a piece of bread and butter and the last of the stewed fruit. Then she played with him for an hour, until he fell asleep. She could always put aside her own grief or anger when Harry needed her, and she made sure that the child had a lot of attention and love – from his mother at least.

Afterwards she examined everything she owned, looking for hiding places for her money. There must be several places from now on, so that Robert could never again find it all. Her petticoats, of course, and the belly of the toy dog she had sewed for Harry, perhaps. Oh, yes, her hoard should be well scattered from now on!

Robert came back in the early hours of the morning, flushed with success. He shook her awake and poured a pile of guineas on to the bed. "Didn't I tell you? Here, take back what you lent me and put it in your box. And take some more to pay for our rent and food. Only don't be mean with the food this week. We all need feeding up if we are to look our best for London. Now, go and put that sponge thing in. I need you."

"But Robert, I'm tired!"

He gripped her arm fiercely. "With or without the sponge. Your choice!"

She did as she was told, though she got no pleasure nowadays from this parody of love. She had long realised that a successful night brought him home with this urgent need upon him, while a bad patch left him uninterested in his wife's body. She had come to resent this blind need, which had nothing to do with love or tenderness, and was only a wild lusting for relief.

Five

The Perrimans went up to London the following week by stagecoach. The driver grumbled at the amount of luggage they had and charged them extra for it, after a few sharp words with Robert. Harry, fretting at being kept captive upon his mother's lap, alternated between roaring with frustration, wriggling like an eel (to the annoyance of the other passengers) and sleeping like a golden-haired cherub. After one of their stops for food, he was sick all over his mother, so that for the rest of the journey the other passengers complained about the smell. By that time, Helen was too weary to care.

Robert took no part in anything to do with his son and didn't address a single word to Helen unless she spoke to him. He might have been a complete stranger, just another traveller, and one who was very disapproving of the fractious child at that.

In London, however, he brightened up and took charge again. He summoned a cab with one flick of the wrist, which put him in a better humour, then deposited his wife and son at a seedy inn, where he seemed to be known.

When he had changed his linen and smartened himself up, he said casually, "I'll have to leave you for a while." He was already moving towards the door without waiting for a response.

Helen moved over to bar the way. "Robert, wait! Where are you going?"

"I need to go out, make a few inquiries about finding work."

He didn't look like a man searching for employment. He radiated what Helen thought of as his eager gambler's air. But it would do no good to say that. He'd only turn sulky. When he had gone, she sighed and turned her attention to Harry. After cleaning him up, she took him downstairs to the dining-room where she bought herself a meal and shared it with him. There she tried and failed to make friends with the landlady, a shrewish woman whose stringy body spoke the truth about her own cooking even before Helen had sampled it.

Back in their dingy bedchamber, she also did all she could – without success – to keep Harry quiet, expecting Robert back at any minute. In the end, she took the child out for a walk to distract and tire him. Not that he could walk properly yet, but he loved to go out, as he was a very inquisitive child. He was heavy to carry and she was still run down after nursing her husband, so when she returned, she was feeling more tired and depressed than ever. But at least the fresh air made Harry sleep, so she could rest. And she had bought some bread while she was out, secreting it under her cloak, so that the landlady would not notice it. She ate a slice dry for her supper, not feeling able to summon up the energy even to toast it on the fire, to add a bit of taste.

Robert did not come back at all that night and she kept waking up, worrying that he had deserted her and the boy. That she could even think such a thing showed, she thought despondently, how far apart they had now grown, how very unsuited they were. And, saddest of all, she felt that she could hardly blame him if he had deserted them. He was the last man on earth to settle down happily to marriage and to raising a family. She realised that now. The ignorant girl who had tumbled headlong in love with a handsome face now seemed like another person to her.

And yet this hasty marriage had brought some benefits to her. She had escaped her family and the threat of marriage to a man who turned her stomach, and for a time she had been very happy indeed. And whatever happened now, she would always have her son. All Robert had gained were two extra mouths to feed and the responsibility for two other lives which he had never sought. She wondered if he had ever really loved her. She rather thought not. She wondered if what she had felt for him had been true love and decided in the dark hours of that long night that she had only ever craved affection – something she had never known from her family – and that her feelings for Robert had been nothing more than that.

She wondered, as she sometimes did, if she should have obeyed her parents and married Mr Wintermaine. At least with him she would have had a comfortable life, and her children would have had a roof over their heads and good food in their bellies.

Yes, but they might have resembled Mr Wintermaine, said the stubborn voice which sometimes spoke inside her head when she tried to lie to herself, *and then you might not have loved them as you love Harry!*

She felt absolutely sure that the curate's children could not possibly have been as beautiful as Harry, so the fantasy of a secure home never lasted for more than a minute or two.

She slept well and in the morning things seemed a little brighter, the landlady a trifle less surly and even the food more palatable. Her gown had dried overnight and she thought the smell had gone from it now, so Robert would not feel ashamed to be with her. She would not have bothered to buy breakfast for herself, but the landlady clearly expected her to spend some money and, besides, Harry was hungry.

As she sat in the busy common room of the inn, watching the other travellers – and they were a seedy, furtive lot – Helen told herself she had been foolish to fret away the night with black thoughts. Of course Robert would not have deserted them. Of course he would come back today.

When they went back up to their room, she washed her hair and some of Harry's clothes, bribing the chambermaid to fetch up some water. Then she played with her son and tried to wait patiently for her husband to return. It was so hard to be patient, when she was eager to get out and see something of London! When worries would keep creeping into her mind.

Robert sauntered in around noon, looking very pleased with himself.

"Oh, I'm so glad you're all right!" exclaimed Helen. "I was worried when you didn't come back!"

He patted her shoulder, noting with approval that she was looking a bit better today. She'd done her hair and changed into a clean dress. She had looked awful yesterday, and smelled awful, too. He'd been ashamed to be seen with her. "I met a few friends. We had some drinks. I'm afraid I had a bit too much, for we cracked on till quite late. In the end, I felt decidedly bosky, so I slept on their couch. Cabs can cost a lot in London, especially late at night, and it's dangerous to go out on foot alone after dark."

His expression was at its airiest as he added, pretending to have a sudden afterthought, "You'll get used to my staying out overnight sometimes in London, I dare say. It's so much safer than walking back through the dark streets."

She nodded, wrinkling her nose, trying to trace the smell. Was it hair oil? It had a very flowery aroma to it, not the sort of perfume men usually wore. She hoped Robert had only borrowed some from a friend, for she could not bring herself to like it on him. "Yes, I suppose so," she said, seeing he was expecting some comment.

"So, wife, I've been busy on our behalf," he announced, lounging in the one comfortable chair and looking very smug.

He had not, Helen noticed, even looked at Harry, let alone said anything to him. But it would be no use pointing that out. You couldn't force a man to love his son.

"I think I've done rather well for us." He began to tick the items off on his fingers. "First, I've found us some lodgings. Two rooms, so that Master Harry can have his own sleeping place – or I can. Whichever we decide."

"How nice!"

He didn't even notice the sarcasm in her voice. "*And* I've found you some work. Same as before. Sewing costumes and all that."

She stiffened. "How kind of you!" He was supposed to have been looking for work for himself. And what was she to do with Harry while she worked?

He appeared quite unaware of her anger. "I thought you'd be pleased. Now you'll be able to hoard up your pennies again."

"Will I?" And for how long would she be allowed to keep them? He was avoiding her eyes, she could tell, which meant he had something to hide.

"And finally, best of all, I've heard of a couple of chances for me. My friends think it suits me to have lost some weight. It can only be a matter of time before I pick up a good part. With a better theatre company this time. The Marlborough was a bit run down and Roxanne was well past her best. A more skilful whore than actress, she was."

Helen dug her fingers into her palms. He was deliberately goading her. He loved to get her angry. In this mood, he was like a boy tormenting a puppy, or pulling the wings off a fly.

"But you've found nothing definite for yourself?" she pursued.

"My dear girl, after only one day back in town? No one is that lucky! You have to meet people. Show yourself around.

That sort of thing. Which reminds me, do I have a clean shirt?"

"Yes." She got it out without speaking and when he pulled a face at its wrinkled condition, she set her hands on her hips and looked him straight in the eyes, daring him to say anything. He didn't. The victory was small, but it gave her some satisfaction.

When she had packed their things, he summoned a cab to take them across London to their new lodgings. The vehicle smelt of unwashed bodies and mouldy straw, and Helen wrinkled her nose as she got into it. But she looked out of the window eagerly, amazed at how many people there were and how the streets went on and on and on.

As the journey progressed, Robert cheered up, for she kept asking questions about the places they passed and he clearly enjoyed the feeling of superiority as he explained them to her.

When she saw the lodgings, she was unstinting in her praise. Here, Robert had done well for them. A pleasant landlady, who picked up Harry for a cuddle. And two rooms, as well as the use of the small garden. One room was hardly bigger than a cupboard, but it was large enough for Harry and, as it abutted the kitchen chimney, it was warm, too. This proved a godsend, because April blew in cold and windy, coal was expensive and Robert still had no regular work.

Helen, however, had work in plenty, mending and altering the costumes for the New Moon Theatre, a nasty little place which produced melodramas so like each other that the same costumes could be used again and again, as long as they were kept mended, retrimmed from time to time, and altered as necessary to fit the constantly changing leading ladies. To Helen's relief, the landlady was happy to mind Harry for a shilling or two more.

Helen soon found out that the theatre also acted as a place of encounter for a better class of prostitute than those who haunted the street corners and that the actresses themselves were much in demand with the patrons, but when she complained of that to Robert, he stared at her as if she had lost her wits.

"What the hell does that matter? You earn your money honestly, don't you? No one's asking *you* to go a-whoring." He tittered as if the mere idea of anyone paying for her services was ludicrous in the extreme.

"But—"

"Anyway, you're not that much better than them, if it comes to that."

She gasped, so shocked at this accusation that she could not speak for a moment.

"After all, you used your body to trap me, didn't you? I shouldn't be surprised if you didn't fool me about being a virgin, too!"

Tears filled her eyes.

He smiled. It was fun to tease her. Still so naïve about everything – though that could be quite useful in a wife, of course, if a fellow wanted to find himself the odd bit of fun elsewhere.

"You know better than that," she said quietly, not even trying to wipe the tears away.

He felt a sudden shame, but refused to give in to it. "Well, I think you should just mind your own business at the theatre and let others mind theirs. Unless you want to earn a bit of real money for yourself the same way?"

She turned white and drew herself up. "I'd kill myself first."

"Pity. There's more money to be earned on your back than by plying your needle." But he hadn't really expected her to be sensible about that, even though one of his friends, who'd seen her, had said she'd do well.

When he went out, Helen sat down and covered her face with her hands, shuddering at the memory of that conversation. He had not been joking. He would have let her do anything for money. And no doubt blamed her for it afterwards, as well.

She rather thought later, as she tried to understand her changing feelings, that it was this conversation which wiped away the last traces of her love for him. But she was still tied to him, however much her morals were offended. She knew too little about London, and she and Harry would be vulnerable without a male to protect them.

But at least after that, Robert's sniping remarks lost much of their power to wound her, and she found that if she kept her face expressionless when he mocked her, he soon turned to some other topic of conversation.

Helen had to work long hours at the theatre and when the landlady was busy, she took Harry with her because she would not have trusted Robert to look after his son. In fact, he only came home nowadays for the occasional meal and she began to worry that he was on the verge of leaving them for good. He slept at the lodgings two or three nights a week, made love to his wife if he had been lucky at the gaming tables and had nothing better to do, and changed his linen there regularly, getting angry if there was not a clean shirt always waiting for him.

He was out gambling nearly every night, and was not even trying to find a job in the theatre but, luckily for her, he seemed to be doing quite well. Every now and then he would toss her a coin, even a whole guinea sometimes, and say mockingly, "Here you are, wife, for you and the boy."

A few weeks passed, then he began to do less well and the coins became few and far between. Some weeks he didn't even give her enough to pay the rent. She came home from the theatre one day with a tired, grizzling Harry to find her belongings scattered all over the room and her workbox lining slashed to ribbons. Robert had found the coins which she had deliberately left in there and a couple more she had sewn into her spare petticoat, but that was all.

She smiled grimly as she began to tidy up. *You'll never take my last penny again, Robert Perriman. If you won't think of your son, then I must.*

She said nothing to him about the incident when he came home again two days later, and he didn't mention it either.

When she felt she could face her friend again, Helen wrote to Roxanne via the lawyer, delivering the letter to his rooms herself one afternoon when the theatre had no work for her.

She enjoyed the walk across the city. Harry tottered along beside her on unsteady legs and from time to time she picked him up and carried him on her hip. She talked to him and he tried to form sounds in reply. They both enjoyed themselves very much indeed. He had learned to be quiet inside the theatre, and play with the toy dog she had sewn for him, but out of doors she encouraged him to talk and run about as much as he liked.

On the way back from the lawyer's she bought them both a hot potato from a street vendor and then, on a sudden impulse, called in at a little church near their lodgings to pray for a few moments. She had not been to church for a long time and was feeling increasingly guilty about it.

A lady was arranging a very small bunch of flowers on the altar and, when Harry went over to watch her, finger in his mouth, she began to talk to him and then to Helen. She was a plump woman, plainly dressed, with kind eyes and a ready smile.

"Are you new to the area, my dear?"

"We've been here for three months now. We have lodgings nearby. I – I haven't been to church for a while."

"That's a pity. I think you'd enjoy my husband's sermons. He's beginning to be well thought of in the district." She stared at Helen when she spoke, obviously assessing her status. "I'm sure my husband would welcome you into our congregation."

"Would he? Even though my husband is an actor?" asked Helen. Her own father would not have welcomed an actor's family into his church.

"What difference does that make? Our Lord was not too proud to associate with Mary Magdalene! And an actor is not dishonest in his occupation, however much some people disapprove of the theatre."

Tears filled Helen's eyes. "I'm no Mary Magdalene! Just a foolish parson's daughter who ran off to marry an actor and was disowned by her family!"

The woman made a soothing sound and shook her head in sympathy.

Helen suddenly realised why her son was quiet and dived to stop him. "No, Harry! No! Naughty!" Gently she disentangled the remains of some flowers from his chubby little fingers. "I'm so sorry! He doesn't understand. Let me see if I can do something with these."

Deftly her fingers rearranged the flowers, remembering the old skills acquired during the years of helping her mother to decorate the church with whatever could be found in the woods or in the parsonage garden.

"My dear, they look beautiful! Much better than I can ever manage! I wonder – would you like to help me with the flowers sometimes? I should be very grateful."

"Oh, I'd love to!"

After that, to Robert's loudly expressed amusement, Helen took her son to church on Sundays and helped arrange the flowers on the altar every Thursday, if she could manage it. Sometimes she would take a cup of tea with the incumbent's wife and perhaps chat with Paul Hendry himself when he had time to spare away from his busy parish.

Helen even confided in her new friends the dreadful fact that Harry had not been christened. Robert had no interest whatsoever in religion, no belief in anything but the urgency of his own needs. He had refused to bother about his son's christening and she had been too embarrassed by his attitude to go and see a clergyman on her own.

A small private ceremony was arranged to remedy this omission and "make a Christian of the boy" as Mr Hendry joked. But that raised the vexing question of who would stand as godparents.

Just as Helen had given up hope of finding anyone, Roxanne turned up again in her life, a plumper, richly dressed Roxanne, who spoke warmly of her Jack and seemed not to miss the theatre at all. She had received Helen's letter and had come to invite the family to take tea with her.

"Will you stand as godmother to Harry?" Helen asked on the first visit. "The poor boy has not yet been christened."

"Me?" Roxanne gave one of her hearty laughs. "What the devil do I know about being a godmother?"

"You know a lot about being kind and that's what matters." Helen tried to think of some way of persuading Roxanne, because her worst fear in the world was that something would happen to her and then, she was sure, Robert would abandon Harry without a second thought.

It took Helen a while to persuade her friend but, in the end, Roxanne agreed and even promised that if anything ever happened to Helen, she would look after the boy.

Paul Hendry volunteered to act as godfather, seeing Helen's shame and despair at being unable to produce one, so the formalities were more or less attended to. If only Robert had attended the ceremony, thought Helen wistfully, it would have been quite perfect, for dear Harry was so good, not crying at all when the man splashed water on his head, but laughing and trying to reach for the water in the font by himself, all the while observing everything with his bright little eyes.

Afterwards, Roxanne took her and the Hendrys out for a meal

at a respectable inn and bought a bottle of good red wine with which to toast the boy's health.

As she was leaving, Roxanne looked at Helen. "How about you and Harry coming over to tea sometimes? Got to keep an eye on him now, haven't I?"

"Oh, Roxanne, I'd love that."

"Good. I'll send Jack's carriage to pick you up on Monday. Can't have my precious godson walking all that way and tiring himself out, can I?" It was Helen's tiredness that worried Roxanne though, for her friend was thinner, and seemed nervous and slightly on edge all the time, as if waiting for something bad to happen.

Autumn came and Robert still had not found regular work in the theatre. Nor was he doing well in other ways. His luck had deserted him utterly, he complained, and he became very morose, staying away from home more and more, then reappearing gaunt and dirty. He would eat all the food Helen had, as if he had not been fed for days, then he'd sleep for a while and change his linen, before vanishing once again. Now he had completely stopped making love to her – to her great relief.

Harry stayed at the other side of the room when his father was around, staring wide-eyed at the strange man who snarled at him to be quiet if he so much as opened his mouth.

Helen now left most of her savings in Roxanne's care, for she had lost money a few times. Once, when the theatre was closed for redecorating, this arrangement had left her and Harry without much food for a day or two, because Robert stayed at home and she did not dare get out her hidden money.

Mostly, however, she managed to support herself and her son by her needle and her flair for designing costumes. "Seamstresses are ten a penny," the manager of the New Moon Theatre told his owners, "but Mrs Perriman knows what's needed on stage and can make a bit of cloth go a long way, changing a gown completely with only a few touches of trimming." That was why he paid her the princely sum of fifteen shillings a week. Yes, indeed, she had saved them all a lot of money with those costumes. She was worth more than fifteen shillings, if she only knew it, but thank goodness she didn't.

* * *

One day Robert came back and told Helen curtly that they'd have to move. "I can no longer afford such luxurious rooms."

She stared at him in puzzlement. "But it's very cheap here – and besides – I usually pay the rent, not you!"

"Well, I help out sometimes, don't I?"

"Not very often."

"Well, it'll be less often from now on."

"What do you mean by that?"

He began to look shifty. "I mean, I've got a few debts. I can't afford to help you any more. And," he didn't meet her eyes, "you'll need to move so that I'll know you're all right."

"We'll be all right here on our own, don't you worry!" She managed to speak without bursting into tears. She'd been expecting this news for a while, but it did not make it any easier to face. "I'd much rather stay here, though."

"Well, you'll have to move, for your own safety. And the boy's."

She gaped at him, one hand at her throat. "I beg your pardon?"

"You heard me. I meant what I said. You'll be *safer* elsewhere." He gave a short bark of laughter. "Oh, you're so naive! I owe money, you fool. There are some people who wouldn't scruple to try to get *you* to pay up. They might even take your possessions in lieu. Or your body. You'd fetch quite a bit as a whore if they dressed you up."

She looked at him in horror, tears filling her eyes.

"Don't look at me like that, you silly bitch! It's only a temporary setback. And I came to warn you, didn't I? I didn't leave you to face things on your own." Because she might come in useful again one day. After all, her quarter's income would be due in another month.

He tried to speak more persuasively. "Look, I'll help you to move, find a cheaper room. That's all I can do for you at the moment. When I come back—"

She pushed him away. "You're leaving us!" So it had come.

"Not exactly," he said soothingly, as if she were a child.

"What do you mean by that? Either you're leaving us or you're not! It seems quite straightforward to me."

"I don't know what I mean. I can't read the future, can I? Things'll improve again, then maybe I'll be able to come back.

I'll let you have something for the boy when I can, too. So I'm not exactly leaving you." He found, to his surprise, that he didn't want to lose touch with Helen completely.

She turned away from him and went over to stand by the window, staring out blindly at the grey sky and the whipping clouds. It would rain soon. Which seemed appropriate to her mood. "Just take your things and go. I'll find us somewhere else to live."

He shrugged. "I'll send for them this evening, then. You can pack my trunk. I'm no hand at that sort of thing. Leave word where you're going at that damned church. If – when things get better, I'll come and see you, let you have some more money. For the boy's sake." He stared across at the child, who stared back just as solemnly. Funny thing, having a son, he thought, but there was no doubt the lad was his with that hair.

"And that's the only reason I'll take it – for the boy. Go away! Leave us alone! I want nothing more from you, Robert Perriman."

He forgot Harry as he scowled at her. "It'd have been different if I'd been able to get a proper job in the theatre. We'd have been all right then. This is all Roxanne's fault."

"I don't think so. You'd have found some other excuse to leave us. You prefer your gambling to your wife and son."

Silence lay between them, thick with the ice of unspoken recrimination. "Please go, before Harry starts to cry," she prompted at last. Helen did not weep until her husband's footsteps had faded into the distance.

With Mrs Hendry's help, she found herself another room, a much smaller one in a house without a garden, but at least it was in a respectable street and it cost only half of what the other rooms had cost, so she could manage it quite nicely from her wages.

When she got back from looking at the lodgings, she found that Robert's things had gone, and so had another of her little hoards – also Harry's silver spoon. That upset her most of all, but she did not allow herself to give in to her grief until the child was fast asleep.

A week later she saw Harry's spoon for sale in the window of a pawnbroker's shop, so she took out some of her savings and bought it back again. She knew it was a foolish extravagance, but it was the only thing the child had to show that, on her side at least, he came of gentle stock. But she left the spoon with Roxanne afterwards – for safety.

One day, when the manager was paying out the wages, he shook his head when she went to collect her earnings. "Didn't your husband tell you? He came and picked your money up yesterday. Hey! You all right?"

She could feel her face turn white. It felt quite frozen with shock.

"He didn't tell you, did he?" the woman next to her said sympathetically. "Buggers aren't they, husbands? What did you give it to him for, Percy? She's the one who bloody earned it."

Helen waited till the others had gone, then begged the manager not to give her husband any more money. But he and Robert were cronies and every now and then he did so, for old times' sake.

"Why did you do it?" she would plead. "How am I to feed my son if you don't give me the money I've earned?"

"Oh, you seem to manage. It's just once in a while. I wouldn't do it too often. I know you need the money. But surely you don't want poor old Robert to starve?"

In the end, Roxanne found out about this and, after raging at Helen for not asking for help sooner, she spoke to her Jack about the problem. He went and saw the theatre manager, and he also traced and spoke to Robert.

Helen never found out what Jack had said, what threat he had used to stop Robert preying on her, but it was effective and, after that, her wages were not touched again. But the manager seemed disapproving, somehow, as if she was denying a natural law, and he would slap the money down on the table with a sarcastic, "There it is! Every penny."

She began to wonder how long he would keep her on at the New Moon now . . .

From then on, Helen managed well enough. Without Robert to feed, her money went a lot further. She never cared what she ate herself, having been brought up simply to clear her plate, whatever it contained. Harry was too small to eat a lot and she made his clothes from scraps of material she picked up cheaply. She was even saving a little money, just in case she fell ill, or Harry needed something.

One day, perhaps, she would have enough to set up a shop,

or maybe keep lodgings for gentlemen. Her ambitions for herself went no higher.

If Robert leaves you in peace, said the sharp little voice in her head. *If he doesn't turn up again . . .* "Well, if he does, I'll have nothing to do with him," Helen angrily responded aloud.

Hah! it replied.

Six

Helen celebrated her nineteenth birthday with Roxanne and, a few weeks later, in March 1838, she celebrated Harry's second birthday. Her life was hard, but not unpleasant, she decided that morning when taking stock. And she not only had her son but she had found a good friend in Roxanne. That was more than she'd ever had before.

She had heard nothing further from Robert since the day he left and he never sent her any money. Not that she had expected him to. She didn't try to find him. All she wanted was for him to leave her in peace, so that she could bring up her son decently – if not to be a gentleman, then at least to be an honest person.

But in July of that year, soon after the new young queen was crowned, Helen's peace came to an abrupt end. She and Harry came home laughing together one sunny evening, after a walk around some nearby public gardens, to find a figure collapsed across the doorway of the house in which they now lodged.

"Robert!"

He was thin and haggard, with hectic spots of colour in his cheeks. She hesitated, then went to help him into a sitting position.

"There you are at last!" he said in a husky whisper, coughing and spluttering as he tried to get the words out. "Where the hell have you been at this hour of the day? That damned dragon of a landlady wouldn't let me into your room."

"We've been out for our walk." She waited for him to look at his son, but he didn't.

He began to cough, long hacking scrapes of sound that made her throat contract in sympathy.

"What's the matter, Robert?" she asked when he stopped. "Why have you returned to me?" She knew something must be the matter to have brought him back.

"Been ill. Still am. If you . . . won't help me . . . it's the workhouse," he rasped, fighting against the need to cough.

She closed her eyes for a moment, but knew she could not turn him away. Roxanne would call her a fool, but she could not, she just could not turn away a sick man. This skeletal figure was the father of her son. Her husband.

"We'd better get you inside, then. You go up first, Harry, and open the door." She supported Robert up the stairs, amazed at how light he felt. She must have grown since they got married, too, for he was now the same height as she was. Quite a small man, in fact. Why had she not realised that before?

Climbing the stairs took all Robert's energy and when they got into Helen's room, he collapsed on the bed – without a word of thanks for her help – just lying there, gasping for breath. And he still hadn't even looked at his son. That hurt her most of all. She made him a warm drink, helped him sip it and soon he fell into a light doze.

Harry waited until Robert's eyes had closed before he spoke, for he knew, from the time he spent with his mother at the theatre, that he must not interrupt her when she was with other people. "Who's the man?" he asked then, in a piercing whisper.

"Shh! He's your father. He's not well, so he must sleep now. You sit quietly by the fire and play with your doggie, darling." She'd made the toy herself and it was the boy's favourite, for he loved all animals. One day, if things went well, she would get him a real dog, but not until they had a house of their own and a garden for it to play in.

"I'll find us something to eat, shall I?" she asked a few minutes later, realising she had been sitting there worrying about what Robert's return would mean. She tried to keep a cheerful tone in her voice, though she felt sick and apprehensive. She knew, somehow she knew, that this did not bode well for her and her son.

Grimly she did her evening chores, then set about preparing a makeshift bed on the floor for herself and Harry. Luckily the child thought this great fun, and rolled about on the bed with his toy dog until he fell asleep.

Helen woke Robert, fed him a little bread and milk, then lay down on the floor beside Harry.

But the worrying continued, thoughts going round and round in her head in the darkness. She would not share a bed with Robert again, she decided as the long hours dragged past. She had no love left for him now. She wondered if he would try to force her, but she didn't think she would have much to fear from this husk of a man. He was far too ill. And anyway, he only wanted her body after a winning streak. Not when he was losing.

She was bitterly sorry he had come back into their lives. She would not have cared if she had never seen him again.

It was a week before Robert was fit to talk about the future. After his initial collapse, he did nothing but sleep and eat. Sometimes he lay watching Helen with a look of puzzlement on his face; at other times, he watched his son, with the same faintly puzzled air, as if he could not believe that the sturdy little boy with the honey-coloured curls and rosy cheeks was his.

Harry scowled across the room whenever he noticed "the man" staring, and avoided going near him at all times.

Helen looked after her husband as well as she could, but refused to miss her work in order to stay with him, or to leave Harry alone with him at any time.

"You must manage as best you can during the day," she told Robert coldly the first day. "If I don't go and earn some money, we'll all starve."

He nodded, seeing the sense in that, and snuggled down under the covers. "Y're a good wife," he breathed as his eyes closed.

But she didn't feel like a good wife. She'd have been happy never to have seen Robert Perriman again as long as she lived.

Roxanne scolded her furiously when she found out from Harry that Helen had allowed Robert to come back into her life. "Have you run completely mad?" she demanded. "He left you to fend for yourself. He even stole the child's christening spoon – not to mention your wages, until my Jack put a stop to that. You've had no word from him for nearly eighteen months! Turn him out, for heaven's sake! Let him fend for himself! Best of all, run away. Go somewhere he'll never find you. I'll help you."

Helen sighed. She'd been very tempted to do just that. "I can't."

"Of course you can."

"No. He's still my husband, you see. I vowed in church to take him for better or for worse." At least, she knew she must have made those vows, for she could never remember much about the actual wedding ceremony. She gave her friend the ghost of a smile. "Blame the way I was brought up, Roxanne love. I can't lightly dismiss my sacred vows, even if he does."

"There's nothing sacred about vows made to Robert Perriman! You have to think of the boy now. Throw the scoundrel out. Or come and live here with me for a few weeks till he's gone."

But Helen shook her head. "No. I can't do that. I gave my solemn word, in church. I find – I find that I can't break that word now, however much my common sense tells me it would be the best thing to do."

"He'll just sponge off you until he's better, then he'll vanish again, probably taking everything you own with him."

For a second time, Helen shook her head, then she said slowly, "I don't think he will get better, Roxanne. Or not for long. He has – I'm almost sure of it – developed consumption. I've seen the disease many times. I had a lot of practice at visiting the sick when I lived with my parents. Robert's more ill than he realises."

"If he's that ill, think about Harry! You don't want the boy to fall ill, too, do you? Get rid of Robert for the child's sake, at least, even if you won't do it for yourself! Please, love!"

But underneath her quiet exterior, Helen remained stubbornly convinced that her duty was to look after her sick husband. "Harry never goes near his father. He doesn't like him. And Robert – well, he just lies there quietly and does as I ask. If he tried to – to cause trouble, hurt the boy, then I would leave him. I think he understands that. But he doesn't do anything." She sighed again. "He's so thin and tired. You would hardly recognise him."

Roxanne just sniffed and told her again that she was quite mad.

The next day Robert said abruptly, "They say it's consumption."

"Oh? Who are 'they'?"

"I went to see a doctor. A while ago now. Before my luck turned and I lost all my money. He said – he said it might help me to go and live in a warmer climate. The illness is in the early stages, you see. So I stand a fair chance of recovering if I can get away before the winter. I even thought," he laughed, a dry laugh that turned into a cough, "I thought I'd make it. I was on a good winning streak. But my luck turned. Amy, the woman I was living with, well, she nursed me for a while – then, when my money ran out, she left. The cursed landlady turned me out, too, the next day. They're all harpies, landladies are. Well, look at this one you've got here. Won't give me the time of day."

Helen ignored the reference to another woman. She didn't care about him in that way now, certainly not enough to be jealous. "How did you find me?" She had wondered, for she had told the Hendrys not to pass on her new address.

"Through the theatre. Knew you still worked there. Kept my eye on you, in my own way."

Only in case you desperately needed money, Helen thought. But he hadn't, so she'd had her godmother's money to herself. They'd lived very comfortably, really, she and Harry. Not grandly, but with warm food and clothing, and a roof over their heads. It was all she asked of life.

He stared at her for a moment. "Didn't think you'd take me in like this. But there was nowhere else to go. So I took a gamble. And I won." He smiled at her and nodded several times. "I reckon my luck must have turned again." Another pause, then, "Why did you do it? Why did you take me back?"

"Not because your luck had turned!" Her voice was sharp and for a moment it reminded her of her mother's voice, the last time Helen had seen her. That made her shudder and try to speak more gently, as she added, "I did it because you married me. Or had you forgotten? And because of the vows I took. I meant them, you know. *For better, for worse.*" There was silence, then she said thoughtfully, "It's been mainly for worse with us, though, hasn't it?"

He flushed and closed his eyes. His face was pallid and covered with sweat. His hair had lost its lustre and hung damply on his forehead, like dirty smears of butter. After a while he said stiffly, "I never meant to – to hurt you, you know. I didn't even set out to seduce you." Well, not exactly. "It just – happened. You were – you still are – very lovely."

She patted his hand, feeling more like his mother than his wife. "And I was too ignorant to realise where it would all lead." She let out a bitter laugh but couldn't hide her pain and her laughter soon turned to sobs. "I didn't even know how babies were made in those days. What a stupid little fool I was!"

To Helen's surprise, a tear of sympathy trickled down Robert's face. "But you were so very beautiful, with your hair spread across your shoulders. I can still remember those woods."

It was a while before either of them spoke again.

He jerked into a more upright position. "Helen, this is the second time you've saved my life, nursed me better. Perhaps I have got lucky again. And if it doesn't work out – going to the sun, I mean – then you'll be rid of me for good one day."

She put down her sewing. "It'll do you no good to get maudlin." She spoke quietly but firmly, and her words jerked him out of his self-pity and back into a state of dull resentment at how unfeeling she was. It wasn't much fun when a woman was so sensible.

"Better to concentrate on ways of finding the money to send you to a warmer climate."

He stared at her. "You'll still help me – do that?"

"If I can." But she didn't intend to go with him.

He swallowed convulsively. "I'll not go without you, though."

She could not believe her ears. "Why ever not?"

"Because – because I think you're lucky for me. I should have stayed with you before." Helen felt herself tense up, unable to utter a single word. Another long heavy silence, which always seemed to punctuate their conversations, followed. When Robert eventually spoke again, his voice was gentle. "And because you saved my life. I think – I really do think – that if I leave you again, I shall die. With you, I stand a chance of living." His only chance.

Her head was bowed over her work. She did extra personal sewing and mending for some of the actors. In fact, she sewed in every spare minute she could find and her fingers were always roughened where she had pricked them with the needle. Looking down at the sewing, Helen hoped Robert couldn't see the dismay on her face. She had learned the hard way how much importance gamblers placed on their luck. But she did not stop sewing, even though this was such an important conversation. "I had not thought to go with you," she managed at last. "Nor had I desired it."

"Well, I'm not going anywhere from now on without you!" He might have been a child, clinging to its mother's skirts. "Besides, I don't even speak the language over there! You do! You speak excellent French, thanks to that blasted mother of yours."

"But we haven't the money to send *you*, let alone the three of us!" And I don't want to go, she thought, oh, I don't! I'm happy here, with just me and Harry. But she did not say the words aloud.

"Only wait till I'm better! I've still got my signet ring. I always keep that for when the next run of luck starts. I'll pawn it and get a stake. You'll see. The guineas will start rolling in again."

His cheeks were poppy red, his eyes glittering feverishly. She did not dare excite him more by arguing with him. "We'll see," was all she could manage.

He captured her hand. "Just help me to get me better, Helen, then I'll look after you, both of you. I know you won't leave the boy." It was as if Harry were no connection of his.

That night she lay awake on the makeshift bed, not feeling the hardness of the floor but agonising over the decision she might have to make.

So torn was she between conscience and common sense that on the way home from the theatre the next day, she called in to beg Mr Hendry to advise her.

Gravely, he listened to the full story of her marriage, while Harry played outside in the garden, then he bent his head in thought. When he raised it, his eyes were sad. "My dear, it's not easy, but you must keep your marriage vows. You took the man for better or for worse. In sickness and in health. For richer or for poorer. Those phrases are quite explicit. I only wish I could say something different, find a solution which would be easier for you – and better for the boy."

She looked down at her clasped hands, seeing only a pink blur. "I knew the answer really. I just – didn't want to admit it."

When she managed a smile, he thought it one of the saddest he had ever seen.

"I don't care for myself," she went on. "It's Harry I worry about, you see. I can accept the consequences of my own foolishness—"

"Ignorance," he corrected. "And the ignorance was not your fault."

She shrugged. "Whatever you care to call it – I can keep the promises I made before God, but it's hard to see a child suffer."

As Mr Hendry showed her to the door, he offered the only comfort he could. "Margaret and I will both pray for you. But, at a more practical level, if you are ever in need – well, we can always offer you the shelter of our roof."

"Thank you."

That offer warmed her as she walked home. How kind! How very kind! And there was Roxanne, too. Helen was sure her friend would help her if she were ever in need. God had been very good to her.

When Harry was asleep the next evening, Helen took her sewing over to the bed. "We need to talk, Robert."

"Come to tell me of your decision, fair gaoler?" he asked, trying to make a joke of it.

But she could see the fear lurking in his eyes. She could see it quite plainly and that made her decision easier, somehow.

"Yes. I've decided to do as you wish. I've decided to stay with you."

"Ha! Told you my luck had turned." His voice was triumphant. He tried to take hold of her hand, but she moved it away. "You won't regret it, Helen. I promise you won't regret it. Things'll be different this time. I know they will."

She took a cloth and wiped his forehead. "There is just one condition."

"Anything!"

"I could not share a bed with you again. I – just could not! Not after the other women."

He scowled, forgetting his gratitude. "I'm not poisonous! I'll recover, you know. And there weren't that many other women. I'm not diseased."

"Yes, I believe you. But my feelings won't recover, not in that way. I don't love you any more, Robert. So I must warn you that if you ever try to – to force me, then I shall leave you. Immediately. Within the hour. I cannot do that sort of thing without love."

He shrugged. "If that's the only condition, you've no need to worry. I've never forced myself on a woman yet. Besides, we couldn't risk having another child, could we?" He scowled across at Harry. "One's more than enough."

She did not make the obvious retort, that he had never looked after Harry in any way, never shown any interest in being a father. *I feel* as if I have two children, Helen thought, looking at her husband. What had happened to the handsome, laughing man she had married? What had happened to her, come to that? She felt old – so very old and tired. But there was Harry – he made up for everything.

Thanks to another lucky gambling streak that had her husband crowing with triumph at the return of his luck, Helen spent her twentieth birthday in Calais. She didn't mention to Robert that it was her birthday. She had nothing to celebrate, after all. It had been a smooth crossing but, even so, Harry had been unwell, turning white and fractious before the boat had even left the harbour.

When they disembarked, they found a cheap *pension*, dined early and surprisingly well, and went to bed. Although Robert and Helen shared a big bed, he made no attempt to touch her, but he smiled wryly when she looked at him watchfully as they undressed.

In the morning they began their long journey to the south of France, travelling by easy stages in the cheapest ways possible, often by carrier's cart. When Robert began to look tired, Helen would insist that they rest for a day or two. It was better for the boy, too. Harry, who was not a good traveller, grew almost as tired of the jolting as his father did. He was a good child in every other way, though, such a joy to his mother, even now. Helen took care to point things out to him, talking about the countryside they were passing through and teaching him a few French words every day. She did not want him to grow up ignorant of the world around him. But she had to hide the pride she felt, because Robert easily became jealous of his son and that made him spiteful. It must be wonderful, she thought wistfully, to have a husband who cared about his child. But perhaps she was expecting too much from life. Her experience had not included that sort of man.

Twice they met up with men who shared Robert's taste for gambling. Twice he came back to their room flushed with success. "See what good luck you've brought to me! Didn't I tell you things would improve?"

Why did he always ascribe his success to her? It made her feel uneasy. Would he blame her for his bad luck, too? Good luck never lasted. She knew that by now.

But some of the recklessness seemed to have gone out of him. He didn't return to the game on the following night on either occasion, but said he'd not push his luck at the moment, just use the money he'd won to continue the journey.

It was cheaper to live well in France than it was in England. The meals at even the poorest *auberge* were usually excellent. A couple of times Helen managed to earn a little money herself, or payment in kind, which was just as good. It was nothing like as much money as Robert had won, but it was enough to pay for a meal or for their room.

Once, when a maid was ill at an inn bursting with guests, Helen helped in the kitchens and served at table. She had no shame in offering her services, but explained quite frankly about her husband's illness and their need to conserve money.

The second time, they stayed on a few days at another inn and she sewed for their keep. The landlady's daughter was planning to be married, the village seamstress had just died and so Helen volunteered her help. Robert was tiring again and needed a rest, so he was very willing to stop. Harry was sent to play with the ostler's children, and seemed to get on with them well, experiencing few problems despite the language differences.

Indeed, everywhere they went, Harry was petted and made to feel welcome. He soon began to use French words without seeming to differentiate them from the English, which annoyed his father, who had no gift for languages. The little golden-haired boy enchanted the women and amused the men with his precociousness. He was also a passport into conversations with strangers and therefore into chances of finding cheaper means of transport or accommodation.

As the weather improved and they drew nearer to the Mediterranean, Helen found to her surprise that she was enjoying herself. It was an adventure. Robert was exerting himself most of the time to be a pleasant companion, and not grumbling too much at setbacks. And Harry, dear little Harry, was thriving on the fresh air and the stimulation of travel, growing apace and enjoying himself hugely.

At Avignon, however, the enjoyment stopped abruptly. They had a disagreement because Robert wanted to make for Nice and Helen refused. This developed into their first big quarrel since leaving England. There would be too many rich people wintering in the sun at Nice, from what she had been told, which meant too many chances for Robert to find a cosy little gaming house or a group of fellows who wanted to test their skill with the cards or the dice.

"If you want to get better," she insisted, "really better, we must go somewhere quiet and live very simply. You still get tired easily, Robert. You know you do!"

He hunched one shoulder and turned partly away from her, as if he could not bear to look at her. "We'll die of boredom if we stay somewhere with no congenial company."

"And you'll die of other things, if you don't give your body a chance to recover! Anyway, I refuse to go to Nice! We can't afford it. So if you go there, you go alone."

In the end, they compromised on a city called Beziers, which a chance acquaintance had praised. It was an old town in the south west of France, large enough to offer Helen a chance of finding employment, yet near enough to the Mediterranean to have a mild winter climate.

When they arrived, Robert was not impressed. "The place is too damned quiet for me. What if it does have a very old cathedral? The place looks ready to fall down to me. In fact, someone ought to knock it down."

But Helen looked round and decided she liked Beziers, especially when they found two tiny rooms that belonged to a friendly widow in a narrow little side street. Madame helped Helen find employment teaching English and soon she had so many private pupils that Robert condescended to teach a few of them as well. He was not good with the younger children, but he was very successful with the teenage girls, and even more so with one or two ladies who had decided to alleviate their luxurious boredom by learning English from "*ce cher monsieur Perriman*".

Helen did not inquire too closely about Robert's linguistic progress with these ladies and closed her ears to any hints of extra-curricular activities. As long as he left her alone, she didn't care if he bestowed his attentions on others. He had regained something of his good looks, only now he was slender, with large brilliant eyes, which somehow made him appear a very romantic figure. He even obtained a commission posing for an aspiring artist as the young David about to kill Goliath. He and Helen laughed together over this, but she and Harry never saw the money he received for it and it didn't stay long in Robert's pocket either.

By the end of the winter, Harry had grown several inches and could chatter in both English and French. The widow with whom they lodged had taken a great fancy to him and willingly looked after him most of the time, for he was the same age as Madame's grandson, whom she only saw once or twice a year. The two of them would do the marketing together, or play long complicated games.

But all the time, Helen felt deep within her that the whole interlude was just a breathing space, a pause before life rushed her on again. She continued to hoard what little she could save and to hide her money very carefully about her person. She would never trust her husband again, however pleasant he seemed. But at least she was feeling well and energetic. And so was Harry.

During the winter, Robert had found new ways of gambling again – very small amounts at first, on card games or even dominoes in the local café. He enjoyed any game of chance and even a small win would put him in an expansive mood. "A fellow needs a bit of fun," he kept telling Helen, "else what use is life."

By the end of the winter, he was out more evenings than not, and they had had several nasty little quarrels when he lost the money he had earned from teaching English, instead of giving it to Helen for their living expenses. Madame tut-tutted at this and slipped Harry little titbits, but sometimes Helen was at her wits' end to find food for herself and her son without dipping into her precious savings.

By May, Robert had made up his mind to move on to Nice, whatever his wife said. The quarrels over this raged for days, and Harry spent a lot of time shivering under the table in Madame's kitchen.

In the end, Helen refused to discuss it any more, telling Robert to go to Nice on his own, if it was so important to him, and leave her where she was. She could, she felt, settle down quite happily in Beziers.

But he would not even consider leaving her. She was, he repeated obstinately, his lucky piece. Without her, he never won for long and he became ill.

One day, driven nearly to screaming point, she shouted, "You don't honestly believe that! You can't!"

"Oh, but I do! That's what makes me a successful gambler. I *know* that I must have you with me. You *are* my luck!"

"You're utterly ridiculous!" And he was *not* a successful gambler, so how he could think she brought him luck, she did not know. But she didn't say that. It would only have made matters worse.

"And you, madam wife, are being as stubborn as a mule! But I *will* get you to Nice. It's the only place to be!"

A week later, Helen came home to find Madame in tears. *"Il a pris mon petit ange!"* she wailed as soon as Helen entered the house.

Helen stopped dead in the hallway, a sinking feeling making her legs seem suddenly too heavy to move. It was a moment before she could even speak. "What do you mean? Where's Harry?"

More tears, with the words barely distinguishable. *"Il est parti!"*

"Gone! What do you mean 'gone'?"

"Monsieur said you knew all about it, that it had been arranged between you. But I knew it was not so, or you would have told me. I tried to stop him. *Ah, mon petit ange, où es-tu maintenant?"*

Helen swallowed hard and asked in a voice which trembled, try as she might to keep calm. "Please tell me quickly what happened!"

"*Eh bien*, your husband, he grow angry, shout at me. And then he take the child away. And the poor little fellow was screaming and kicking." Madame collapsed again, sobbing loudly into her apron. *"J'ai fait tout mon possible!"*

Helen turned and without a word to Madame, ran up to their rooms, dreading what she would find there. No sign of Harry or Robert. One of their two wicker trunks was missing altogether, as were Robert's clothes and some of Harry's. On the floor behind the door she found the toy dog, which Harry took with him everywhere. How would he sleep without Dodo? Where would he be sleeping that night? She picked the limp creature up and pressed it to her breast, but would not allow the tears to start. Not yet. Now she had to think, to make plans to find her son.

First she looked for a note. Robert must have left one, for he would want her to follow. It was ten minutes before she found the tiny scrap of paper he had used. It had fallen off the mantelpiece into the hearth. She had nearly missed it. Her heart went cold at the thought and her hands were trembling so much that she had to spread it on the table to read it.

Harry and I will be waiting for you in Nice. Inquire at Le Chat Gris, near the Town Hall.

No signature, no reassurances that he would look after the child.

She paced up and down the room, feeling quite sick with rage at him and his selfishness. How dare he take her son from her? How dare he? But she soon admitted to herself that, as usual, Robert had got his own way. She must now wind up their affairs here in Beziers and follow him to Nice. And as soon as possible. He was no fit person to be in charge of a child.

Seven

"Bad man!" Harry had said, when his mother found them. "Bad man!" And he continued to infuriate Robert by repeating this catchphrase whenever he was particularly upset by his father's high-handed behaviour.

"About time you taught that young devil some manners!" Robert complained, when Helen arrived in Nice. "Threw his porridge at me this morning, he did. See if you can get my blue coat clean, will you? I have to go out tonight."

Not a word about the way he had taken Harry away from her, let alone a greeting or an apology. "If you ever take my son away from me again," she said, blocking the doorway for a moment and speaking quietly, but with grim determination, "I shall leave you – whether you're ill or not!" She hugged Harry close and he clung to her like a limpet.

Robert snapped his fingers in her face. He was always one for a stupid theatrical gesture. "Been finding out a few things about that, my pet. As his father, I get to keep the boy if you walk out on me, for whatever reason. So don't try anything, or you'll be sorry! Now, have a look at my coat, for heaven's sake, or I'll be late."

Horror made her blood run as cold as ice water in her veins. She closed her eyes for a moment and bit back further threats. What was the use? Robert had changed, even in a few days. He was not only more confident, he was feverishly intent on his own concerns. He had made friends with a set of "good fellows", who preyed upon the rich visitors to Nice and these new companions seemed to have brought out the worst in him. He might never have had an acting career. All he thought of now was, as he phrased it, "living off my wits".

The Perrimans spent the whole summer in Nice. As there were

a lot of foreigners there, it was not as easy for Helen to obtain employment teaching English. Instead, to Robert's great annoyance, she offered her services as a seamstress.

"What does it look like, *my* wife taking in sewing?" he raged. "What'll people think?"

"No one knows us here, so they won't *think* anything."

Harry sidled behind his mother and hid his face in her skirt. The time he had spent alone with his father had upset him very much indeed and he had hardly left Helen's side since her arrival.

"They know *me*! How can I play the part of a gentleman if you insist on taking in sewing?"

"You'll manage somehow." A gentleman! He was the antithesis of this ideal.

"And anyway, there's no need!" He flung a coin at her, catching her on the finger and cutting it. "See! I've plenty of money. So you don't *need* to work!"

She picked up the coin and sucked the blood from her finger. "I prefer to work. For when your luck turns again."

"Damn you, don't talk like that! You'll *make* it turn!"

She shook her head helplessly. You couldn't reason with him on the twin subjects of luck and gambling. She tried to turn the conversation to something less fraught with conflict. "Shall I look around for some other rooms? These are nice, but they're expensive – and it's not a good place for Harry. It's very noisy."

"Certainly not! I like it here. It's very convenient for me. I'm the head of this family, and it's about time you started doing what I say."

It was convenient for his gambling, he meant. She found the place very noisy and there was nowhere outside for Harry to play safely. "Well, as long as you can pay the rent, we'll stay," she said, as quietly as ever. "But if you can't, I shall find somewhere else. I can't afford to keep up a place like this."

"It's *me* who is paying and I *can* afford it!"

There was just no reasoning with Robert since he'd come to Nice. And it was certainly the longest winning spell she could remember. But she knew – oh, yes, she knew in her bones – that it couldn't possibly last.

Whenever she had time, Helen took Harry for walks or to play on the beach. He was tall and strong for his age and he possessed, like his father, she was forced to admit, a great deal of charm. He had his father's wavy hair and bright blue eyes, too, but he also had, she thought, a certain strength of character, young as he was. Anything he started to do, he must finish, and he wept bitterly if he failed. He was devoted to his mother but disliked his father, who rarely did anything but shout at him to keep quiet.

And although for the whole of that summer, Robert's wits and his luck served him well, he regained none of the weight he had lost and his cheeks were rarely without a hectic flush. He grew tired easily, too. She had no need to worry about him pressing his attentions upon her, because he was always exhausted when he came home. They didn't share a bed, because he often slept badly, sweating a lot and blaming it on "this damned heat".

In the autumn there was a fight and some sort of scandal at one of the cafés which had a back room devoted to gambling. Robert came home looking dishevelled, with a bruise on his cheek and announced abruptly that they were going to winter further south. She'd better pack. He'd got them tickets for the following morning on the early stage coach to Milan.

"Milan! But – what shall we do there?"

"I have a position waiting for me if I want it. I've been thinking about going for a while now. I'm fed up with Nice, and they say Milan is a big city, very modern."

Stunned, she could only stammer, "But – neither of us speak Italian! How shall we manage?"

"Oh, you'll learn the lingo soon enough. They tell me it's very like French, and look how good you are at speaking that!"

"But how shall we—?"

"How, how, how," he mimicked, smiling knowingly. "We shall manage as we always do, you fool. By using our wits. Though I've got quite a bit of money saved this time."

That was news to her. He'd been short of money only two days ago.

He gave her a push. "Stop worrying and start packing! I've got things all worked out."

Helen looked at her sleeping son and wondered how she could get him away from this uncertain life, where they never stayed more than a few months in one place. To think that she had once longed to travel!

As if he read her thoughts, Robert came over to stand beside her and stare down at the boy. "Don't try anything stupid, my pet! Remember, the law is on my side. Even the clothes you're wearing belong to me, legally."

"Why can you not let us go? You don't love us. We're just a burden to you! I can support Harry and myself." She touched his arm, her eyes pleading with him. "Please, let us go, Robert. You'll be happier without us."

He threw her hand off. "I've *told* you why I need you. You're my luck! So I'll put up with the boy. And if you ever try to get away from me, I'll make sure that you don't see him again. I'll put him somewhere you'll never be able to find him. A father has very wide powers over his children, you know." He began to cough, a racking cough that went on for a long time. "Must have caught another damned cold," he muttered, when it subsided.

Silently she handed him a drink of cold water, and he raised it in a mock toast to her. She watched him sip it. "You need to rest, Robert. Can we not postpone our departure?"

"I'll rest when we get there. We're better off away from Nice at the moment. I don't know why the French want to get it back from Savoy. It's a very overrated place, if you ask me."

What had he done now? Why must they leave in such a hurry? Feeling sick with worry, she set about packing.

They had to get off the stagecoach before they got to Milan, however. Robert's cold settled on his chest, the cough worsened and the other passengers complained. At the next stop, a small town about fifty miles from their destination, the coachman threw their luggage off and them with it. Feeling sorry for the tired-looking woman with a child so young and a husband so sick, he gave them back the balance of their fare. It was obvious this man would not make old bones, then the poor woman would have to shift for herself.

One of the passengers, who spoke a little French, told her there was a convent in the town, a nursing order. They should go to the good sisters for help.

The innkeeper took one look at Robert and refused to take him in, but he did make signs that he would let Robert wait with the luggage in a corner of the stables. Robert, dizzy with exhaustion and fever, sat slumped on his trunk.

"*Suore,*" repeated the innkeeper several times. "*Il convento è là.*" He shook Helen's arm and pointed. Then he pointed to Robert. "*Ospedale!*" He shook his head. "*Molto malato.*"

If she followed correctly what he was saying – and it did resemble French – the nuns and the convent were in that direction, and there was a hospital. She took Harry's hand. "*Grazie, signor!*" She had already picked up a word or two, of necessity. "Come along, Harry. Let's find somewhere to stay."

"Bad man!" said Harry, scowling at the hunched figure of his father.

"Shh!"

The convent was bare and immaculately clean. Its quiet and sense of peace made Helen long to sink into a chair and sleep for a week. Instead, she had to try to explain what was wrong to an elderly nun, who kept pinching Harry's cheek in a way he obviously disliked.

"Doesn't anyone speak English?" she asked after a while, when she didn't seem to be making any headway. "*Inglese.*"

"Ah!" The nun clasped her hands together. "*Un momento.*" She vanished.

Helen sat there and the minutes ticked away. She began to worry. Surely the sister wouldn't just have left them here? Then, another nun appeared, a rosy dumpling of a woman. "Sure, they said there was an English woman here," she teased, by way of a greeting. "And that's nearly as good as being Irish."

At the sound of her native tongue, Helen burst into tears and Harry immediately followed suit.

To the kindly nun, Helen at last managed to explain what the problem was. She wept harder in sheer relief when the sister agreed to help her fetch Robert to the hospital. "You poor thing. You're exhausted! Come on, my dear, leave your husband to Sister Clara. I've told her what's wrong. Let me find you and the boy a place to rest."

Oh, the relief of being put to bed and cosseted, of having the burdens lifted from her shoulders, even if only for an evening! Helen was installed in a small, very simply furnished bedroom, with a truckle bed set up beside her for Harry. She was fed hot soup, then a plate of something called pasta, covered in a delicious sauce.

Later, Harry was bathed in a large bowl in front of the fire by the same plump nun, whose name was Sister Concepta. No sooner had she seen him fall asleep, toy dog clutched to him, than Helen relaxed into a deep sleep herself.

She did not awaken from it until the following afternoon. There was no sign of Harry, no noise and bustle, no sewing to be done, no jolting coach and best of all, no demanding husband. She sighed and lay there drowsily, reluctant to get up and break the spell.

Sister Concepta tiptoed in a little later. "Ah, you're awake now, are you? Good! I'll fetch you something to eat."

"Harry?"

"Eating a piece of bread in the kitchen and playing with the kittens. That's a fine child you have there, my dear."

"And – my husband?" She wished she didn't have to ask this, wished she need never see or think of Robert again.

"He's in our hospital. We're doing all we can for him." When Helen just stared at her, she asked delicately, "Do you – er – know how ill he is?"

"Yes."

The sister patted her hand. "It must be hard for you, to see your husband gradually getting worse . . ."

"The hardest thing," said Helen bluntly, "is that he *is* my husband! He is not a – a kind, or even an honest man. And he's a gambler."

"Ah. Like that, is it?" The sister squeezed her hand. "Well – the Lord's will be done."

"Yes. The Lord's will. I've kept my marriage vows, but it can be hard."

"It will be for the best in the end. You'll see."

Helen could not imagine how anything that had happened could possibly be for the best, but later, as she sat thinking, she realised that only Robert could have given her Harry, and Harry was worth everything she had suffered. Everything. So perhaps that was what Sister Concepta had meant.

The next day Helen was summoned to see the Mother Superior, an austere-looking woman who questioned her curtly about her circumstances, with the help of Sister Concepta. The Mother agreed not only to let Robert stay in the hospital, but also to give Helen and her son the use of a room, in return for Helen's help with whatever tasks there were.

"Some of them will be dirty," warned Sister Concepta.

"I'm no fine lady. I've always had to work hard to feed and house my son. As long as he's all right, I care little about myself. I'm a good seamstress, and I can scrub a floor. Whatever you need." She said nothing about the coins sewn into her petticoat.

She found the convent a very soothing place to stay and took to sitting in the chapel when her day's work was over. Sometimes she prayed; sometimes she just sat and let the peace wash over her; and sometimes she listened to the sisters' exquisite singing. The voices soaring up into the darkness of the vaulted roof were so pure and beautiful, they often brought tears to her eyes, and even Harry, young as he was, would sit quietly and listen with her.

After two weeks, Robert began to improve, confounding all the sisters' dire prognostications. But he was even thinner than before and he didn't lose the cough completely. He hated the convent, was often rude to those caring for him and, as soon as he possibly could, he left, dragging his wife and child off to Milan.

"If I don't turn up, they'll give the position to someone else," he kept saying. "Why did you get off that coach? I could have rested in Milan just as easily."

The position he had spoken of so glowingly was in an establishment totally devoted to gaming. The hard-faced proprietor found it useful to have an English "gentleman" available to chat to the visitors from whom he took so much money. He claimed it lent a better tone to the place.

Robert seemed to feel that he could play the part of a gentleman to perfection, but his tales of the tricks used against the hapless visitors disgusted his wife. How had she been so blind as to marry this man? Why had her parents kept her so ignorant of the world? She would not, she vowed, keep Harry ignorant. She would tell him everything about their lives as soon as he was old enough to understand.

It was a hard winter in Milan, and the colder it became the more Robert coughed. In February, even he admitted that they must move on again to a milder climate. "Damned nuisance, this cough! But I haven't caught another cold, have I? I'm over the worst now. If I can only get away from these biting winds, I'll be fine. You'll see."

Helen made no attempt to argue with him. If he wanted to

fool himself, then let him! Anything to make him easier to live with! For as his health deteriorated, Robert's temper became more uncertain. He had hit her several times recently, in sudden fits of rage – and once, once only, he hit Harry.

When that happened, she had seized a knife from the table and threatened him with it. "If you lay one finger on my son again, I'll kill you."

He laughed in her face. "You're not the sort."

She pushed her face right against his and spoke softly but viciously. "Try me, then. I promise you, I mean it. I'll do anything to protect Harry from you. Anything, including murder."

For a moment everything hung in the balance, then muttering something about she-wolves and vixens defending their young, he swung out of the room.

After that, he left the boy alone and took his ill humour out on her alone. That upset Harry almost as much, anyway.

Again, they had to move suddenly, still heading south. Rome was cold and dirty, also very expensive. Robert took another of his dislikes to it and they left after only a few days, to Helen's relief.

During the following two weeks, they made their way further south by easy stages, moving from one small town to another. Robert won small amounts here and there, and Helen occasionally helped out at the inns, or used her sewing skills. It was a pattern they had followed before, but now it was irking her. They could have stayed on in Beziers, lived in modest comfort. Robert just didn't understand how hard it was for her to keep them all clean while moving so often. Nor did he sympathise with the problems she had keeping a very small boy amused on tedious journeys, though he soon complained if Harry made too much noise.

They came to a place called Serugia by accident, having misunderstood what the man driving the carrier's cart had said. It was a slightly larger town than most of those they had passed through, built around a small, semi-circular bay, with large white houses on the hills above the tight central cluster of red-roofed houses that scrambled over one another to cling to the lower slopes of the hills around the bay. The inhabitants fished, catered for summer visitors or carried on a multiplicity of small trades, growing their own wine and olives on the slopes behind the town.

Helen fell in love with Serugia on sight, but she had learned by now that whenever she made a favourable comment about any place, Robert would discover nothing but faults there. So she made a slighting remark about the narrowness of the streets.

He scoffed at her. "Nothing ever satisfies you, does it? You'd complain if I took you to heaven."

They lodged for a night or two in a small inn, whose owner spoke a little atrocious French but who was very willing to help Helen improve her small store of Italian phrases.

Robert went out for a couple of short strolls, but spent most of the time resting. On the third morning, he said, "I like it here. My cough's much better."

"I don't think—"

"Just shut up and listen, for once, and let me do the thinking! I want you to find us some rooms. It'll be cheaper than staying at an inn."

Helen enlisted the help of the innkeeper's wife, who had taken a fancy to Harry and who kept irritating him by stroking his honey-gold curls and clasping him to her ample bosom. Francesca found them a whole house to themselves, at a ridiculously cheap price, because it was winter and there were few tourists at that time of year. It was a small house, by most people's standards, with two rooms and a kitchen on the ground floor and two tiny bedrooms and an attic above. It was sparsely furnished, but clean and attractive, and it was the largest place the Perrimans had ever had to live in.

Harry adored the attic, from which you could see the sea, and took immediate possession of it. "Me an' Dodo like this house," he declared, dancing the dog up and down on the windowsill.

The prospect of having a house of her own reduced Helen to tears. In her halting Italian, she confided in Francesca that never before in her married life had she had a whole house to herself.

Francesca, who disliked Robert as much as she liked his wife and child, tutted sympathetically. She had established herself as Helen's friend and protector and now proceeded to organise things for her. She had a cousin who would move the Perrimans' luggage to the house, another cousin who would supply them with fruit and vegetables very cheaply, a brother who was a butcher and a female cousin who might be able to help signora Perriman to find some pupils who wanted to learn English or French.

Serugia was, it appeared, getting quite a few foreign visitors nowadays and it was useful for those tradespeople who wished to make money from them to learn English.

Francesca's cousin Maria was housekeeper to il Conte, whose house this was, Francesca said with pride, and Helen made suitable noises to show that she was very impressed. Il Conte was the largest landowner in the neighbourhood and he lived in the biggest of the white houses on the hill overlooking the town.

"Un bel palazzo! Magnifico!" enthused Francesca.

"Magnifico!" echoed Helen.

Robert graciously allowed his wife to arrange their move and joined her at the house only when it was all over. She wished he had not, for his ill humour seemed to mar the happy atmosphere of the small dwelling. She wished, as she had wished many times before, that he would just go away, the further the better – and never return.

Eight

Thanks to Francesca's help and volubility, Helen learned Italian with remarkable rapidity.

Robert said languidly that he'd known she would come in useful and condescended to learn the numbers from her. "If you know the numbers and a few other phrases, you can play cards or throw dice in any language. But why the devil are you feeding us so much of that damned pasta stuff? I need some real meat."

"We can't afford a lot of meat. I haven't got much work yet, only the two pupils."

He sighed. "Well, at least that stuff is filling. When I've recovered from this damned cold, I'll find some way of picking up a bit of money and then we can eat properly. There must be a few fellows around who like a game of cards."

And sure enough, since he was tired of poor men's food, Robert made it his business to hunt around for kindred spirits. He soon met "a good fellow, Italian, but speaks a little English". Paolo introduced Robert to some others with similar tastes. "Rum bunch, but they know their cards. That Conte they all fawn over comes down to play sometimes, they tell me. Useful, eh? He won't be short of money. He owns half the town."

As usual, Robert was successful at first, then more and more unsuccessful. Helen had enough students by now to cover the cost of the little house and the food for herself and Harry – but only just. She entrusted her small emergency fund to Francesca, explaining that her husband was a gambler. She flushed as she added that he sometimes took her money, and that she wanted to save some "*per il piccolo* Harry".

Francesca swore that the devil could tear out her entrails before she would surrender one single coin to signor Perriman. And if they were ever short, she would personally see that Harry should never go hungry again. Helen could not help hugging her. It was wonderful to have a friend once more. She wrote a letter to Roxanne and another to the Hendrys, telling them all where she was and trying her best to sound optimistic.

The seasons passed and summer came again. Robert's brief run of luck was long past now. He was becoming very nasty about the food she served him and he had gone through her things several times searching for money. She retaliated by refusing to make him an evening meal unless he gave her the money to buy food.

She was very embarrassed when she visited Francesca one week, because of a bruise Robert had given her, when he slapped her hard on the face. Her friend fingered it, clicked her tongue in dismay and found her some evil-smelling ointment to anoint it with.

Harry now went and hid in the attic whenever his father was in a bad mood.

One hot summer night, Robert came home in the foulest of tempers.

"Is something wrong?" Helen asked. It must be money. Surely, oh surely, they wouldn't have to move again! She didn't think she would be able to cope if this were the case. She had grown to like Serugia and to love her little house. And there was Francesca, too. Not to mention some boys with whom Harry had made friends.

"Oh, no, everything's wonderful!" Robert sneered. "What do you think it is, you fool? The damned cards won't fall for me lately. Never had such a bad run. Never!" He started gnawing on a piece of bread which had been intended for Harry's breakfast. "Not even a smear of jam to put on it! What sort of a housekeeper are you? I don't know why I keep you around, I really don't!"

"You're very welcome to leave us. Go and try your luck elsewhere!"

"Oh, yes, you'd like that, wouldn't you? Like to get out of all your marital duties."

She tensed. Was he going to demand that she share his bed? Because she wouldn't. Whatever he said or did, she would not willingly lie with him again. She couldn't bear him to touch her and she was not risking him fathering another child on her, for it was hard enough to feed the one they'd got.

"Don't worry. *I* don't want to touch you! But I do think it's about time you helped me."

"What do you want me to do?" she asked, puzzled.

"See that chap for me – il Conte."

"Why?"

"He's getting a bit nasty, that's why. We'll see if *you* can soften his heart a little. Play the poor little woman who can't feed her child. That might get him. Though I wouldn't rely on his being sympathetic. He's no gentleman, I can tell you, whatever stupid Italian title he gives himself!"

"Do you – owe him money?"

"Some. Nothing I can't pay off, if he'll only give me more time."

Her heart sank.

"So," he said, with what she recognised as assumed casualness, "you'll have to go and see him for me tomorrow. It's a long way up that hill. It'd make me cough." He avoided her eyes. "And anyway, your Italian is quite good now. Think of that damned brat. Play on il Conte's conscience."

She was horrified. "I won't go! Why should I? The debt is your concern."

"Will you not, madam? Will you not?" He raised his fist to her. "You'll do as you're told!"

She backed away. "But I don't even know the man, Robert! And it's *you* who owes him money!"

"Doesn't matter. Wear something pretty. That green thing. Go and weep buckets all over him. I'll look after the boy."

"No."

"You will go, you know. He's expecting you. I sent him a message. And he replied to it. He's expecting you tomorrow at three."

They argued for a while longer. The situation was becoming more and more heated, and, then, Robert finally snapped. He turned violent and started to hit Helen. She could hear Harry sobbing quietly in his room and, in the end, she capitulated, for the boy's sake and also because she didn't want to move from Serugia. But she refused to leave Harry with his father. She would never trust Robert again. She left the boy with Francesca and, face burning with embarrassment, she asked her to hide Harry if his father came looking for him. Thank goodness, her friend couldn't see the bruises on her body.

Francesca watched her walk away up the hill. "*Poverina!*" she said without thinking.

"*Papa è cattivo!*" announced Harry, whose Italian was coming along fast. "*Picchia la mamma.*"

"To think a child of his age should know such things!" Francesca told her husband later. "What a villain that man is! To beat an angel like the Signora!"

Helen arrived at the *palazzo*, feeling ashamed as well as hot and tired. It was a hard pull up the hill and she knew that her face was red and her skirt dusty, though she tried to shake off the worst of the clinging white dust before she went in. There was no one at the tiny gatehouse, so she walked slowly and reluctantly up the drive to the big house. She summoned up her indignation at having to come here and that helped her to overcome her embarrassment and her strong desire to run away.

At the big house, she pulled briskly on the bell. "*La Signora Perriman,*" she said loftily to the footman who opened the door.

He grinned, a knowing grin that sent a shiver of apprehension up her spine. Did even the servants know why she had come? To her surprise he led her towards the stairs and she hesitated for a moment. Surely the *salone* couldn't be up there?

"*Il Conte L'attende,*" said the man, using the polite form of address, but still leering at her in a way that was definitely not polite.

She hesitated, then followed him, but stopped dead on the threshold when he tried to show her into a bedroom. "No!"

Without more ado, he pushed her inside, threw a piece of folded paper after her and slammed the door.

She heard a key turn in the lock and, with a gasp of horror, she ran across to bang on the door and shout to be let out. It was a very solid door and didn't even shake under her blows. Nor was there any noise from the other side of it.

Catching her breath on a sob, she flew across the room to the window, but that, too, was locked. What was Robert up to now?

As she turned round and began to pace up and down the room, the crackle of paper underfoot reminded her that the footman had thrown a piece of paper at her. She bent to pick it up, smoothed it out and icy horror shivered along her veins. The paper bore Robert's handwriting. Why should he need to write her a note when she had just seen him? It was a moment before she could bring herself to spread it out and read the message.

> If you want to stay in Serugia, be sensible for once. Think of Harry and be kind to the Count. R.

Disgust and panic held her motionless, then she looked at the large bed and had to gulp back a sob. She did not want to believe that Robert would offer his own wife in payment for his debts, but he had broached the matter before and why else would she have been sent to the *palazzo* and locked in this bedroom?

She walked across the room to rattle the handle of the big French window that led out on to the balcony, but it held firm. Should she try to break a pane of glass? But she could not see a key on the other side, so what good would that do? For a moment, she leaned her head against the coolness of the glass, but she could not seem to think clearly.

When a voice behind her spoke, she jumped in shock and, with a sudden movement, twisted round.

"He say you shy, but not that you go back on your word."

A thin, grey-haired gentleman whom she recognised as il Conte, though she had never spoken to him, stood there. He inclined his head as she stared at him.

How had he got in? She looked round, saw an open door behind a curtain, connecting the room to another one and, with a sob of desperation, she ran towards it, only to be tripped up by the long cane upon which the Conte had been leaning. She lay there for a moment, winded, then struggled to her feet, keeping as far away from him as she could.

"Please – why have I been brought here? I don't understand."

He frowned at her, looking intently at her face. Something he saw there made the frown deepen. He rapped the cane on the floor. "There is something wrong, I think. Please to come with me." Seeing how she hesitated, he bowed to her. "We talk. I not touch you. Is some mistake, I think."

She swallowed hard, then followed him next door into a sitting room. She did as he asked, sitting with her trembling hands clasped tightly together in her lap and waiting for him to explain.

He limped across to another chair. "I sit, too. Bad leg." He studied her, still looking puzzled. "You are the wife of il Signor Perriman?"

"Yes."

"He send you here?"

"Yes. To speak to you. About the money."

"Your husband owe me much money. Play cards. No luck. Say you pay in other ways."

Helen blushed a fiery red. "I knew nothing of this, Conte, nothing!" Her voice broke. "I can't believe that even *he* would do such a thing. Or that you would want a reluctant woman!"

"I am bored. Is nice to have a young woman. But I do not," he struggled to find the right words, "take woman who not want me." A look of pride appeared on his face. "I never need to force women."

She let out a long shuddering breath of relief. She believed him. Suddenly she could not look at him, at anyone. Robert's behaviour had embarrassed her so deeply that she could only cover her face with her hands and try to hide the tears she could no longer hold back. "I'm ashamed, so very ashamed! And I have no money to give you." Her voice came out muffled, but she could not bear to see the disgust he must be feeling for her.

"No." His voice was slow and thoughtful. "But I am a lonely man. You shall give me company instead. I like you to share a *merenda* with me – same as the English tea."

The wary look was back in her eyes again.

"How old are you, signora?" he asked gently, tapping the top of the cane with one fingertip.

"Twenty-one, sir."

"And I am – near to sixty – and lame. My wife, she is dead long time. My daughters are marry. My son," he snapped his fingers in a gesture of dismissal, "he prefer to live in Roma. I have think – you are like your husband. *Ma non è vero*. You are what the English call – a lady. Is true?"

She smiled reluctantly. "I was brought up a sort of lady, Conte, but my family are very poor. And since my marriage I have not led the life of a lady."

He nodded. "Not with that one. You make bad mistake, to marry him, I think."

"Yes." Useless to deny it.

"So. You teach English – and you sew to earn money for your child."

He laughed at her surprise. "I stay home much, but news come to me. I know many thing. How much you charge for teach English?"

She named a modest sum. "Per hour, sir."

"Good. You come teach me – two times a week, two hours each time – speak English, take *merenda*. I pay." He tapped her hand lightly with the end of the cane. "Not look like that. Is not trick to get you in bed. Bring the son too. We talk about," he shrugged, "life, books. You read much books?"

She felt suddenly more at ease with him. "When I can." Which was not often lately. You didn't buy books when you could barely afford food.

His eye fell on a small table with a board set open on it. "You play chess?" His voice did not sound hopeful, but he brightened visibly at her response.

"Yes, sir. But I have not done so for a long time." Strangely, it was her mother's one passion, chess, and the two women had played it sometimes when her father was out of the house.

"Good."

She shook her head. "I can't come here like that, Conte. People will – will say—" She could not finish the sentence and she could feel how flushed her face was.

His face fell. "Ah." He leaned his head on one side like a bright-eyed bird, then snapped his fingers together and beamed at Helen. "I know. My housekeeper is *very* respectable. She sit with us, tell everyone what happen. Then all town know you are respectable. Maria play with boy. You talk English with me – play chess, too. I pay you for this."

Helen bowed her head and tried to wipe away the tears that had filled her eyes at this offer. "Sir, you are generous indeed."

He smiled and shrugged slightly. "So. I get value for money, I think." The smile became a smirk. "I still like other sort of woman, too. Not too old for that. But you, we keep respectable."

She chuckled. She could not help liking him. Then she remembered the debts. "You must take the money I earn off what my husband owes you, Conte." She hated having to say this, for she found it hard to manage on what she earned. But the debt still lay between them.

"No. Not so. I make your husband to work for me. I send him off to deliver messages, do small businesses for me. He pay back debts like that. You keep money you earn." He looked down at her arm and frowned.

She glanced down and saw that her sleeve had risen up her arm enough to show one of her bruises. She was grateful when this kind Italian nobleman did not comment on it.

And though Robert railed at her for her squeamishness and even beat her again, il Conte had his way. Twice a week, Helen and Harry walked up to the *palazzo* and took tea with a lonely and somewhat mischievous old man. And his housekeeper, Maria, sat in the corner of the room each time to lend respectability to the proceedings.

At first deeply suspicious of Helen, Maria gradually relaxed and decided that her cousin Francesca was right. The poor *signora* was quite respectable. During the visits, Maria would sit with Harry on her ample lap, playing quiet little games with him. Sometimes, on fine days, when Helen and il Conte sat out on the terrace, she would walk ponderously up and down the nearby gardens with the boy and together they would infuriate the gardeners by picking flowers for his mother, for Harry loved to give her presents.

Often Maria loftily told her cronies in the town that *la Signora Perriman,* unlike her *scellerato* of a husband, was a lady of the first respectability – even if she was English. And if they said anything different, they would have her anger to deal with.

By now the Perrimans had become a fixture in the town. The agent who hired out their little house on il Conte's behalf had not raised the rent during the summer, as he had threatened to do, and it had begun to feel like a real home. Helen would never have guessed that the count was behind this, but she was very relieved. She could not have afforded to pay more.

Her husband had no illusions on this point. Il Conte had clearly taken a fancy to Helen. But Robert said nothing because, if the old villain wanted to throw his money around without getting any real return for it, why should they refuse the largesse? He didn't even hint at what he suspected to his wife, because her damned silly scruples might cause her to decline such help.

The two of them had been living in a state of armed neutrality ever since her first visit to the *palazzo*. In the quarrel that followed her return, he'd tried to intimidate, then beat her into submission, and for once she'd fought back, hurling at his head any projectile that came to hand. When he threatened to take her son away, she warned him that she would go to Il Conte. This put an end to his menacing behaviour for a time but, after a while, it started again.

After a few weeks, Helen confided her worry about this to Il Conte. He spoke to his lawyer, who had a quiet word with Robert, and not a single threat was made again.

During that summer, Robert's health grew no better, but became no worse. Serugia, he said, agreed with him.

As soon as winter started, however – even the mild southern winter – Robert visibly began to weaken, and then he could speak no good of the town. The evenings when he stayed home, either because he was too tired to go out or because he could not find anyone to gamble with, became another ordeal for Helen, who had to sit through sly innuendoes about her relationship with the count, open abuse directed at her inadequacies as a wife, and cruel taunts about Harry's lack of future "in this God-forsaken hole".

Robert would have moved on again, were it not for the debts and the intervention of Il Conte's lawyer, but this time he was well and truly trapped.

Il Conte still sent Robert on errands out of town from time to time, especially when he saw Helen growing weary, with that look of dumb endurance in her eyes. Besides, as he said cynically to his lawyer, he might as well get his value out of the man – in one way or another.

In fact, Robert enjoyed being away from Serugia, with the expenses of his journeys paid – though not generously. He began to stay away longer than was necessary and to gamble with any fellow travellers he met. In November he set off happily to go to Rome with a pile of letters to deliver personally and a list of purchases to make. He was to stay at the house of il Conte's son.

He was brought home again a few days later by the son's second coachman. He had a raging fever and was delirious.

Helen had to stop her teaching to nurse him. Alternately moaning, feeling sorry for himself and cursing her in a wheezing whisper of a voice for bringing him to this plight, Robert fought for life with a tenacity that surprised everyone but her. She had seen him recover before and would not be surprised if he did so again.

One night she fell asleep in a chair by his bed. When she woke, she saw him staring at her with a malevolent expression on his face. "I'll get better just to spite you, you bitch!" he whispered hoarsely. "You'll see. My luck'll turn. It always does."

She saw to his needs and then went to get an hour or two's proper rest on her bed, but she could not sleep. She knew she could no longer stay with Robert. She did not dare. Since his return his hatred of her was so obvious that she was frightened of what he might do when he recovered. Her only recourse was to beg il Conte to help her get away from him. She would be ashamed to do that, and would hate to leave Serugia, but she would not put Harry in danger ever again.

Bleak despair filled her at the thought of leaving and she felt the hours pass before she fell into an uneasy doze.

She woke with a start early the next morning when people started moving about in the street. Her head was aching for lack of sleep and she was dreading what would surely feel like an interminable day.

In the doorway to Robert's room, she gasped, stopped short. Robert was dead, his face contorted, and his eyes staring sightlessly at the door. It was as if he were waiting for her to come in, ready to berate her for some imagined grievance.

As she stood there, relief flooded through her, and she actually found herself saying, "Lord, I thank you!" – muttering it over and over. Then common sense took over and she covered her husband's face, running lightly upstairs to wake her son.

As he gave her his usual hug of greeting, she said quietly, "Your father's dead."

"Dead? Like Francesca's dog?"

"Yes."

"They'll bury him in the ground and he'll never come back?"

"Yes."

Harry beamed at her. "So he won't be able to hit you again?"

That made her more sad than Robert's death. A son should have good things to remember about his father. A son should not rejoice in his father's death.

Nor should a wife.

Numbly she let Francesca and Maria guide her through the formalities of death Serugia-style.

Robert had to be buried in a corner of the Catholic graveyard reserved for suicides and Protestants, but the priest was gentle with *la Signora inglese* and Francesca accompanied her to the brief funeral.

She suspected that the count had smoothed over any difficulties and when he, too, turned up at the funeral, she was sure of it.

"What will you do now?" he asked afterwards, as they stood together in the shade of an old cypress tree, watching the gravedigger shovel earth into the hole. A short distance away, Harry was playing with the gravedigger's little daughter, showing no signs of grief.

Helen sighed. "I don't know. I haven't thought. I didn't expect him to die. Not yet, anyway."

"Have you money? Did he leave you anything at all?"

"I have a little money. He left me nothing, but I have a small – a very small – income of my own and the next payment is due soon." She brightened at the thought. Now that Robert wouldn't be able to waste it, the annuity would make a big difference to her and Harry. "It's not enough to live off, but it helps. And I still have a few pupils, I think."

His face brightened. "So you stay here?"

"I think so. For the time being, anyway. If you'll let me keep the house on?"

"Of course, of course." He waved one hand in a lordly gesture, then frowned at her. "Your family not want you back – now he is dead?"

"No." She was too ashamed to talk about them, but he had been kind to her, so he deserved the truth. "My parents are very – very harsh people. They disowned me when I married Robert and they won't wish to see me again, whatever happens. I have some friends in London, but I think I'll stay here – for a while, anyway. But not for ever. Harry is English. When he gets older, he must be educated properly, as an Englishman – if I can manage it. Conte . . . ?"

"Yes."

"What about my husband's debts to you? I should prefer to pay them."

"They are paid." He put an arm round her shoulders and gave her an almost fatherly embrace. "I 'ave no need of that little piece of money. And your 'usband – he give his life in my service, so the debts are paid. But you will still come to tea? Give me my English lessons? Maria would miss the boy."

"Yes. Oh, yes!" For he was truly her friend now, and he was teaching her so much. About life, about the world, about people.

"I wish – I wish I could look after you properly," he said tentatively. "Marriage I cannot offer, but money, a nice house . . ."

For a moment she leaned against him, and he wondered if she would weaken now that she was alone in the world. He would like that. She was very lovely.

But she moved resolutely away, smiling at him through a mist of tears. "I greatly value your friendship, Conte, and shall continue the lessons, if you wish. But employment is all I will accept from you."

He shrugged. She might not be willing to become his mistress, but she would still be his friend. And at his time of life, that was not such a bad thing.

"*Bene*," he said quietly and signalled to his coachman to come and help him across to the carriage, for he grew stiffer and more awkward each year.

It was so peaceful in the churchyard that Helen remained there, sitting under a tree, for a long time. She stared into space, enjoying the breeze on her face, listening to the birdsong, not thinking very much. Just relaxing.

After a while, she called to Harry and they went home. She could not quite believe it would be peaceful at home, too, and stood in the doorway for a moment, half expecting to be met by a curse. But the house was quiet.

Only then did she weep, unable to stop, hugging Harry tightly to her. And although she felt shaken by the storm of tears, she felt cleansed, too. She had made a mistake. She had paid dearly for it. Now she was free to make a better life for herself and her son.

Nine

The next two years passed very happily for Helen, though later she was to realise it was not happiness she was experiencing, but tranquillity. The lack of anyone telling her what to do was a wonder to her. For the first time in her life, she had only herself and Harry to worry about. For weeks she felt light in both body and spirit, as if the burden she had shed was physical as well as emotional.

She and Harry continued to occupy the little house behind the church and, without Robert to feed, Helen managed to earn enough for their daily needs, so that she did not have to touch her annuity. She wrote to tell the lawyers to keep the money for her until she came back to England and, if they could, earn her a little interest on it.

That was all she could manage to put by for their eventual return, and for Harry's education, since her other income, like that of most Serugini, fluctuated with the seasons. She worried that Harry's English was interspersed with Italian phrases, but told herself that it didn't matter too much while he was so young. She could teach him standard English quite adequately herself, and had, with il Conte's help, found a supplier of suitable books in Rome. And anyway, the boy was happy here. No more hiding in his room. No more keeping quiet. He had become a normal, noisy child – dirty and exuberant, sometimes naughty. That gladdened her heart.

Il Conte tried to help them in many ways, but Helen was very firm about what she would and would not accept. She was determined neither to take advantage of his generosity, nor to compromise her good name. She would accept vegetables from his gardens, legs of ham from his home farm – the latter, for Harry's sake, for a growing boy needed good meat to build his bones – and even a few bottles of wine from his vineyard, but she would accept nothing personal for herself. The count sometimes grew angry about her fierce sense of propriety, but she could always coax him into a better mood.

It was a devastating blow to Helen when il Conte died suddenly in his sleep soon after Harry's sixth birthday. And although she did not then know it, this was only the first of many changes to come. Even if she had known, she would have lifted her chin and faced up to whatever life brought her. For that was her way. She had gained this strength through hard experience. And she was proud that she had won through, by her own efforts, to a comfortable plateau where life was very pleasant.

The new conte came home from Rome for the funeral and stayed on to settle his father's affairs, but he declined to live in Serugia, which had, he said scornfully to the priest, no scope for a man of business. Maybe one of his sons would like a quiet country life one day. He would wait and see. If not, he would sell the estate.

Shock waves ran through the town at the very thought of that.

Maria came to take tea with Helen and reported, with much flourishing of her handkerchief and dabbing of her eyes, that the new conte was to let the *palazzo* to summer visitors. Let it! How that would have broken his poor father's heart! They were to keep on only a skeleton staff during the winter and hire temporary servants for the summer visitors. And Signora Perriman could guess what sort of workers they would be, people with no love for the house, no real skills, either, or they'd not be available for temporary work!

"Me, I am to stay," Maria concluded, with a scornful toss of the head. "But I ask you, what work is this for a woman like me? I shall be nothing but a caretaker! Me – housekeeper to il Conte for twenty years! I shall give notice," she wound up dramatically. "I shall leave. I have my pride. Others will know how to value me, even if he doesn't."

Helen knew that wild horses would not tear Maria from the *palazzo*, which was as much her home as it had been il Conte's, for she had worked there since she was a girl of twelve. But Helen had lived in Serugia for long enough to know that she could not say this straight out. "Life is hard," she said instead. "And the good are always imposed upon. But – will il Conte rest easily in his grave if you go away? He left his home in your most capable hands – who else could care for it like you?"

Maria sighed gustily. "Who else, indeed!" More sighing, then she nodded her head slowly. "It is a sacred trust." She struck a proud, heroic pose.

"Ah yes," agreed Helen softly, hiding a smile, "a sacred trust."

"I shall make the sacrifice and stay. For il Conte's sake."

No one had ever called the new owner "il Conte" in the same tone of voice – or ever would. They said "il conte Alessandro", as if speaking politely of a stranger, for that was what he was to them now, though most of them had known him as a boy.

To Helen's surprise, the new conte came to call upon her before he returned to Rome. She found him a cold, punctilious man, most unlike his father. She offered him refreshments and introduced her son to him. He refused the refreshments, nodded briefly to Harry and thereafter ignored the boy completely.

"I have come, Signora Perriman, to acquaint you with the terms of my father's will. He has left you a small bequest, and there were instructions that I was to give you this letter personally." He flourished at her a crackling piece of paper, with a great red blob of a seal on one side.

She took it reluctantly. "I didn't expect anything. I have no right!"

He looked bored, judging her reply to be mere histrionics. "It is, Signora, a very small bequest." He waved his arms to encompass the room where they sat. "*Effettivamente*, it is this house. With the condition that if you ever wish to sell it, you must first offer it to me. However, I can tell you now that this will not be necessary. I have no desire to acquire more property in Serugia."

"I – I don't know what to say. I'm grateful, of course, but—"

He held up one hand. "I must ask you to read the letter and tell me that you will accept the bequest." He pulled out a large gold watch and frowned at it. "And I should be obliged, Signora, if you would do so quickly, as I am pressed for time."

The letter brought tears to her eyes, for il Conte had written it himself and it sounded just like him speaking. He begged her to accept this "so small" bequest for the sake of their friendship, which had given him much pleasure in the loneliness of his declining years, and also for the sake of her beautiful son. He would have left her something more valuable, but he knew how foolishly proud she was. This, however, she would not – could not – deny him.

No, she could not refuse a gift made with such loving kindness. She looked across at the stranger. "I shall accept the bequest. And know that I shall always be grateful to your father."

Il conte Alessandro bowed, not in the slightest interested in her feelings. "Then, Signora, I have done as my father wished, and we may now leave it to the lawyers to settle the details." He studied Helen in puzzlement. A strange woman, this last mistress of his father's, not beautiful exactly, but with a face full of character. Too thin for his taste and very soberly dressed. Who did she think she was fooling with her prim governessy clothes and the English lessons she gave?

He paused again as a shaft of sunlight caught the glory of her hair. She might not look bad, though, with that magnificent hair let loose around her shoulders but it did nothing for her appearance so tightly coiled in a chignon. Still, she had made his father happy in his last years, had cost him very little (she must be a fool not to have feathered her nest) and she had made no scandal. What more could one ask of a mistress? He thought the bequest very fair payment for her services.

At the door he bowed again. "I have to thank you, Signora, on behalf of the family, for your many – er – kindnesses to my father, and, above all, for your discretion."

He was gone before she had realised what he had meant by such a statement and there was no one in whom she could confide her indignation, deeply though it burned. She almost wrote to him to reject the bequest but, in the end, common sense prevailed, and the thought of Harry made her swallow her pride and sign the papers the lawyer presented to her a few days later.

She was filled with quiet joy afterwards as she wandered round her house, touching a window frame, a door, a pot of flowers here and there. With no rent to pay, she would be able to save more from now on. But sadness crept in behind the joy. She would miss il Conte dreadfully. Her life would be very lonely without her intelligent, educated friend to talk to.

* * *

The following year brought more summer visitors to Serugia than ever before. The region was becoming very popular with the gentry and nobility of Europe, especially those with artistic pretensions. The *palazzo* was rented first by a family from Rome, then by one from Milan.

Maria complained about all the visitors. They smelled of new money, she said scornfully, elevating her button of a nose and shaking her plump jowls. These holiday-makers were not like il Conte, who had been a true aristocrat. His son, though, was a poor substitute, for he cared naught for the land or for his dependants. He no doubt took after his mother's side of the family!

Helen, however, could not afford to turn up her nose at the Gracchioli family, who hired her to keep their three young daughters company and to teach them some English while they were in Serugia.

The Umbertini came next, from Milan. They had no children, and Signor Umbertini was often away on business. His young wife grew bored and hired Helen as a companion. She made a pretence of learning some English, but she was a very indolent young woman, and spent most of the time in idle gossip, only happy when recounting the social triumphs that her husband's money had purchased for her, or when experimenting with her clothes and hair. Helen, bored by this constant iteration of her employer's social successes, gritted her teeth and reminded herself of the good money she was earning simply by listening.

In the autumn the town became much quieter, though a few visitors still lingered. Helen was able to devote more time to her son and his education, and to spend an occasional hour with her friend Francesca, but she was thinking of returning to England the following year. It would need careful planning, but perhaps she could manage to work something out. It would be best to sell this house, because she did not think she would ever return. But if not, she could perhaps rent it out and let Francesca collect the money for her. No tenants would get the better of her friend, of that she was sure.

One evening, as she was returning home from giving a French lesson, Helen found her way barred by a group of revellers. One of them swept her into his arms and demanded the forfeit of a kiss before he would let her pass. Alarmed, she cried out in English and another of the revellers stiffened.

"*Smettila, Tonio!*" He laid his hand on her captor's shoulder. "Excuse me, Signora, but – are you English?"

"Yes, sir! And I would be obliged if you would tell your friend to let me go!" She spoke angrily, but her voice trembled, for the street was dark and there was no one from the town in sight.

"*Tonio! Non insistere! Lasciala!*"

Tonio tightened his grip on Helen's arm and the other hand came up to fumble at her face, making her squeak in alarm. He then declared in a slurred, stubborn voice that he had seen her first and he would have his kiss.

Helen kicked him in the shins at the same time as her would-be rescuer pulled him away from her. Yelping, Tonio spun round, wobbled mightily and sat down with a bump. Helen too would have fallen had not an arm supported her. As soon as she had regained her balance, the arm was withdrawn and the gentleman bowed to her. The bow was a trifle unsteady, but the gentleman was in no way abashed by that.

"I fear the streets are not safe, ma'am. I shall, with your permission, escort you home."

"There is no need to trouble yourself, sir. But I thank you for your assistance."

Her voice was cool, her tone dismissive. Definitely respectable, he thought to himself. Pity.

The two other men did nothing, but neither did they move out of the way. The one called Tonio, having risen to his feet, brushed down his clothes, then lurched towards Helen again, complaining that it was unfair of Carlo to poach on a friend's preserves.

As he and his companions were blocking her way, Helen could not get past, and she began to feel alarmed again. Why had she not left as soon as the man let go of her arm?

Tonio came close to her, arms outstretched, and of necessity, she drew back towards her rescuer, who offered her one arm and shoved his friend away with the other. He was tall and well built, and it took little effort to push Tonio over again.

"I think, ma'am, you must accept my protection. Permit me to introduce myself. Charles Carnforth at your service."

She had no option but to take his arm, but she could *not* like being seen in company with a stranger at this hour of the night. She hoped she would not meet anyone she knew. "Mrs Perriman," she responded curtly. "And I thank you for your help.

Fortunately, I don't have far to go." She set a brisk pace along the street.

"You're English." It was not a question, almost a sigh.

"Yes."

"On holiday here?"

"No. We live here."

He eyed her black clothes in the light of a lantern at the corner of a street. She looked like a widow, though she could have been mourning for another relative. She had a lovely voice, soft and low. He was getting homesick for English voices, he realised suddenly. But this lady was obviously not inviting any familiarities.

"It's good to hear an English voice again," he ventured. "It's been a while."

"You will find that there are still one or two English families staying in the district. I'm sure they would be happy to meet you and talk to you." She stopped in front of her door.

As you are not, he thought ruefully. But he knew when not to push his luck, so he simply bowed to her.

"Again, I'm very grateful for your help. And now, I wish you goodnight, sir." She whisked herself inside and had turned the key in the lock before he could think of anything else to say.

"You made a mess of that, Charles," he murmured, staring at the closed door. "Nice voice she had, too. A lady's voice. I'm a bit tired of shrieking whores, however generous in nature."

He turned and walked slowly away. Damn Tonio! Stupid braggart! Could he not recognise a lady when he saw one? Somehow the savour had gone out of the evening. Charles took his time to get back to the inn, where he spent the rest of the night sitting in a corner of the main room, wishing that he had someone intelligent to talk to. He was getting tired of drunken revels. He always needed a bit of jollity to wipe out the bad taste of a letter from his lawyer at home, but enough was enough.

Francesca came to him in the corner. The Signor Carnforth was all alone tonight. Had his friends deserted him?

Any companionship was welcome just then, especially that of a respectable woman. In his near-fluent Italian, he told her that, on the contrary, he had deserted them, having no taste for their drunken buffooneries. Doubtless he was growing old.

She nodded sagely and cocked her head, waiting to see if he wanted anything.

"Perhaps the Signora would have time to share a bottle of wine with me?" he ventured. "I would be most grateful to be informed about this charming town. I've been travelling for too long and am thinking of settling down somewhere for the winter. I very much appreciate the excellent comfort you offer here." Which was no lie.

Francesca's face brightened at this prospect. Winter was a slow time. A long-term guest would bring a welcome addition to the profits. "I will send my husband for some of the good wine," she said.

He asked a few questions about the town, for form's sake, then slipped in the question to which he really wanted the answer. "Are there any permanent English residents here, Signora? People who would be here in the winter? It's good sometimes to speak one's own language. Not that Italian is not a truly beautiful language. But I'm sure you will understand that one likes to hear the sound of one's own tongue sometimes."

Very flattered, Francesca explained that they had only one permanent English resident. She went on to tell him exactly who his mystery lady was. He heard about her brute of a husband – God rest his soul! – and the kindness of il Conte, who had treated la Signora Perriman as a daughter, please understand!

"How could it be otherwise?"

"La Signora Perriman is of the most respectable, as everyone in Serugia will testify."

Finally, Francesca spoke glowingly of the Signora's angel of a son – the apple of his mother's eye – with hair of gold and the manners of a nobleman, young as he was.

Charles listened avidly, drank very little more and afterwards thought much about his enigmatic lady. He had been very struck by her sweet face, he admitted to himself. He had a great desire to pursue the acquaintance, but she had made it clear that she did not share his desire. So he would have to win her round. In fact – he brightened at the thought – he would enjoy the challenge of getting behind her defences.

When he eventually went up to bed, his valet and general factotum, Alfred Briggs, found him unusually quiet and almost sober, for a change. He had been a bit worried about his master lately, who only drank to excess when he was unhappy about something. Not that the Captain was ever nastily drunk. No, Charles Carnforth was a gentleman, whether in his cups or sober. He was considerate of those who served him, and was always fair in his demands. He was the best of masters, as he had been the best of officers in the army.

Alfred, who had had the honour of saving the then Captain Carnforth's life at Waterloo and who had left the army with him once Old Boney had been defeated, was totally devoted to his master, so much so that he had followed Charles around the world to some very nasty heathen countries.

The next day, Charles called on Mrs Perriman formally, to tender his apologies for his companions' behaviour. He took a large bunch of flowers with him as a peace offering, and found that he was nervous, as a man of over fifty might very well be when calling upon a much younger woman who had caught his fancy and given him no encouragement whatsoever.

The door opened and she stood there, her hair loose about her shoulders, a chestnut glory in the morning sunshine. "Oh! I thought you were the butcher!"

"No." An inauspicious start. She was embarrassed about her hair, which was not quite dry after being washed. No doubt she would screw it up into a knot again as soon as it was dry. Respectable women usually did, for some obscure reason.

"Ma'am, I've come here to apologise properly for my companions' boorish behaviour last night." He sounded stiff and pompous, he knew. Awkwardly he held out the flowers. "Would you please accept these?"

Helen hesitated, then took them. "There was no need, sir. The incident is forgotten and no harm was done, thanks to your intervention."

He bowed slightly. "Permit me to introduce myself properly. Charles Carnforth, of Ashdown Park in Hampshire, at your service." He handed her his card.

She sighed and took the card reluctantly. What did he want with her? She had no desire to complicate her life with such an acquaintance. But she could not be rude to him, for he had been kind to her and, anyway, it was not in her nature. "I am grateful, sir. And – and it's very kind of you to bring me these. But I'm afraid that you must excuse me now. I have an appointment at eleven o'clock, to give an English lesson," – that would show him she was below his touch, socially – "and I must not be late. Thank you again for the flowers."

Charles Carnforth – noted ladies' man, who rarely failed to charm a member of the fair sex upon whom he set his sights, be she five or fifty – found himself standing once more outside a firmly closed door, as lacking in words and address as the most callow of youths.

As he walked away, he acknowledged the irony of this, if only to himself. He went for a walk along the cliffs, his eyes still filled with a pretty English face and a tumbling mass of gently curling chestnut hair. Or was it the sweetness of her smile that attracted him? Or even perhaps the roughness of her hands, which he had not been able to help noticing? She looked like a woman who worked hard for her living. A woman of determination, who had no time for frivolous flirtations with itinerant gentlemen like him.

"And yet, I want to know her," he said aloud, staring down at the waves breaking on the small half-moon of beach. "I just *have* to get to know her."

Maybe when he did, she would appeal to him less. People did not, in his experience, improve with acquaintance. Or maybe . . . He did not finish that thought. But he set his mind to finding a way to gain her acquaintance.

Ten

Morosely, Charles Carnforth made his way back to the inn. There, he ordered a bottle of red wine and sat in his room, sipping a glass and staring out at the village square. People came and went, but he saw none of them. His thoughts were still filled with the lovely Mrs Perriman.

When Alfred came upstairs, to see if the Captain had any orders for him, any plans for the following day, he found his master uncharacteristically quiet. This raised his spirits considerably. The Captain only behaved in a heedless, roistering fashion when he was upset about something, usually something connected with his family in England. Perhaps the fit of gloom was passing. Alfred certainly hoped so. He was getting too old for these late nights and drunken capers. As was his master.

"Sit down and have a drink with me," Charles ordered abruptly.

"Happy to, sir." Alfred poured himself half a glass and sat back, and prepared for the confidences that usually ensued in this sort of situation.

Quietly, Charles began to talk, confiding in the servant who had been with him so long. They had been under fire together, had bivouacked in some very uncomfortable circumstances, and had quite literally shared their last crust. They were more than master and servant; in all but name, they were close friends.

"She's a beauty," Charles said reflectively.

"Is she, sir?"

"She is indeed."

Alfred had a fair idea of whom his master was talking, but he asked anyway, "And what might this paragon's name be, sir?"

"Helen – Helen Perriman. Our hostess was telling me all about her last night – well, not all, obviously, but a great deal."

Alfred nodded, took another sip, though he thought wine a poor substitute for a glass of good English ale, and waited.

"She's a widow. Was married to an actor fellow. Bit of a gambler, too. He died of consumption two years ago. Good riddance, from what the Signora tells me. Used to ill-treat the lady, so she says."

"Not a gentleman, then."

"Definitely not a gentleman."

Another pause, then, "And she has a son, fine little lad by all accounts. She sounds to be a brave woman. Earns her own living, keeps herself respectable. Damn fine thing, eh?"

"Yes, sir." Alfred frowned. The lady didn't sound at all like his master's usual type. "But if she's respectable, then why are you—?" He broke off, seeing the frown on the Captain's forehead.

"Dashed if I know why. I just – want to get to know her. And damn, I'm not leaving until I do."

"It'll be nice to have a bit of a rest, sir," Alfred said philosophically. "Pleasant little town, this."

"Yes."

After a while, Alfred put down his glass and left quietly. Charles sat on, with his wine barely tasted, for another hour or two, then roused himself to go for a ride.

When his erstwhile drinking friends, who were staying at one of the houses on the hill, came to find him that night, he sent them away, saying he was feeling unwell.

But try as he might, Charles could find no way of getting to know Mrs Perriman and, although he caught a glimpse of her once or twice in the street in the next day or two, she hurried away so quickly that it would have made his pursuit far too obvious if he had run after her.

In the end, it was Alfred who furthered the acquaintance with Mrs Perriman for his grateful master. Four days after the initial meeting, he was in the stables, checking on the Captain's horse, for he didn't trust the groom at the inn to look after it properly. After a small contretemps with the stable boy over the way the stall had been cleaned out, Alfred turned round to find himself being solemnly regarded by a little lad with dark blond hair. Alfred observed him through narrowed eyes. Not many Italians had hair that colour. Could this be the son of the widow to whom his master had taken such a fancy? Yes, surely it must be?

He smiled encouragingly. "Hello, young fellow."

He was rewarded by a tentative smile. "Good morning, sir. Are you – are you English?"

"Yes, young shaver, I am, and proud of it."

"I'm English too, but I'm afraid I don't remember England. We left when I was only a baby."

They studied the horse together for a while, then Harry recalled his manners. "Oh, I'm sorry, sir, I didn't introduce myself. I'm Harry Perriman."

"Are you, now?" Yes, that was definitely the name his master had mentioned. "And I'm Alfred Briggs, young sir. Valet and general factotum to Charles Carnforth, late Captain in the Light Horse."

Harry frowned at him. "If you please, sir, what's general factotum?"

"It's a servant who is prepared to do anything, any job that is needed, my lad."

"I see." Another thought penetrated Harry's mind. "Carnforth, you said? That's the gentleman who called to give my mother some flowers the other day, isn't it? I didn't see him, but I heard his voice and the flowers were lovely. I pick flowers for Mother sometimes, but not beautiful ones like that."

"She's a lucky lady to have a son who picks her flowers. I dare say she likes yours best."

Harry beamed. "She says she does. I help her in other ways too, you know," he confided eagerly. "She works very hard for us both, so I try to do what I can."

"That's a good lad."

There was a companionable silence for a while, as they both continued to study the horse, then Harry said wistfully, "He's a fine-looking animal, sir."

"He is, and has a nature to match. You won't get a show of temper from Jervis here, however tired he is. You can't beat a grey, young fellow. The Captain always rides a grey."

"Can you not? I don't know very much about horses, I'm afraid. But one day I'm going to learn to ride them. My mother's promised me that."

"That's the ticket, Master Harry! A gentleman should always know how to ride."

Another frown from the boy. "My mother says I'm not exactly

a gentleman. We have to earn our way in the world, you see."

"Well, there's nothing wrong with that, as long as you do it honestly."

The bells of the church started to ring and Harry sighed regretfully. "I must go now. My mother will have finished giving her lesson. Will you – will you be here tomorrow?"

"I will."

"Then – may I come and look at the horse again?"

"You may indeed. And I'll show you how to bridle him, if you like."

The boy's face lit up. "Will you, sir? Oh, I'd like that!" He nodded to Alfred and ran off to meet his mother.

Alfred went off to report this useful encounter to his master.

The next day, when he observed from his window the arrival of a golden-haired lad, Charles sauntered down to join Alfred who was working in the inn yard. Soon Charles had the boy standing on a box, while he gave him his first lesson in bridling and saddling a horse.

With a grin, Alfred stepped back and left them to it. The young window was going to have a very difficult time repulsing the Captain, with her son in a fair way to becoming a disciple of his. And no one could deny his master's considerable expertise on the subject of horses, or his knack of passing it on to youngsters. A pity he'd never had a son of his own. He would have made a good father.

Within three days, Harry was following Charles around like a tame lap-dog. His conversation at home consisted mainly of eulogies about Jervis, upon whose back Harry had been allowed to sit while Alfred led the animal slowly round the inn yard and Mr Carnforth corrected his posture. When Harry was not discoursing about horses, he was telling his mother what the Captain or Alfred had said and done.

Helen was torn in her reactions to this new friendship. On the one hand, she had a strong desire to allow Harry to spend some time with an English gentleman, so that he would have someone upon whom to model himself. On the other hand, she had a feeling that she ought to stop the association before her son got hurt or, worse still, she herself got dragged into it. In the end, she decided that she could not help getting involved, if only to keep an eye on her son and to check that he was not making a nuisance of himself.

"Mother's coming to pick me up early today," announced Harry. "She wants to see Francesca, and she wants to see you too, sir."

"See me, eh?" Charles hid a smile.

"She wants to thank you for teaching me about horses. I say, sir, may I hold the reins myself today?"

"'Fraid not. You're too small to control Jervis."

Harry's face fell.

"We'll have to see if there's a pony we could hire for you, then I could really teach you to ride."

Harry looked at him, head on one side, then the small head was shaken firmly. "I'm sorry, sir, but Mother couldn't afford to hire a pony."

"But I can."

Another shake of the head. "That wouldn't be right, sir. We – we don't allow others to pay for us. We didn't allow il Conte to do it, either, and Mother says he was a good friend to us. I used to sit in the corner and talk to Maria – she was his housekeeper – when we visited him, you know. Maria used to give me cake and lemonade."

So the rumours had been wrong, Charles mused. Not that anyone who had the slightest acquaintance with her would have believed that Helen Perriman would behave immorally. But it was nice to have it confirmed from an unimpeachable source.

Charles, realising he had been carried away by his thoughts, saw that Harry was still waiting for an answer, so he searched his brain to remember what they'd been discussing and recalled the question of a pony. "Would you let me pay for its hire if you knew that you would be doing me a favour by keeping me company when I go riding?"

"I – I don't think so, sir. Mother and I – we often talk about things like that. We like to stand on our own feet, sir, and not be beholden to anyone."

Harry's expression, like his conversation, was curiously adult for a lad of seven. *In fact, a nicer and more thoughtful lad I have never met. Though I'd like to make him laugh more. He's a very solemn child.* Without having lost his desire to foster an acquaintance with the mother, Charles had begun to enjoy the son's company for its own sake.

Helen arrived at the *albergo* a little before noon. She allowed Harry to re-introduce her to the man who had so quickly become his idol. "I have to thank you, Mr Carnforth, for the interest you've shown in my son." She smiled at the boy as she spoke and her whole face lit up with love.

She could be a beauty if she were properly dressed, thought Charles. "It's been a pleasure," he said formally. "I've enjoyed his company. You have a fine son."

"I think so."

"Mrs Perriman – would you and your son do me the honour of taking luncheon with me today?"

The warm expression vanished and a wariness replaced it on her face.

How transparent her feelings were, Charles mused. He liked the lack of artifice. He had never known what his late wife was thinking – and after a few months of marriage had not even wanted to know.

Helen was still hesitating. "I don't think . . ."

"I would be very grateful. A man gets tired of eating alone."

His voice had suddenly grown diffident. She sensed a loneliness behind the request, which, if it did not equal her own, then at least approached it. Could it be so harmful to have lunch with a fellow countryman? Just the once? "Well . . ."

Harry tugged at her arm. "Do say yes, Mother! Mr Carnforth was going to tell me about India and what it's like to ride on an elephant."

So, because it was good for her son and because she, too, was lonely, Helen agreed.

They dined in a corner of the inn's public rooms. Charles' private parlour, Helen said gently, when it was suggested, would not be quite the thing. She was still a little worried about what people might say, so she had a quick word with Francesca, explaining her dilemma.

Francesca, who had been watching Charles with Harry, and who already had ideas of match-making, waved away her friend's scruples. "You have your son with you and I myself will wait upon you. Thus, I will be able to refute any gossip, *if* anyone is stupid enough to suggest that *my* inn is not of the most respectable!"

Francesca smiled as she walked away. She would see how the two of them got on. Any fool could tell that Charles Carnforth was very taken with both mother and boy. Poor man! He had told her one night that he had no family of his own. He must be very lonely. Why not encourage him to do something about it? And as she knew Helen would not do any encouraging, Francesca had every intention of interfering.

What a delightful time the three of them had! The inn's temperamental cook produced a marvellous meal, and Francesca's husband Paolo was persuaded to unearth from his cellars one of the special bottles of wine that only the most favoured customers were allowed to know about.

Pressed by Harry, Charles told them something of his travels, not only in India, which he had visited after his wife's death, but in other parts of the world.

"I'd had enough of killing after we beat Boney at Waterloo, so I sold out of the regiment and went off to see a bit of the world instead."

Harry's eyes were round with wonder, and he fired off so many questions that conversation never flagged. And Charles had many fascinating tales to share with them. Three whole hours had passed before Helen realised it.

"Oh!" she exclaimed, when the church bells rang. "I hadn't realised how late it was. I have a lesson to give."

"Leave the lad here with me," Charles offered.

By now she trusted him enough to do that. "Are you sure?"

"Very sure." It was not the only thing about which he was now sure.

"She's the one," he said quietly to Alfred as they stood watching Harry feed the horses some wrinkled apples.

"The one, sir?"

There was a sad expression on his master's face as he explained, "She's the one I should have met when I was a young man."

The Captain did not need to explain to Alfred what he meant by that, because his manservant had seen for himself how very unhappy the marriage was.

When Helen returned to collect Harry, Charles persuaded mother and son to stroll down to the fishing harbour with him, and they enjoyed one of those golden late autumn days, with the mildest of breezes and a memory of flowers in the air.

Helen had never had the pleasure of a gentleman's attentions before. Her father had had a harsh idea of how a Christian gentleman should behave, even in polite company, and her brother had followed the paternal example, especially with regard to his sister. Her husband had never attempted to cosset her in any way, but had simply expected her to serve him. But Charles had fussed over the menu, deliberately chosen subjects of conversation which would be of interest to her, and listened to her opinions with flattering attentiveness.

And now, as they walked along, he was handing her over rough bits of ground as if she were a piece of precious china. That made her feel warm and cherished. So she did not hurry home, just allowed herself the utter luxury of this one golden afternoon.

That evening, she hummed as she prepared a simple meal, for Harry was always ravenous. She could not remember when she had spent a happier day. And Charles had spoken of seeing her the next day. Seeing her and Harry, of course. She knew already that she would not refuse another invitation.

For Harry's sake, she tried to tell herself – then she blushed in the darkness of her room as she realised that it was also for her own sake. She really liked Charles Carnforth.

It was a whirlwind courtship. Charles wooed both mother and son, taking infinite trouble to arrange the most delightful little excursions, sometimes with Francesca as chaperone, to that lady's secret delight. And as it was the quiet season, Helen had time to spare, conversation to share.

Within a month he had decided to propose marriage and he spent some time thinking what to say to her, how to make utterly certain she couldn't refuse him.

It happened on a windy day in early November. The three of them had gone for a brisk walk along the cliffs above the town, where public gardens and walks had been laid out to please the summer visitors.

After a while, Charles turned to Harry. "I wonder if you'd leave us alone for half an hour, old chap. I have something very important to discuss with your mother."

Harry, already primed by Francesca to expect something of the sort, nodded and whispered, "Good luck, sir!" then ran off.

Helen allowed Charles to lead her to a stone bench, and sat there with her head bowed. Her heart was beating fast and her thoughts were in a whirl. This could only mean one thing – and she had persuaded herself that Charles was just enjoying their company for a short time until he moved on. But if it meant – if he . . . Colour flooded her face.

He sat down beside her and took her hand very gently in his. "My dear Helen, you must have guessed how I feel about you. I'm not one to make you fancy speeches, but – would you do me the honour of becoming my wife?"

She took a deep gasping breath and looked up at him. "I – I don't know what to say!"

He could hear the near panic in her voice. Gently, Charles, he said to himself, take it gently.

"At least you haven't refused me, my dear. No, let me finish first, then think it through before you answer. I've not got much to offer you. Spent most of my money. Got enough left to keep you and the boy in reasonable comfort, though."

She didn't inquire what he meant by that. To her, reasonable comfort meant a roof over their heads, a warm fire in winter and enough to eat. "I – don't care about money."

"No. I know you don't. You're not like that. But it does come in useful, and damn, you'd be a lot better off than you are now. The boy too. He needs a father. And I – I'd like a son."

When she still said nothing, he added painfully, "Know I'm a lot older than you are, but – well, you're never too old to fall in love. Fell in love with you that very first evening."

She raised her eyes and gave him a troubled look. "I – I'm not in love with you, Charles. I don't think I could ever fall in love again. My first marriage was a – a total disaster." She had sworn never, ever to imagine herself in love again.

"I know you're not in love with me. Strange if a chit of a girl like you were to fall in love with a crusty old wanderer like me. Just thought you'd like to know I loved you."

"Chit of a girl, indeed! I'm twenty-five!" And felt much older sometimes. It seemed an eternity since an ignorant young woman of sixteen had allowed an actor the freedom of her body without realising what she was doing. She hardly even recognised that foolish young Helen now.

"And I'm fifty-four," he went on. "More than twice your age."

He sighed. "I feel it too, sometimes, but other times – well, other times I feel as frisky as a colt." How difficult this was! He seized her hand. "You may not love me, but – you do *like* me, don't you, Helen?"

"Very much!" She didn't pull her hand away and she smiled as she spoke, for he looked boyishly anxious, his expression very like her son's when he wanted something desperately. And Charles's soft thinning hair always seemed untidy and windswept. What did it matter if it were grey? She had a sudden desire to push it back, out of his eyes. Without thinking, she let go of his hand for a moment to do just that and the smile they shared seemed to form a tangible bond between them.

He smiled at her. "Liking me very much will do fine for me. In any case, I sometimes think there are many shades of love. There's the love you feel for your son, and the love Alfred and I feel for one another—" He saw the surprise in her eyes and added, "We've faced death together several times, Alfred and I. It forms a strong bond."

She liked him all the better for admitting how close he was to his servant.

"So if you like me enough, my dear, I feel we're well on the way to reaching an understanding."

When he took her hand again and clasped it in both of his, she let it rest there. It felt so comfortable. So safe.

"And the boy likes me too," he added softly. "You heard him wish me luck."

"Yes. I know he does." If Harry had not liked Charles, she would not be here now, listening to her first real proposal of marriage.

"That's important. For him and for me. I never had a son. I should have liked one very much. It wasn't to be. My wife and I never had any children. But I would consider it a privilege, a very great privilege, to help you raise your son. I promise you, I'd be a father to him in every way I could."

She could think of no better father for Harry.

They both looked across at the small figure on the headland. The boy was tossing pebbles over the edge of the cliff, concentrating very hard on hitting something below, by the looks of him.

"Fine lad, that!"

"Isn't he?" She looked at Harry proudly. He made everything she had suffered worthwhile. Even Robert, for only Robert could have given her this son.

"Forgive me for saying this. Not the sort of thing a gentleman should mention to a lady. But – what future is there for you here? Giving English lessons to fools! What sort of a life is that? And – you're short of money. Can't help seeing that, however neatly you darn your clothes. Damned black things! Why do you wear them? I'd like to dress you in bright jewel colours!"

She blushed and put her hand over the darn. She could not afford new clothes, and it had suited her to wear black. She knew that widows seemed more respectable, somehow, to potential clients.

"So – wouldn't it be better to accept my offer, Helen, my dear? I'm not rich, you'd not be marrying a fortune, but I could look after you, get a good tutor for Harry, teach him to ride and to—"

"How could I take advantage of your kindness like that?" she whispered. Ah, the temptation to say yes!

He put his hand gently under her chin and forced her to look him in the eyes. "There's nothing wrong with an honest bargain, Helen, my dear."

She felt suddenly breathless. "Please, Charles – you shouldn't tempt me!"

The arm tightened around her. "Why not?"

"Well, because – because I should be taking advantage of your kindness."

"Good! I'd like that! Ah, Helen, Helen, why didn't I meet you when I was young? It's me who'd be taking advantage of you!" What if she later met someone whom she could truly love? No, he would not let that happen.

Her hands were trembling so much that she had to clasp them together. "I – I . . ."

He smiled at her, and reached out to trace a line down her cheek. Suddenly he felt optimistic enough to press the point. "Well, my dear, won't give me my answer? Can you stand to marry me?"

"Oh, Charles, I shouldn't – I – you—"

He kissed her and then, as she sighed and laid her head on his shoulder, he repeated, "Say yes! Go on, say it!"

And it seemed the most natural thing in the world to say, "Yes, Charles, I will marry you."

"You'll not regret it, my little love. I'll make sure you don't regret it. We'll have such fun together!" She deserved some happiness. What she'd told him about her earlier life made his blood run cold. He'd thought he had uncaring parents, but he'd had his nurse, and a whole variety of friends to make up for their indifference. And later on, Alfred. She'd had no one.

He hugged her tightly, then threw back his head and let out a whoop of triumph that made Harry stop in his tracks, look towards them and start running down the hill.

He arrived to see that Charles had folded Helen in his arms and that the two of them were staring into each other's eyes as if they'd never seen one another before. "Why are you cuddling my mother, sir? Are you all right, Mother?"

Seeing Helen's blushing confusion, Charles answered for her. "She's just agreed to marry me, young fellow. People always cuddle each other when they agree to get married."

"Oh, I see." Then Harry frowned at them. "Will that make you my father, sir?"

"Yes. Well, stepfather, anyway. Same thing, as far as I'm concerned. How do you feel about that, eh?"

Harry left them in no doubt. He flung himself upon them, burrowing between Charles and Helen and trying to put his arms around both of them at once. "It's splendid! Just absolutely splendid! Wait till I tell Alfred and Francesca! They said my mother would marry you."

Charles chuckled and gave him a rib-cracking hug.

Helen, watching them with tears in her eyes, thought that here, surely, was another shade of love, the love of father and son. She had no doubt that such a love was already growing between these two.

"There you are, Helen, my dear." Charles pulled her closer. "Your son approves, at any rate. Don't you, my boy?"

"Oh, yes, sir." Harry let out a shout of joy. "Hurrah! Hurrah!"

"What's that in aid of?" Charles asked indulgently.

"If you're my stepfather, we shall be able to hire that pony, shan't we, sir? So I'll be able to learn to ride properly now!" He jumped off the seat and did three forward somersaults, yelling happily, "A pony! A pony!"

Charles grinned down at his betrothed. "There you are! Knew there was a good reason for us to get married!" And they leaned against each other, laughing helplessly.

Eleven

The wedding of Helen and Charles was very quiet, for it took place in Rome, where Helen had no acquaintances and where even Charles had very few – of the respectable sort, anyway. She had wanted to get married in the little church in Serugia, but Charles was adamant that this would not do.

"When you become Mrs Carnforth, my dear, the ceremony must be conducted in such a way that no one can ever challenge the validity of the marriage. A wedding in an obscure Catholic church is not good enough. If anything ever happens to me, you must be securely established as my wife. So that means Rome and the presence of the British Ambassador, or one of his aides, at least."

"Don't talk about – anything happening!" she said involuntarily.

"I must. Always face facts, even if you don't like them, and you'll find you can cope with most things in life. I'm much older than you and therefore likely to die first. It's how things are, so why pretend otherwise?" He kissed her cheek. "Not that I won't do my best to hang on till a ripe old age! But," he placed his forefinger gently on her lips to stop her interrupting him again, "we shall do everything openly and correctly, and we shall plan carefully for all eventualities – for both you and the boy."

She kissed his finger, then stood on tiptoe and shyly kissed his cheek. It was still hard for her to show affection openly, as he did, but the smallest gesture pleased him so much that she was fast learning to do so. She still felt guilty sometimes, especially when lying in her comfortable bed at night, that she could not love him in the same way he loved her. He seemed more like a friend, an uncle almost, than a lover, though she did not dislike his touch. Definitely a different type of love to what he felt for her. But if he was content with that, she was too. He was such a dear man.

"And that brings us to your wedding dress, m'dear."

"I can make myself a . . ."

"No! You can't make the wedding dress yourself. The eyes of the English community will be upon you. The dress must be of the very highest standard made by one of Rome's top dressmakers. If there were time, I'd get one in Paris, but I don't want to wait that long."

"But the expense!"

"Is necessary."

So they said farewell to their friends in Serugia, took up residence very correctly in two separate hotels in Rome, called upon the British Ambassador and made their preparations for the wedding.

"Is – er – is there anyone in England you should inform?" Charles asked one day.

The hurt look he so hated to see came into her eyes.

"Ah, my darling, forget I ever asked!"

"No. You're right. I think perhaps I should write to Lord Northby, who is a distant connection of the family. When I informed him of Harry's birth, he sent a silver spoon, so *he* has not disowned me. It was the only christening present my poor boy ever received, and even that . . ." She told him the sad little tale of how Robert had stolen it and how she had redeemed it and thereafter left it with a friend in England for safekeeping. "My parents didn't even reply to my letter then, so I shall not write to them now," she finished wistfully.

"Want me to write to Northby for you? Knew him at Oxford. Pompous old fool he turned into but, as you rightly say, it won't hurt to inform him of the marriage."

"You may write as well, if you wish, if it's the correct thing to do, but I shall do so myself. I don't shirk my duties, Charles." Then she brightened. "Oh, and there's Roxanne, too. I must write to her. She's – she's not exactly respectable, but she was good to me, and she is Harry's godmother."

Charles frowned as she told him about Roxanne. Where his wife-to-be was concerned, he was surprisingly straight-laced. "Don't like the connection, m'dear." Then he admitted reluctantly, "But you can't drop her acquaintance if she was kind to you and the lad."

"No, Charles. There are Mr and Mrs Hendry, too, but they're

very respectable, I promise you. He's a minister of the Church of England. He became Harry's godfather, because I – I didn't know anyone else."

He gave her a hug. "Well, now you've got me as well." But it worried him that she would only really have him and he spent a long time with an English lawyer recommended by the Ambassador, drawing up a new will, and settling part of his unentailed income on her and Harry immediately. When that was done, he felt better. She would be safe now, whatever happened. He had copies of the will sent to his family lawyer in England and then he put all such gloomy thoughts out of his mind. He wanted his little love to enjoy herself. Damn, he was going to make sure she enjoyed herself.

The wedding gown was a masterpiece of white *gros de Naples* silk, handsomely trimmed with several flounces edged in expensive lace. Helen did not feel she should wear a veil for her second marriage, but she did allow Charles to help her choose an elegant bonnet, trimmed with silk flowers and lace, whose brim curved down over her ears, forming a low oval frame for her face.

She could hardly believe her own eyes when she saw herself in the mirror before she left the hotel to go to the Protestant church patronised by many from the English community in Rome. A maid from the hotel had dressed her hair in gleaming coils and loops, and she thought in wonderment as she stared into the mirror that she had never looked so well. Over the gown, for the weather was now cold, she wore a pelisse in a palest pink velvet, trimmed with swansdown. She looked elegant and fashionable, a fit wife for an English landowner.

And no one could see the butterflies that were currently careering round inside her stomach and making her feel so nervous that her hand trembled in that of her new husband as they were pronounced man and wife.

After the simple ceremony, they entertained the Ambassador's aide and his wife, who had come to witness the ceremony at Charles's invitation, to a gourmet luncheon at the hotel. Then at last they were able to escape to a secluded *albergo* which Charles knew of, only twenty miles outside Rome.

Harry was left with Briggs in a pleasant *pensione* on the outskirts of the city. A pony had been hired and riding lessons were to begin at once, so Harry waved them goodbye quite happily.

"You'll look after him, Briggs," Helen said before they left.

"With my life, Mrs Carnforth."

She nodded, still feeling strange to be addressed by that name.

It seemed to Helen, then and thereafter, that Charles's love was a very tangible thing. He surrounded her with every comfort and attention the inn could provide. A trunk full of clothes awaited her in their bedroom, as a "little surprise", and there was a present for her every evening of that memorable week.

Best of all, to her, was his tenderness. She had not known that love could be so very beautiful. And yet, this was not the rapture of her first months with Robert, and she could not lose herself in Charles's love as she had done when she was a girl. Rather, this was a love between two friends, or between an old and a young relative, on her side at least, though she tried to love him as he deserved.

It made her feel very guilty at times that she had not tumbled head over heels in love with him, as he clearly had with her. But she found that the deep affection which grew steadily within her was enough to make him happy, and he never reproached her for not offering him more, as she had feared he might.

She also found that with him she enjoyed making love. With Robert she had enjoyed it for the cuddles, but Charles made every part of it a pleasure, touching, caressing and wooing her with words as well as deeds till she felt ready to explode with joy.

Something dark and painful that had dwelled inside her all her life began to melt, and little by little, happiness took its place.

Charles would look at her sometimes and feel tears well up in his eyes as he saw how she had been transformed by his love. Then he would have to cough and find something to do for fear of making a fool of himself.

After the honeymoon, they rejoined Harry and Briggs and headed for Venice, which Charles wanted to show to his young wife. He continued to shower her with presents and was, with difficulty, restrained from finding her a lady's maid.

"Charles, this must stop!" she scolded one day. "You're too extravagant. I don't need all these things!"

"I like to buy you things. You've got so little, m'dear. It gives me immense pleasure."

"But you said – you were not rich. I would hate us to get into debt . . ." She faltered to a halt.

He stared at her, suddenly realising what she was thinking. "Like your first husband did?"

"Yes."

"My dearest girl, I've been living well within my income ever since I met you. In fact, I'm saving money for the first time in years. I don't gamble now," he pulled a wry face, laughing at himself, "and I don't miss it at all." He saw her face brighten. "I don't waste my substance in riotous living, either. You've been very good for me." He pressed one hand to his chest and said in a melodramatic voice, "Behold, the reformed rake."

She frowned, as a dreadful suspicion occurred to her. "But – but Charles, if that's so, you must be much richer than I ever dreamed."

"Does that make me ineligible, my dearest goose?"

"N-no, but it makes me even more ineligible," she said in a low voice. "People will say that I – I married you for your money."

He roared with laughter and swept her into his arms, waltzing her round the room. "My own love, if it makes you feel happier, I will give the money away and live with you in abject poverty."

She tried to frown at him. "Now you're being silly!"

"Just teasing you a little, my dear. You've never learnt to laugh at the world and its follies, have you?"

"No." But her expression was still worried, so he guided her over to a plump sofa set invitingly in front of a crackling log fire. Time to face up to a few more things.

"Let's talk about my finances," he said, in his usual decisive way. "After which, we'll forget about the whole damn thing and go to the theatre. It's time you learned to enjoy plays from the other side of the stage." He kept hold of her nearest hand.

"Now, Mrs Carnforth, if you're imagining that I shall be leaving you a rich widow, you're going to be sadly disappointed! I was the younger son, so I have my mother's money, which I may leave to whom I like – in this case, you. Shh! You must listen carefully! When my brother died childless – my generation of Carnforths haven't been good breeders – I inherited an estate which was most strictly entailed upon the male line. I may not leave even a square yard of my land to you, or to anyone else. It all goes to my heir, who's a sort of second cousin, one Daniel Carnforth by name."

He looked into the fire, his eyes veiled by memories. "I also have some of my first wife's money left, but not much, because I spent most of it after she died." The grip on her hand tightened. "I went into the Army when I was young and, later, I married Gertrude to please my family – and I did my duty by her, however reluctantly."

He grimaced. "She was a pious shrew, and she hated me even touching her, so we lived fairly separate lives after the first year. When my brother died, I tried again to provide an heir for Ashdown. But Gertrude and I never managed to have any children. I would very much have liked some, but it was not to be. I couldn't even blame her. I've had plenty of – er – romantic adventures, and never, to the best of my knowledge, have I produced a child."

He sighed. "Ah, but she was a cold, proud woman, Gertrude was . . . not like you . . . and she grew very bitter as the years passed! Like living with an iceberg, it was! The two of us could not have been more ill-suited. When she died suddenly – well, I knew that I could not face another such marriage and I suspected that it would be useless anyway, for I felt then that I'd never father a child."

He was clutching her hand as he spoke and she could feel the tension in him, the pain, too.

"I refused the pleas of my venerable relatives to marry again and set out to enjoy my declining years. That's why I went off to India. They couldn't catch me there. Two glorious years I spent in that country, though I suspect Briggs may not consider them in the same light, poor fellow. He's not fond of foreign parts. It's a harsh country, India, but fascinating. If I were younger, I'd sweep you off and we'd travel round the world. But I must confess that I haven't the stamina or the digestion I once had, so we'll stick to Europe, eh?"

She looked down at their linked hands and confessed, "I think I'm not as adventurous as you are, Charles. Europe will suit me fine. But please go on. I want to know all about you."

"All! That's a big order. And I don't think I'd want you to know some things. I'm not proud of everything I've done. We all make mistakes, and I've made more than my share. But to continue this tale – I got in a land agent to run Ashdown when I set out to see some of the world, and he's still there, as far as I know. I haven't been back since. The family lawyer deals with things for me."

He planted a kiss on the softness of her cheek. "But never, wherever I've gone, whatever I've done, have I been as happy as I am with you, Helen m'dear! I was a rackety young fellow – young officers usually are – and then there was Gertrude, poor woman, to whom I was not always true, I fear." He gazed at her solemnly, "But I swear I'll be true to you, my dear love."

"I know that, Charles." He had hardly strayed from her side and most nights he left her in no doubt about his love.

"This is the best, the very best time of my life."

She nestled against him. "And of mine."

"So, to come back to the point that worries you – when I die, most of my fortune will pass to this distant cousin, Daniel Carnforth. You will have the Dower House to live in, if you choose, for the rest of your life, and you'll have what's left of my money, which will be enough to live on, but not by any means a fortune – and that's all."

She sighed in relief.

"Yes," he said, speaking almost to himself, "my cousin Celia's son will inherit Ashdown. Never met the chap, but it's to be hoped that he doesn't take after his mother. She's a drooping daisy of a woman, always fluttering her hands at you or weeping over something. But she has a vicious streak, too. I never could abide her! No wonder her husband turned into a brandy-guzzler. She'd drive a parson to drink, that one would. Son's bound to be a twiddlepoop!"

He scowled. "I got a damned impertinent letter from her a couple of years ago, saying that as my heir, this Daniel of hers ought to get to know the estate and the tenantry. She practically ordered me to put him in charge. Soon nipped that in the bud. Told her straight that he could get to know everything after I was dead and, until then, he'd better stay away from Ashdown."

"Shall we go to live there ever?"

"No. It's a deuced miserable sort of place and I don't like the English climate. I'll take you over for a visit one summer, if we've nothing better to do, but I'll not live there again, even for you, m'dear. Ashdown has got nothing but unhappy memories for me. Tell you what, though, we might find ourselves a house somewhere we do like and settle down for a bit. How'd you like that, eh? I've had enough of hotels. Where would you like to live? Nice?"

Now it was her turn to shudder. Those months in Nice had left her with only painful memories. "Oh, no!"

He gave her an extra hug to take away the sadness. "In the Kingdom of the Two Sicilies, then. Some white villa on a hill, with views of the sea. How'd you like that?"

"Very much indeed."

"Good. So would I! But one day I must show you Paris in the spring!" He nodded at the thought. "And we'll buy some more horses. Time you learned to ride."

"Me! I'm too old now!"

He grinned wickedly. "Nonsense! One's never too old to learn new tricks! I'll teach both you and Harry myself. It'll be fun!"

And it was fun! Life suddenly became one great glorious feast of pleasures. Charles's favourite sound was the merry peal of his wife's long-repressed laughter at the antics of her husband, her son, the pony, or the little dog Harry acquired in Naples and smuggled into the hotel, with disastrous effects upon the smooth running of that august establishment.

In England, the news of Charles's unexpected second marriage brought varying reactions.

Helen's brother Edward was informed of it by Lord Northby. He was much relieved that she had seen the error of her ways and become respectable, and he felt it incumbent upon him to write to her once, at least.

> Sister,
>
> I am in receipt of a letter from Lord Northby, informing me of your second marriage to Charles Carnforth of Ashdown. I must congratulate you upon this marriage and I assume that you have seen the error of your former ways.
>
> I regret to inform you that our parents have both passed away: our father of a seizure three years ago, and our mother, soon afterwards, of the influenza.

I hope things go well for your future comfort, but, given our differences, I propose no further communication.

Yours,

Edward Merling, Parson, Middle Wotherton

Comfort! Helen thought. Future comfort! What was wrong with the word happiness, for heaven's sake? She did not reply to the letter, nor did she show it to Harry. A few days later, however, she received another letter from Lord Northby, which she did show to her son.

My dear cousin Helen,

I am writing to offer you my hearty congratulations upon your recent marriage. I have the honour of being acquainted (slightly) with your husband, who comes from an old and well-respected family in the next county. It's an excellent match and I wish you every happiness.

Yours sincerely,

Basil, Lord Northby

Mrs Celia Carnforth also wrote to Charles and he did not show this letter to anyone else.

My dear cousin Charles,

I read your recent communication with great surprise. I do hope that, at your age, you have not taken an unwise step in marrying a woman over twenty years younger than yourself. And that you have chosen carefully one who will be a helpmeet to you in your declining years.

Your heir, my dear son Daniel, has asked me to join his felicitations with mine.

Your loving cousin,

Celia Carnforth

"How the devil did she find out how old you are?" Charles demanded irately after telling Helen about it. "The woman's an inveterate gossip! I told her nothing about you, except that you were a widow with one son and connected to Lord Northby." He screwed up the letter and threw it on the fire without showing it to Helen. "To hell with her! And to hell with her son too! He might be my heir, but I mean to make him wait a long time to inherit."

Helen put one arm round his waist. "Poor Charles! It's not worth getting angry about. I assure you your cousin's attitude doesn't worry me."

"Nor me. We shall not concern ourselves with the Celia Carnforths of this world, m'dear, not now or ever! There are too many other things – and people – to enjoy!"

But in her pleasant house in one of Bath's elegant terraces – not Royal Crescent, but one as close by as she could afford – Celia Carnforth continued to concern herself with her cousin Charles and his new wife, for she was ferociously protective of her son's inheritance, which might now be jeopardised by a late heir.

When she received Charles's curt note, informing her of his marriage, she first succumbed to an attack of the vapours, then, when this got her nowhere, she summoned her son from his country estate on "a matter of direst urgency".

While she waited for him to arrive, for he was used to her fusses and panics and did not turn up for several days, the imprudence of Charles Carnforth's second marriage was her only topic of conversation, and her friends grew quite tired of it. She cast doubts upon the marriage's validity. She worried about the foolishness of a man of Charles's age marrying a woman so much younger. (What a piece of luck it had been to meet the brother of the ambassador's aide and find out something about this woman! They were now forewarned.) She also, very delicately, hinted that this female must have a dubious background. Why else would she be living by herself in an obscure Italian town? What was she hiding?

Daniel Carnforth came to Bath reluctantly, for when his mother took a pet about something, she could be a most uncomfortable companion.

"Read this!" she announced dramatically the minute he entered her parlour, picking up a crumpled piece of paper and thrusting it in his face.

He took it from her, sighed, and read the letter slowly. "Surely you didn't ask me to come here just because of this? I got a letter from cousin Charles, too, as is only proper, so I know all about it. Really, Mother!"

She stared at him open-mouthed, horrified that he could just accept this *mésalliance* so calmly. When he handed back the letter to her, sat down and leaned back with a tired sigh, Celia jumped to her feet and began pacing up and down the room, accompanied by the fretting and yapping of her little dog. "But what are you going to *do* about it, Daniel?"

"Do? Nothing."

"You must do something!"

"What can I do? Charles has a perfect right to marry whoever he wishes. It's none of my business."

"But she's young enough to have children! You could find yourself cut out of your inheritance by some puling infant! Oh, I could murder him! He was ever a fool!"

Daniel shrugged. "There's absolutely nothing I can do, or wish to do, Mother, but accept a *fait accompli* with dignity." He wondered how soon he could leave her and get back to his estate. He had no love for town life, especially in Bath. Whenever he visited, which he only did out of duty, his mother would not leave him alone, but expected him to squire her around and devote every minute of the day to her.

For her part, Celia was wondering how she could persuade him to stay for a while and meet the latest heiress, who was said to be as rich as a nabob and not too ill-favoured, though not, of course, a lady of the highest breeding. But the Carnforths were not rich and it behoved Daniel, as the last of the line, to mend the family fortunes by a judicious match.

By dint of a determined campaign of weeping and pleading, she managed to hold her son with her for two more days, and even to introduce him to the heiress in the Pump Room. But to no avail. The girl was not ugly, certainly, but she was astonishingly silly, with several annoying mannerisms. And Daniel had never been one to bear fools gladly, even if they were rich.

He had been such a serious little boy, a real cuckoo in the nest, she sometimes thought, and had stayed serious as he grew up – except for a deplorable sense of humour, which betrayed him into foolish pleasantries at the most inappropriate moments. He had displayed real brilliance at school and had continued to shine academically at university, to his mother's great horror. She didn't know where he got a taste for Latin and Greek from! There was no one like that on her side of the family, thank goodness! She blamed the Carnforths for that. And for much else.

However, since his father's death, Daniel had given up all that sort of book rubbish and had settled down, devoting himself to farming the small estate which was all that was left of his patrimony and had been his mother's dowry. And who, pray, was interested in farming, except for a few cranks? A gentleman should employ an agent to deal with such mundane things. A gentleman should marry money, not make it, and then get himself an heir. And so she had told Daniel. Many times. But had he listened to her? No. He had not. She did not know where he got his wilful nature from.

Daniel, who had realised with a shock just how perilously close to bankruptcy the estate was after his father's mismanagement, kept silent about the real reason for his sudden devotion to matters agricultural and applied himself to restoring the family fortunes in his own way. He not only succeeded beyond his wildest expectations, but discovered in himself a love of the land and a flair for the business of farming.

While his mother bought herself a small house in Bath and indulged her taste for an indolent, gossipy sort of existence, her son stayed quietly and happily at Bellborough. He sometimes wondered whether he should marry. His mother certainly said he should. She said it often. But for quite a while he had had a pleasant liaison with a very obliging widow, and life was so comfortable that he had just drifted along contentedly.

He'd get married one day, when he found a peaceful sort of a woman. And now that the widow had found herself another man, one who seemed likely to marry her, he might look around for a wife. There was no hurry.

Daniel, like Charles, was a true Carnforth in appearance – a large man, tall and broad-shouldered. His hair was brown and wavy, his face tanned from an outdoor life and his hands, as his mother complained every time she saw him, vulgarly roughened, real "cowman's hands". His eyes were the brightest of blues,

"Carnforth eyes", she always said scornfully when he had upset her. Celia Carnforth, unhappy in her marriage, was scornful of anything to do with her husband's family and never stopped harping on the fact that Daniel had Bellborough from her side of the family.

And at least he took after her side of the family in his attitude towards money. The Bells had always been noted for their frugality and good management, unlike the Carnforths! If his poor dear father had not passed away so young (her side of the family was also noted for its longevity, she was thankful to say!), heaven alone knew what would have happened to Bellborough. That was one of the few things Daniel agreed with her about.

The one mistake her dearest papa had made was in her marriage contract. He should have tied up her inheritance so that her husband could not scatter it to the four winds, as he had done with his own. If her papa had known what Stephen Carnforth was really like, he would never have allowed her to marry him – though to be sure, poor Stephen had been disastrously handsome, like all the men of that family, as she knew to her cost!

His son had a great look of him at times, which was very upsetting to a woman of her sensibilities. And behaved like him too! Stubborn as a mule. Only think of the eligible females to whom she had introduced him, and would he look twice at any of them? No! He would not! It was more than time he settled down and set up his nursery. Good heavens, he was turned thirty now!

Daniel gritted his teeth, endured two days of his mother's company, sometimes retaining his sense of humour enough to be amused by her foolishness, sometimes feeling like strangling her. When the latter occurred, which was more often than the former, he found silence to be his best weapon, for it infuriated her. After that, he decided that he had more than done his duty and escaped back to Bellborough.

He would be sorry, though, if he did not inherit, for he had visited Ashdown Park covertly once or twice and found it beautiful. A pretty manor house set in stunning grounds, with fertile, though much neglected, land attached, too. That agent did not know his business.

In Bath the gossip about Charles Carnforth's second marriage gradually died down, though Celia continued to fret about the possibility of him producing an heir. But her spite could not reach Helen, who had no idea at all of how her husband's only close relatives felt about her.

And her husband, watching fondly as she bloomed and grew even prettier, intended to keep it that way.

Twelve

Fifteen months after their wedding, Helen became aware that Charles was having stomach trouble. He said it was nothing, refusing to let a "touch of indigestion" incapacitate him. Then one evening, when he and Helen were sitting on the balcony of their villa after dinner overlooking the Bay of Naples, he experienced a much sharper pain than he'd ever had before. As he was taking a sip of wine, he grunted, letting the wine glass drop and he doubled up, gasping in agony.

"Charles! What is it?"

"Pain. Stomach. Must have – uh – eaten something!" He waved her away and concentrated on breathing deeply and not crying out. He would not shame himself before her.

She went quietly to the other side of the room and rang for Alfred, who came and helped his master upstairs. She had great faith in Alfred's common sense, as well as in his devotion to his master. She also guessed that Charles would prefer to suffer in private. He was rather sensitive to anything which put him in a bad light in front of his young wife. As if she could think anything but well of him, whatever he did. She might not be in with love him in a romantic way, as she knew he still was with her, but she loved him dearly, nonetheless.

After a while Alfred came down to report that his master had been sick and was now lying in bed, feeling somewhat easier. "He says he don't want a doctor fetched, Mrs Carnforth, but I – well, that is, I . . ." He faltered to a halt.

"But what? Please go on, Alfred!"

"Well, I don't want to seem disloyal to the Captain, but he's had a few sharp attacks of indigestion lately, really sharp, which he's hidden from you and – and that ain't something he's ever suffered from before, not even in India, where they put pepper in everything! So I thought – well, if *you* sent for the doctor, there'd be nothing the master could do but see him."

"Indeed I shall! Thank you for confiding in me, Alfred." She never called him Briggs, which seemed so impolite to someone who was very much part of the family.

The doctor arrived half an hour later, having judged a rich Englishman to be of sufficient importance to warrant an emergency home visit so late at night. With much grumbling, Mr Carnforth submitted to an examination and enumerated his symptoms. When the doctor came downstairs, he refused very politely, but firmly, to discuss his diagnosis with Helen. "That is for your husband to tell you, Mrs Carnforth." He bowed his way out again as quickly as he could.

Cold fear crept into Helen's heart. The fear darkened to an icy dread when Alfred came to tell her that His Lordship would like to be left alone for an hour or so. "He's sorry to keep you from your bed, ma'am."

His face was so wooden that fear shot through her. "It's bad news, isn't it?" she whispered. When he just looked down and said nothing, she pleaded, "Don't keep it from me! I can bear anything but not knowing." When he raised his eyes to meet hers, she could see that they were full of tears and the fear gripped her even more tightly.

"I fear so, ma'am. But he wishes to tell you about it himself and I think we should do as he asks." Alfred's face looked pinched.

She nodded, afraid that if she tried to speak she would burst into tears. And that would help no one. "Let me know when he's ready to see me," she managed at last, and her voice sounded strange in her own ears, far sharper than usual. "I shall be out on the *loggia*."

Helen huddled there alone, staring at the reflection of the moon on the water, but not seeing the beauty with which she was surrounded. Crickets twittered away in the gardens and moths came to flutter around the lamps, but she paid them no heed.

At one point, the housekeeper came to see if her mistress needed anything but, when Helen didn't even raise her head, the woman tiptoed out again. Briggs had threatened all manner of reprisals if Giuliana did not leave them all alone.

It was well past midnight when Alfred came to summon Helen to join her husband. She was running up the stairs almost before he had finished delivering his message. At the door to the bedroom, however, she slowed down, straightened her spine and walked in. Charles, looking pale and drawn, very unlike his usual self, was lying on the bed. He held out his arms to her and she ran into them.

"What is it? Oh, Charles, don't hide anything from me! What did the doctor say?"

He stroked her hair and held her close. "It seems – I have a growth in my stomach. He's pretty certain that's what it is. Says he can feel it quite clearly. It's not – there's nothing they can do about it. It will – grow bigger and I shall not recover."

She clung to him convulsively, but she did not have hysterics, or burden him with noisy grief, as he had half feared. "Oh, Charles – is he sure?"

"'Fraid so, m'dear. Sorry to keep you out of the bedroom, but – well, the idea took a bit of getting used to!"

After a moment, she managed to ask, "What must we do?"

"Nothing we can do. That's the hardest part. There's nothing at all anyone can do about it. The enemy occupied the fortress before war was even declared. So all we can do is – enjoy the last few months as much as we can."

"Few months? Is that all?"

The doctor had been rather more pessimistic, but Charles would not tell her that yet. He intended to spare her as much as possible. "So he says."

"Couldn't we – see someone else? There are other doctors."

"We could – but he seemed very sure of what he said. And I don't much care for being mauled around by other doctors. What this one says makes sense." He felt the death sentence was unfair, so soon after he had found happiness, but no one promised you life would be fair.

Tears were trickling down her cheeks, for all her brave resolves, but she said as steadily as she could manage, "Then we must make sure that you – we – enjoy every minute of what's left to us."

He raised her chin and kissed her wet cheeks. "That's my dear brave girl!" She nestled against him and they stayed there for a long time, each trying to come to terms with the horror that had crept so stealthily into their lives.

Two months later, Charles Carnforth lay in his bedroom, watching the late afternoon sun flood everything with light. He refused to let them keep the curtains drawn and usher him out of the world in a darkened room.

Earlier that day, the housekeeper had crept into the bedroom with some fresh water, tutted to herself and tried to draw the curtains, so that the sun should not fall on her master's face. Alfred was dozing in a chair in a corner of the room and didn't notice Giuliana come in. Tired as he was after a bad night, he did not like to leave his master alone, and Mrs Carnforth was also exhausted and trying to sleep for an hour or two.

Alfred woke with a start as the Captain spluttered into life.

"Leave those curtains alone, you fool of a woman!" The voice was a mere echo of his master's former parade-ground roar, but it made Giuliana give a little yelp of shock.

Alfred jumped up and rushed over to the window. "Get out! *Via! Via!*" he shouted, waving his arms at the housekeeper and pushing her towards the door. He could speak very little Italian, for Alfred was stubbornly English and seemed constitutionally incapable of getting his tongue round silly foreign words, though he understood a great deal of what was said. But his signs and waving arms were perfectly clear to Giuliana and so emphatic that she panicked and fled.

Alfred pulled back the curtain, so that the view was in no way obscured. He adjusted its folds with an air of triumph. "That woman is a fool," he said conversationally. "There y'are, sir. Lovely day it's been, ain't it?"

Charles burst out laughing. "Did you see that fat old hen run?" But the laugh turned into a fit of coughing and choking, which went on and on, and brought Alfred rushing back to the bed. It also brought Helen hurrying in from the next room, where she had been snoozing on the sofa.

When the coughing fit had subsided, she sat down by the bed and took hold of the invalid's hand. "When will you learn to stay calm, Charles Carnforth?" she asked reproachfully. "You know how bad it is for you to get excited!"

"Never will learn now, I expect," he whispered, irrepressible as ever. "Damned shame if a fellow can't have a bit of a laugh now and then!"

"Oh, Charles!" She sat down by the side of the bed, smiling as cheerfully as she could. Why try to change him? What did it matter if he lived a few days more or a few less? The main thing was for him to get as much pleasure from his last days as he could. "Let's watch the sunset together, shall we?"

He squeezed her hand, then lay back with a sigh against the carefully arranged pillows. His once-powerful body made the slightest of bumps under the heavy silk counterpane, and Helen had to blink very hard, so that he should not see the tears that sometimes came into her eyes at the sight of his wasted limbs. He would not tolerate pity from anyone, least of all from his young wife. Once he had come to terms with his "sentence", as he persisted in calling his illness, he had resolutely maintained an air of cheerful acceptance of his fate, and had insisted that his household and family do the same. He still shared a bed with his wife and only a week or two previously, he had managed, with her assistance, to make gentle love to her, though the effort had left him white and gasping.

"Worth it," he had said when he saw the expression on her face afterwards. "You have a beautiful body, my dear. It's given me much pleasure."

Although the invalid's eyes flickered shut and he fell into a sleep, Helen did not dare move away in case she woke him up again. He had slept so little for the past few days. Besides, he would be gone soon enough, and then she would have no hand to hold. She could rest all she pleased then.

She smiled down at him fondly. The wayward lock of hair had fallen over his forehead again. Sometimes, when his eyes twinkled with mischief, he looked like a schoolboy dressed up as an old man. Such blue, blue eyes he had! Age had not faded them in the slightest, nor had illness dimmed their brightness.

She sighed and the smile faded. She did not know what she would do without him, but she would not burden him with her fears, as he had not burdened her with lamentations about his illness. So she rarely discussed her own future, unless he raised the matter, but concentrated on making her husband's last weeks as happy as possible. She had coped well enough when her first husband had died. But in spite of the money, it would be much harder this time, for she would miss Charles dreadfully.

During the past week, he had gone downhill very rapidly, for he could not hold anything solid down now. He was, quite literally, starving to death.

As the room grew darker, Helen sat on beside the bed, still lost in thought. She had no fear of death, for she had grown used to deathbeds from a very early age. All she wanted was to be with Charles at the end.

"What are you thinking of?" The whisper startled her out of her reverie.

"Charles! I didn't know you were awake. Let me make you more comfortable! Would you like something to drink?"

He submitted to her ministrations with a faint smile. "Avoiding my question, Helen?" he asked as she sat down again.

She took his hand and smiled at him. "Not at all! I was remembering the first time you invited Harry and me to share a meal with you. Such a lovely day!"

"You were wearing a black dress. Darned, too. Black doesn't suit you. You should always wear rich colours, with your complexion. Don't wear mourning for me! Promise!"

This time she couldn't keep the tears back. "Don't – don't talk about that, Charles! It won't matter what I wear if you're not there to see it."

He grinned. "Watering pot!" he said provocatively. "Think it'll make it all go away if we don't mention it?"

She shook her head mutely.

His cheerfulness faltered for a minute. "Ah, lovely girl of mine, if it wasn't for leaving you, I'd not mind half as much. I've had a good life. And there are worse ways to die than being nursed by a beautiful woman, with a view like that outside my window." He returned obstinately to the question of mourning. "Promise me!" he repeated. "No damned weeds! No drab clothes!"

He was getting excited, sweat pearling his brow. What could she do but promise what he asked? "Very well. I won't wear black more than I have to. But there are times when people would be s-scandalised," she had to pause for a moment to swallow back a sob, "if I wore colours. For both our sakes, Charles, I must wear black then."

"Very well. I don't want them thinking badly of you. But at other times, no black. No grey, either. Or lilac. Or any of those damned faded colours. I won't have you drooping around. You've had enough of that in your life! More than enough."

"I promise." She saw with relief that he was relaxing again.

He squeezed her hand and settled back with a sigh. "Thank

you, love." A little later, he said, "We've had a bit of fun together, haven't we?"

"A lot of fun. More than in my whole life before."

"Not sorry you married me, then?"

"Not for a minute!"

He nodded in satisfaction and presently he drifted off into sleep again. He rarely stayed fully awake for long now, because of the laudanum he was taking for the pain. She looked at him affectionately. No, she was not sorry at all that she had married him, even if they'd only had a short time together. He had taught her to be happy, given her so much. And the money was the least of that.

Later that evening, Harry, now nearly nine years old, came to sit with his stepfather, as he always did, to chat about his day's doings. This time he had a cut on his lip to display with pride. He sometimes had difficulty with the boys of the village. "So I hit him, sir, just like you showed me, and he fell over. And when he got up and tried to hit me back, I thumped him harder. He won't dare to call me *un maledetto inglese* again!"

"Good lad! Good lad! Always stand up for yourself – and for your mother. I shall count on you to do that when I'm gone. I'll tell Briggs to teach you how to box, eh? Give him something to do. In fact, he can be your groom and your mother's general factotum then. Can't have him idling around, can we? And he can teach you to ride better, too, once you're in England. You'll need to learn to jump, so that you can hunt."

"Yes, sir." Harry's lips might be trembling, but he knew better than to cry in front of his stepfather, who had explained his illness to him, and how important it was, for his mother's sake, to stay cheerful. And as he had a vague memory of another invalid, one who hadn't stayed cheerful and who had made his mother cry, he tried very hard to do as Charles wanted. His stepfather was a very wonderful person.

The next day, the small household was thrown into confusion by the arrival of Charles's English lawyer. Mr Samuel Napperby drove up to the door in a cab just after midday, asking, in a loud, slow voice, for Mr Carnforth – *Carnforth.* Speaking like that was, he was convinced, the best way to make foreigners understand what you wanted.

Not knowing then who the visitor was, but having been told that the gentleman had come all the way from England, Helen felt impelled to see him herself in order to explain why it was impossible to trouble her husband with anything less than a very major crisis.

Mr Napperby, who had been admiring the view from the window of the drawing-room, turned to greet his employer's wife, hostility evident in his face and rigid bearing. Samuel Napperby had not liked the sound of this marriage, nor the generous arrangements Charles Carnforth had made for his young wife in the new will. He had heard echoes of the rumours spread by Celia Carnforth and felt there must be some truth in them. This young woman had married a much older man for his money. And as Charles was his friend, as well as employer, he very much resented that.

However, he blinked in confusion at the pale beauty who greeted him quietly, and who looked so tired and drawn. Dark circles under her eyes bore mute testimony to sleepless nights, but she was magnificent. No, he corrected the thought, not magnificent, for she was not tall enough or flamboyant enough for that. Her pure beauty reminded him of a little medieval statue of the Virgin Mary he had seen in a church once.

"I'm Mrs Carnforth," she said quietly. "How may I help you?"

Her voice removed another of the misconceptions Samuel had built up. His friend had previously favoured blowsy, buxom women – actresses usually – who could share a joke, a romp in bed and a bottle of wine with him. In fact, Samuel had been required to pay one or two of them off, for Charles had ever been generous. But this one – why she was a lady through and through! You could see that just by looking at her.

Helen wondered what he was thinking about as he stared at her. If she had known, she would have shrugged, not caring whether he thought her a fortune hunter or not. All she cared about just now was her dying husband.

"My name is Napperby, Samuel Napperby," he answered, bowing over her hand, "Mr Carnforth's lawyer – indeed, the family lawyer, for my family has served the Carnforths for three generations now."

"Oh dear! I hope nothing is wrong. My husband is in no state to – to . . ." Her voice faltered for a moment and her eyes filled with tears. "I'm afraid that Charles is very close to death, Mr Napperby. I can't allow him to be worried about anything. He is very weak."

He bowed again. He had not missed the signs of her distress. She obviously cared deeply for her husband. She looked done-up, too. She'd probably collapse when it was all over. He'd seen it happen many times. People kept up a brave front till their loved one was dead, then – bang! It hit them. Well, Charles had done the right thing in sending for him. He would know how to look after the poor young widow, who seemed to be about the same age as his own daughter.

"There's no bad news to trouble Mr Carnforth with," he said soothingly, "but I think it would be better if you let me see him. You see, it was he who sent for me. Urgent, he said it was."

"Oh." There was a pause. "I think it would be best if you saw him after sunset, then. He loves to watch the sun go down over the bay and he's always very calm afterwards. You see, any exertion makes him cough and splutter – and that isn't good for him. He's so weak now that anything may – may – precipitate a crisis."

"You may trust me to do nothing to disturb him."

She nodded acceptance at this statement. She had taken a liking to the lawyer, such a sturdy, solid sort of man. "Yes, I'm sure I may. In the meantime, I'll have a room prepared for you."

"I couldn't trouble you at such a time. There must be an inn where I can . . ."

She gave him a singularly sweet smile. "It's no trouble. And if Charles – if you are needed suddenly, it will be more convenient for us all if you are here." She rang a little bell and a plump Italian woman surged into the room. "*Per favore*, Giuliana, *una camera per il Signor Napperby. E l'avvocato di Mr Carnforth. E forse, una tazza di tè.*"

She turned back to Mr Napperby. "Giuliana will prepare you a room, and I've asked her to bring you a cup of tea." Again that sweet smile. "And I've taught her how to make it to the English taste, too."

Mr Napperby's expression lightened. He had no head for the rough red wine the innkeeper had pressed upon him the previous night, and he was not overly fond of the coffee they seemed to serve everywhere abroad. "That would be splendid,

Mrs Carnforth!" he said with real enthusiasm. "I must admit to a longing for a cup of good English tea."

She inclined her head. "Good. And now, if you'll excuse me, I'll go and sit with Charles. I don't like to leave him for too long."

She left the room before he had time to reply. What a quiet person she was! And how beautiful! No wonder Charles had remarried! Samuel had cordially disliked Gertrude Carnforth, who had treated him and all other employees of her husband as if they were ignorant scullions. He was already sure that Charles had found some happiness with this young woman, and glad of it, too. They had played together as lads. And even when his old playmate had come into the inheritance, he had not ceased to treat Samuel Napperby as an equal and a friend.

One week later, Charles Carnforth died. Typically of him, he died laughing.

The housekeeper, a clumsy woman at best, though well meaning, had come into the bedroom chasing a kitten that had somehow strayed into the house. Apologising profusely and incomprehensibly in Italian, she had attempted to catch the creature, then, when it scratched her, had become a veritable Diana in its pursuit. Since Giuliana's generous body was not built for a rapid chase, the affair had degenerated into a farce, the sort that Mr Carnforth had once loved to watch at the theatre. He began to chuckle. Then, when Giuliana tumbled head over heels, exposing her fat pink arse to his amused gaze, he had burst into roars of laughter.

A moment later, the laughter stopped.

It all happened so suddenly that he could have felt no pain and Helen, smiling by his side, took a moment or two to realise why the room had become so quiet. And when she did realise, she could not help but be glad that it had happened in such a way. He had died as he would have wanted to, enjoying life.

Contrary to Samuel's expectations, Mrs Carnforth did not immediately give way to her grief. In fact, he never saw her lose control of herself or her household, and only once did she weep in front of him. Her eyes were indeed reddened, but she did her grieving in private.

As Samuel spoke not a word of Italian, it was she and Briggs who had to organise the necessary preservation of the body, for Mr Carnforth had expressed a desire to be buried among his ancestors in the family vault – if that was not too much trouble – and had summoned his old friend and lawyer to see to that, and one or two other matters as well.

Except for the public occasions, when they escorted the casket to the docks, or when they disembarked at Southampton, Mrs Carnforth did not wear black. She told Samuel of her promise to her husband, and admitted to a feeling of guilt about it.

"Only," she said, with her gentle air of dignity, "I promised Charles and I should not like to break that promise, for he never broke a promise to me."

The sole occasion on which Helen did become agitated before they left was when Samuel gave her the main facts about Mr Carnforth's will. Her husband had left her everything which was not entailed, every single thing he could, and she also had a lifelong tenancy of the Dower House at Ashdown Park in Dorset.

"Oh, no, no!" Helen exclaimed in distress. "I could not! I had never realised . . . Charles did not tell me it would be so much! I can't take all that money, Mr Napperby. How can I? I didn't marry him for his money. Truly I didn't!"

Harry rushed to put his arms around his mother and scowled at the lawyer. "*Cara mammina*, please don't cry!"

But it was several minutes before she was composed enough to continue listening.

"Ahem!" Samuel looked at her guardedly. "There is – one more thing you need to know about."

"Yes?"

"Your son – Harry."

Harry began to scowl again. He was jealous of this fat old Englishman who was taking up so much of his mother's time.

"Charles was much concerned for the boy's future. As you know, he adopted Harry formally, so he has made a father's provisions for your son. He has left some money in trust for the boy, for when he is twenty-one, and he has appointed his heir, Daniel Carnforth, and myself to be joint guardians to him."

"But Harry can need no guardian! He has me! I'm his mother!" Helen drew her son possessively towards her and he wriggled uncomfortably in her arms.

"Ahem. You can be assured that I shall not – not interfere in his upbringing. But Charles was more concerned that Master Harry should have a – a gentleman to sponsor him into society. Later on, you know. He felt that the legal obligation would ensure that Daniel Carnforth did this. He said – he said that even Celia's son would not neglect the sacred trust imposed on him by a dying man, er, especially Celia's son. The – er – the lady is rather addicted to death and its ceremonies."

"How could he do it?" she repeated, not at all interested in Celia Carnforth's peculiarities.

"He was very fond of the boy. Said he regarded him as a true son. Wished he could leave him the whole estate," Samuel offered as a palliative.

"But he need not have saddled him with a guardian whom we've never even met!" she said bitterly. "What if he – this Daniel person – tries to take my son away from me?"

"There was no turning Charles from this point," Mr Napperby said unhappily, for that had occurred to him, too. "I did try, believe me. But he began to grow agitated – and I didn't dare press the point."

Helen sighed. "Yes. I know. Charles was a dear, but he could be very stubborn at times."

"Yes, Mrs Carnforth. But – I did manage to persuade him to set up a joint guardianship, as a safeguard. In that way, if Daniel Carnforth neglects his duty, I can see to the boy. I do not have his connections, but I believe I am quite well respected in the county. And, with the permission of both of us needed to do anything against your wishes, he will not be able to take the boy away from you. I shall see to that." He blinked at her earnestly from his round grey-blue eyes, his plump jowls quivering sympathetically.

She took a deep breath. What couldn't be cured must be endured – and with dignity. Charles had taught her that. After a moment, she even managed a half smile. "Well, if there is no help for it, I suppose I had better just accept it. Is there anything else I should know, Mr Napperby?"

"No, my dear lady. The other details can wait."

"Then I'll go and attend to my packing. I shall be happy to settle into my new home."

She hoped the new owner of Ashdown would be pleasant

to deal with, though Mr Napperby had hinted that the family had not been best pleased by the marriage. But it was no use worrying about that now. She had dear Charles's last wishes to fulfil.

Thirteen

Daniel Carnforth paced up and down the drawing-room at Bellborough and cursed his own stupidity. What mental aberration had made him send word to Bath informing his mother that Charles Carnforth was dying and had asked the family lawyer to go to see him in Italy, when he heard from Mr Napperby? She had come hotfoot to join him in the country and had been with him ever since, driving him mad with her complaints and affectations.

"Daniel, dearest one, are you *listening* to me?"

"Yes, Mama. I mean, no. I'm sorry. I was thinking about the old water meadows."

"Farming? At a time like this? When you may hear at any moment that you are the new owner of Ashdown? An ancient manor house, a family which can trace its line of descent from a Norman baron." She sighed ecstatically, for her family had no noble ancestors.

As if Daniel cared about that! It was the land that mattered. A larger estate, that was the inheritance that mattered to him. Land. "I need to put in some new drainage," he said apologetically, then grew angry with himself. Why did she always make him want to apologise?

She shook her head sadly. "You will become quite unbearably bucolic if you do not take care, my dear boy."

He resumed his pacing.

But she could never bear silence for long. "If only we *knew*!" she sighed for the twentieth time that day. Her pale eyes were fixed hungrily upon her son's face, as if she expected to see a change in it signalling his ownership of Ashdown. In her hands she was clasping a volume of sermons, which he knew she had never read, because he had seen the uncut pages, but which she always displayed prominently upon any sad occasion – or when she was particularly displeased with her only child.

"Well, we don't know and we can't know, Mama, so there is no use fretting, is there? Why don't you let me take you out for a drive? It's a beautiful day and the fresh air would do you good."

Celia smiled bravely and dabbed at her eyes with a lacy handkerchief. "Ah, if I only had your stamina, my son! But you know how sad news oversets me. And I *cannot* go out driving when, for all I know, my poor dear cousin Charles may be lying on his death bed! At this very moment! And I not in mourning! How shocking that would be!" Her voice throbbed with emotion and the handkerchief was wielded again, though it remained dry, Daniel was sure.

Silence reigned for a few moments, broken only by the loud ticking of a very large and ugly gilt clock, which Daniel had always hated. He had banished it to the attics once, but his mother had unearthed it on her next visit and given him a lecture on respecting family heirlooms. Rather than endure prolonged homilies upon the subject, he had allowed her to place it upon the mantelpiece again. When she had gone this time, he would, he vowed, take the damned thing outside and break it into tiny pieces. It was driving him mad.

When it came to his home comforts, he must learn to be as stubborn as her – but in a quieter way. A man needed a bit of peace after a hard day's work. Heaven preserve him from the upsets his mother seemed to thrive on!

Feeling that her son's attention was not upon her, Celia sighed and fluttered one hand at her brow.

Daniel's scowl deepened. This theatrical gesture never failed to irritate him. He suspected, no, he *knew* that the headaches to which she was prone were pure fabrications, for they only seemed to come upon her when her will was crossed, never when she had something she considered pleasant in prospect.

Another sigh whispered through the air.

Daniel gritted his teeth. As for his mother's delicate health and her air of drooping fragility, that was another myth, he thought, glaring at her thin back and wispy hair as she stood up and tottered over to the window. She was the heartiest eater he had ever seen! And it was no wonder she could spurn food in company and plead a lack of appetite; she never stopped nibbling from the time she got up to the time she went to bed. Why she wasn't as fat as his best sow, he could not understand! Even now there was a dish of fresh shortbread set temptingly on a small table next to her, and the sofa bore distinct traces of crumbs.

When she sat down again, he stood up. Anything rather than sit facing that reproachful gaze.

Up and down the room he went, unable to sit still. From the window, he watched her select another piece of shortbread and nibble at it as delicately as a mouse. Desperately he began to cast round for an excuse to dine away from home that evening, or at least to escape after dinner. He could not face another barrage of complaints. Why did she always make him feel so inadequate? Why could he not cope better with her vagaries?

His friends thought him mad to put up with her as he did. But they did not know what an unhappy life she had led. He could never forget how badly his father had treated her or how, when he was a boy, she had often shielded him from his father's drunken anger and even from physical violence. And he usually managed to see the humorous side of things. Though not today.

When the gong rang to dress for dinner, he opened his mouth to offer his apologies and invent a prior engagement, but she forestalled him.

"We'll have such a cosy little chat over dinner this evening, my dearest. I'm *so* glad you're not going out again tonight!"

How in hell's name had she found that out? The cook, probably, he thought gloomily. She and the cook were as thick as thieves, for Mrs Banning loved to bake for someone truly appreciative of her skills. But now he had to face another evening in his mother's company! Her idea of a "cosy little chat over dinner" was to describe with relish and the utmost detail all the deathbeds at which she had ever been present, or the illnesses she had encountered in herself and her acquaintances. He knew the intimate details of his own father's death by heart, but that did not prevent her from going through it again at regular intervals.

However, no excuse would have availed to free Daniel from his mother that evening, for just after the gong had summoned them down to dinner, there was a knock on the door and a messenger was revealed, bearing a letter from Rome. This was carried ceremoniously into the dining-room by the maidservant who waited at table, her awed expression showing that she realised the import of the missive.

"Oh, my dearest, dearest boy," Celia breathed, clutching her son's arm. "Steel yourself! It may be the news for which we have been waiting." She fumbled for her handkerchief and released her grasp so that he could stretch out his hand for the letter.

He stared at it. Mr Napperby's handwriting.

"Are you not going to open it, Daniel dearest?"

He pulled off the seal, unfolded it and scanned the contents.

> My dear Daniel,
>
> I regret to inform you that your cousin Charles passed away last night. The end was sudden, and a merciful release from pain.
>
> I shall wait here for a few days and escort his widow back to England myself, together with her young son. The lady wishes to take up residence in the Dower House at Ashdown Park, as is her right.
>
> Mr Carnforth wishes to be buried with his ancestors, so we shall also be bringing back the Captain's body for interment in the family vault. I would be grateful if you would go to Ashdown – which now belongs to you of course, under the entail – as soon as you receive this, and make all the necessary arrangements for a suitable funeral.
>
> It is my duty to inform you that . . .

Daniel stopped reading the letter aloud.

"Ah!" declared Mrs Carnforth with great satisfaction. "You are now the owner. You can style yourself Carnforth of Ashdown Park. It has a very noble ring to it, do you not think? I'm so glad we didn't call you John, as your Aunt Susannah wished. It would not have done your position justice." She turned to her son. "Why have you stopped reading? What else does Mr Napperby have to say, pray?"

But she had to wait to find out, for her son had forgotten her presence entirely. Face flushed with annoyance, he was re-reading the last part of the letter, holding the paper as if it were a snake about to bite him. He muttered something which sounded suspiciously like an oath, screwed the letter up and threw it on to the floor. Then he bent and snatched it up to smooth it out and read it again.

"I'll be *damned* if I will!" he exclaimed, and thumped the table to emphasise his point. "How *dared* Charles do such a thing? Without even asking me!"

It took Celia five minutes to calm him down enough to divulge what had enraged him. By this time she was so anxious to know what it was that she even refrained from pointing out to him the shocking nature of the language he had used. "What is it, my son?" she cooed.

"If you must know," he was still having great difficulty in speaking calmly, "Charles has named me as guardian to that woman's brat, whom he had apparently adopted! His dying wish. Foisting such a child on me! And I'll be *damned* if I'll do it!"

She shared his outrage at once. "Guardian! But – he can't – can he? I mean – you weren't asked, so it can't be legal. And even if it is, you must certainly refuse! She's bound to be the most *vulgar* person. He had a deplorable taste in women. Not even good actresses!"

"Of course I mean to refuse. You may set your mind at rest upon that point! I have no intention whatsoever of taking on such an onerous task. What do I know of schoolboys? Or wish to know?"

"Quite right." Doubt seized her even as she spoke and her hand fluttered to her brow. "But – 'dying wish', did you say?"

"Yes. That's why he summoned Mr Napperby. And it's as outrageous as everything else about the man. Well, if he thinks I'll be coerced into accepting the task merely because it's his dying wish, he's wrong. Was wrong. You know what I mean. I'll have enough on my plate with Ashdown Park, from all accounts. The estate's quite gone to pieces. Shamefully neglected, in fact. The agent will answer to me for that, I can tell you!" Nothing was so heinous a crime in Daniel's eyes as the neglect of one's land.

"Dearest, if you would but sit down and discuss matters *peacefully*. You know how such tirades give me a headache."

Daniel flung himself into a chair. "What is there to discuss? I shall refuse to become a guardian to some hobbledehoy about whom I know nothing and care even less!"

"Is there – is that all the letter says?"

"What? Oh, no. There's more. I am, if you please, to ensure

that the Dower House at Ashdown is cleaned, aired and made ready to receive Mrs Carnforth and her son. How old is the brat, anyway?" Thump went a clenched fist on the table again. "I am also to hire whatever servants are necessary to look after the place. And finally, I am to make suitable arrangements for the funeral." He ground his teeth quite audibly.

"Precious one! Your teeth! You *know* how I hate that sound!"

He ignored her. "I shall have to arrange the funeral, I suppose. As the heir, I can do no less. And I suppose I must do something about the Dower House, too. It is her right to live there. But those are the only things I shall do! Guardian, indeed! Not so much as a by-your-leave! And to the son of a fortune-hunting harpy, who took advantage of a sick old man to worm her way into one of the oldest families in Dorset!"

Neither Charles nor Helen would have recognised this description of him, let alone her. Daniel, who had never met his cousin, was basing his judgement on his knowledge of his own mother, who was roughly the same age. He simply assumed that a gentleman in his fifties would be elderly, in ill health and susceptible to flattery – or whatever wiles that woman had used. Probably an actress, as his mother had said.

Celia gazed at her son with fascination. She had never seen him so angry before. Indeed, she had always considered him to be a rather phlegmatic man, not to say bucolic, with his passion for farming and his disdain for polite society. And he had a most reprehensible sense of humour, too, for he laughed at the strangest things sometimes. Though he had not done so in her presence for the past year or two, so perhaps he was growing out of that habit. She herself considered levity to be rather common.

"I shall come with you to Ashdown Park, my dear son," she announced suddenly. "You cannot know how to organise such an important funeral," her tone became enthusiastic, "but I, alas, am very experienced in such matters." Not only experienced. Funerals were her passion. She attended any she could, even of the most distant relatives or the merest acquaintances.

"There's no n—"

She ignored his interruption. "Besides, I haven't seen the place for years, not since you were a baby. I wonder if the Chinese Room is still there? Such a marvel it was reckoned in my younger days! And the house has a very elegant facade – featured in several guidebooks to the county, you know."

"Yes, you told me."

"I do recall, however, that I found the woods very depressing. Such dark, gloomy places, woods! Perhaps you could cut them down! My sensiblities are so acute! I must have peace and beauty around me, or I pine." She saw that Daniel's attention was wandering again and cut short her reminiscences.

He was torn between annoyance at the thought of having to continue suffering her company and the knowledge that she was right about his inexperience when it came to organising a funeral for a major landowner. He shrugged. He had better take her with him. "Very well, Mama. I shall be grateful for your help with the funeral."

He tried to be optimistic. No doubt she would return to Bath as soon as the obsequies were over. She had very frequently voiced her detestation of rural life. Personally, he was more concerned with seeing in what heart the estate was, for to him Ashdown Park meant the land. So much land, too, not a toy estate like Bellborough. He would make its restoration his life work. His eyes gleamed at the thought.

Daniel's pleasure in his inheritance diminished the moment he caught sight of it. Ashdown Park was in a far worse state than last time he had visited the district. Grimly he followed the elderly agent round the neglected acres. The old-fashioned barns and cow byres were so badly in need of repair that he thought it would be easier to knock them down and build new ones. He dreaded to think of the cost of that. There had better be some money left from the Carnforth fortune, or he did not know how he could afford to bring things up to scratch.

On and on it went! He was downright ashamed of the state of the cottages, in which the estate workers were housed, and could hardly bring himself to acknowledge their salutations. And many of the lanes were so deeply rutted as to be almost impassable after even a light rainfall, while as for the hedges, they were overgrown and . . .

The more the new owner investigated the way the estate had been allowed to be run down, the angrier he became. And could not help showing his scorn about the mismanagement. Within two days, he had accepted the agent's resignation, not caring to employ a man who had allowed this to happen. If his employer had refused to allow improvements to be made, the agent should have gone after him in person and *made* him understand what was needed. Daniel would have done that in the agent's place. Instead, this man seemed to have settled for a quiet life and had simply let things fall down or moulder away.

Until he knew how he was left financially, Daniel decided not to employ another agent, but to take matters into his own very capable hands.

Once that decision had been taken, his mother saw little of him, for he was out from dawn till dusk, checking that the work he had put in train was being carried out properly and sometimes even helping with it himself. This soon began to win him the grudging approval of his tenants, in spite of his brusque way of speaking.

He got to know every copse and thicket on his land more quickly than anyone would have believed possible, as well as learning about the people who depended on him for their livelihoods. He never forgot a name or a face. And he accepted that things needed to be done without complaining or blaming anyone for the neglect, though he sometimes said bluntly that he could not yet afford this or that, but would have to put it on his list.

"He'll do," they said in the village inn. "He's like his grandfather, this one is. A farming Carnforth, not a roistering Carnforth."

Unlike his mother, Daniel fell in love with the woods around the house, though this did not blind him to the fact that a lot of work would be needed to set them in order – dead trees cleared and saplings planted to replace them. It galled him to have to wait upon the lawyers before he could make a proper start on that, or on anything else.

In the evenings, Daniel usually joined his mother for a hasty meal, listened to her complaints for an hour or so (many of them concerning the lack of servants and the dilapidated state of the house), then escaped to shut himself up in the estate office and go through pile after pile of dusty papers. Had no one ever thought to file them away neatly? This task took him longer than he had expected, for the papers afforded him fascinating glimpses of the history of the Carnforth family. How he wished he could have grown up here and learned about his inheritance properly!

For once, Celia did not protest much about her son's neglect, for she was enjoying herself enormously, going through all the cupboards in the house, re-arranging the furniture and ornaments, and planning the most splendid funeral the district had ever seen.

She was also pleased to receive visits from the other families in the neighbourhood, though they were not so pleased with her. Plain folk, most of them, so long established in the area that they neither wanted nor needed titles and honours to bolster their self-esteem. Celia's airs and affectations were not at all to their liking.

Of the middling people, the parson and his wife were the first to call and offer a welcome to the new heir. Since the living was in the gift of the Carnforths, they could not afford to offend the new owner. However, the parson, one Henry Morpeth, took an instant aversion to Mr Carnforth's mother and, when she developed a habit of driving over to the parsonage to discuss her latest ideas about the funeral (and these changed almost hourly, causing notes to be sent as well as visits to be made), Mr Morpeth took to slipping out of the back door of his house and taking refuge in the vestry.

He had one or two close shaves but, fortunately, Celia's vacuous blue eyes were very short-sighted and she was too vain to wear spectacles. Sylvia Morpeth nobly took the brunt of these visits and, by dint of agreeing with all suggestions but declaring her inability to act without her husband's authority, she managed to put a stop to some of Mrs Carnforth's wilder extravagances without giving offence.

Daniel assumed that his mother would see to the cleaning of the Dower House and the hiring of servants, while she conveniently forgot the need to make it ready for the new occupier. Why should she put herself out for such a woman? And, anyway, Daniel must have set matters in train, since he had not repeated his request.

But Celia did not forget to drop a few poisonous remarks about "that wicked woman who preyed on my poor cousin in his declining years" into her conversations. And, although people had little time for her, the idea stuck that Charles Carnforth's widow was an ill-bred harpy who had married him for his money.

Mrs Morpeth did wonder whether something should be done about the Dower House but when she mentioned the matter to her husband, he shuddered and begged her to do nothing that would bring "that dreadful Carnforth woman" down upon them again.

"Depend upon it," he said vaguely, "they are waiting to hear from the dowager or Mr Napperby about the exact date of their arrival, and will do what is needed at the proper time."

Fourteen

Three weeks later, on a rainy afternoon in early August, an imposing procession of carriages passed through Asherby village and brought the inhabitants to their windows or doorways to stare through the driving rain and speculate about the passengers in the mud-splashed vehicles.

"They've brung him back, then," said one villager.

"Who else can it be?" her neighbour agreed.

"Poor soul, he didn't make old bones," sighed a woman who remembered Charles Carnforth as a rather handsome young fellow who had once stolen a kiss from her at harvest home – when she had been young and rosy, still with all her teeth.

Many eyes noted all the details to be discussed at leisure later: the smart travelling chaise; the coach full of luggage; and the hearse, drawn by four exhausted black horses. Yes, they agreed, it could only be him.

As it had been pouring down for most of the last three days, reducing the roads to quagmires and making the farmers shake their heads about the prospects of a good harvest, the people in the carriages were only blurs seen through the hissing rain. Even the horses looked tired and dispirited and the coachmen were huddled in their greatcoats, not looking to right nor left.

"They'll be tired out," said Mrs Bagham, comfortable in her warm cottage near the green. "'Tis dreary work travelling in this weather. Pity we ha'n't got one of they railways to the village, ent it? That'd make things easier. Though they'd still have to get a carriage to take him to the big house. We're old-fashioned here, that we are." Mrs Bagham was all for progress and had actually ridden on a railway train when she went to visit her sister, who was in service in London. Since that time, she had not stopped boring her friends and neighbours with the details of this wonderful modern invention.

Men plodding home from their day's work paused to take off their hats and bow their heads as the hearse passed by. Respect paid, they strained to catch a glimpse of the wicked woman who had married poor Mr Charles, but all they could see was a veiled figure in black.

Inside the carriage it seemed almost as damp and chilly as outside and Helen sighed as she tried to wriggle some life into her numbed toes.

"Nearly there now, my dear," said Mr Napperby encouragingly.

She managed a tired smile, for he had been very kind to her throughout the long sea journey, then she tried to move her cramped arm without waking up her son, who had not proved a good traveller. Harry had not complained, but he was so wan and weary from the sickness, which had embarrassed him at regular intervals on the ocean, that he had at last fallen asleep from sheer exhaustion. He lay now with his head on her lap, like the boy he was, not the brave man-child he had tried to become since his stepfather's death.

Mr Napperby followed her gaze. Good as gold, that lad had been, he thought, and he was only nine, too. He had several grandchildren of a similar age, and, fond of them as he was, he could not imagine Tommy or naughty little Paul bearing up under such adversity as Master Harry had done – or being so sensitive to their mother's needs.

With a quick apology to Helen, Mr Napperby let down the window and leaned out to direct the driver to turn left. He was a little dubious as to whether to take Mrs Carnforth and her son to the big house, or whether to go straight to the Dower House. In the end, he concluded that it was only polite to go to the house first, where, no doubt, she and her son would be invited to stay until after the funeral.

It did not take him long to realise his error.

A sloppy-looking footman opened the door to Mr Napperby's knocking. Daniel had been too busy to engage new servants, but his mother was working on him about staffing the place properly and, above all, getting himself a proper butler. She had, in the meantime, co-opted a few people from the estate into filling some of the many gaps. "After all, Daniel dearest, if you are to settle permanently at Ashdown, you cannot continue to live like a gypsy and dine in the breakfast parlour, now can you?"

The footman, a man not known for his quick wits, just stood and goggled at the carriages for a moment. Then he recollected one of the phrases that had been dinned into him. "Er – I'll inquire if the master is at home, sir," he managed, feeling pretty pleased with himself for getting it all out without a mistake.

"Well, surely you don't expect us to wait out here on the doorstep while you go and ask, do you?" snapped Mr Napperby, who was not only chilled to the bone, but hungry as well. He glanced back at the carriage, where a white-faced Helen was sitting patiently and his heart went out to her.

After a moment's hesitation, the footman, who had been a gardener two weeks previously, opened the door wider and said he supposed they might wait in the hallway.

"Wait in the hallway, you impudent fellow! What do you mean, wait in the hallway? I have Mrs Carnforth sitting outside in a chaise. Were you actually intending to deny her entry into her late husband's home?"

The man muttered something inaudible and fled in search of help. He had heard old Mrs Carnforth say several times that she was not prepared to receive "that woman" into her son's house and he dared not announce the visitors to her.

Mr Napperby turned to find that Helen and her son had already alighted from the chaise, for it helped Harry's travel sickness to walk about and take the air whenever they stopped, however cold and damp that air might be.

Tutting with annoyance and embarrassment at this appallingly rude reception, Mr Napperby ushered them into the hall, a large, echoing apartment, with suits of armour and dim family portraits set stiffly around its perimeter. There was a fire burning sluggishly in a monstrous grate at one end, but it seemed to do little to dispel the damp chill. Nonetheless, they all gathered around it, for the flames were the most cheerful thing about the place.

"They – er – they seem to be a bit short of staff," he offered in apology.

Helen, who knew how bedraggled she looked and also how near to tears she was, shrugged and held out her hands to the warmth.

The footman returned with the housekeeper (formerly the caretaker's wife) who had received specific instructions on how to deal with "those people" from Celia Carnforth. Only, to Mrs Mossop's dismay, "those people" included Mr Napperby, with whom she was well acquainted owing to his years of supervising the estate. She became flustered as she tried to deliver the set speech she had conned carefully.

"If you please, the master's out an' the mistress is indisposed. There's a bier set ready in the library to hold the coffin and the Dower House is down the North Drive."

Helen, who was urging her shivering son to warm himself before the fire, stiffened in shock and outrage. Before Mr Napperby, who was equally stunned by this rudeness, could reply, she had taken Harry by the hand and was walking back to the front door.

The footman reported later to the other servants that her eyes "dug right into you, they did an' she weren't half angry". But she hadn't screeched at him, like the old lady did. No, just spoke her piece quietly, like.

"Thank your mistress for her kind offer and welcome," Helen said with icy dignity, "and tell her that we shall not trouble her. I came but to pay a courtesy call. And, of course, my husband's body stays with me until I can make arrangements for the funeral!" Not waiting for a reply, she pulled the veil back over her face, walked back down the steps to the chaise – with Harry by her side – and opened its door herself.

Mr Napperby turned to the housekeeper, simmering with suppressed fury. "I had not expected you to greet us like this, Jane Mossop!"

"I – I'm sorry, sir! I had my orders. I wouldn't—"

"Who gave you those orders?"

"Mrs Carnforth. The master's mother."

"Where is Mr Daniel Carnforth?" he demanded, interrupting her stuttering attempts to apologise.

"I can't say, sir."

"Can't – or won't?" he demanded, face red with indignation.

"Can't, sir. Truly. He went out this afternoon and he hasn't come back yet. He didn't say where he was going. He never does!"

"Very well!" Mr Napperby pulled a card from his pocket and

asked for a pen. When it was brought to him from the library, he scribbled a message on the back of his card. "Please see that your master gets that as soon as he returns – your *master* and no one else! Is that clear?" Normally he would have been the soul of diplomacy, but he knew Celia Carnforth of old, so to make sure his message got through, he added, "You are not to give it to Mr Daniel's mother under any circumstances. And tell him that I shall wait upon him tomorrow at eleven o'clock in the forenoon, unless I hear to the contrary."

"Y-yes, sir." With trembling fingers Jane tucked the card into her apron pocket, dropping him a curtsey as she did so.

"I–I was only following orders, sir," she ventured, as she escorted him to the door, for she was a kindly soul at heart, and not only had the widow seemed exhausted, but the poor little boy had looked pale and ill.

"Then see that you follow *my* orders just as closely. Give my message to Mr Daniel and to no one else!"

Only when the carriages had pulled away did Jane recall that the Dower House was not ready for visitors. But it was too late then to tell them that.

Five minutes later, the tired shivering horses drew to a halt in front of the Dower House. No smoke rose from the tall brick chimneys and curtains were drawn over the windows, some of which were festooned with cobwebs. The gardens were overgrown, too, with soggy piles of dead leaves lying in the corners.

Mr Napperby was near to an apoplexy by now. "I can't believe this – this rank discourtesy! They have not even got the place ready. My dear lady, let me take you to an inn at once! The Roe Deer in Asherby is small, but I can vouch for its comfort. You can't possibly stay here!"

"I can and I shall!" Helen declared, spots of red flaring in her cheeks. "They shall not drive us away. Charles wanted me to live here, and that's what I'm going to do."

Harry said nothing. Sometimes, when adults were upset, it was best for a boy to keep quiet. He had learned that lesson when he was very young. And, anyway, his head was aching and his stomach growling.

Briggs, who had gone to reconnoitre, pulled open the chaise door and poked his head inside. A blast of cold damp air swirled in and drops of rain splattered the upholstery and the passengers.

"There's an old woman round the back, who says she's the caretaker. She's got a fire lit in the kitchen an' she says she can find us some food. Me and the Captain have managed in worse bivouacs than this one, ma'am." He held open the door of the chaise invitingly.

"And I can manage, too!" said Helen, a martial light in her eyes. "Come, Harry!" She waited for her son to jump down from the chaise and turned to the lawyer, "Shall you not join us, Mr Napperby?"

Sighing, he pulled his cloak around him and got out. He was too old for jauntering about the countryside like this. Not to mention trailing to and fro across Europe. Longingly he thought of his home, his wife's tender care to ensure his comfort and the way the butter melted into his cook's hot crumpets.

As they stood there, the rain ceased and the wind died down a little. "There you are!" said Helen, trying to sound optimistic, for Harry's sake. "The weather is improving already. It's a good sign." She paused for a moment to study her future home and said in tones of surprise, "How pretty the house is! Why did you not tell me that, Mr Napperby?"

He shivered as a gust of wind shook a shower of droplets from an overhanging branch on to his already damp cloak. Muttering something unintelligible, he turned to stare at the Dower House. He had never bothered to visit it when he came to check up on the accounts at quarter day. He did not think it pretty, seeing only the years of neglect: the dull windows; the peeling paintwork; and the unkempt gardens.

Helen, who had become used to the stark white of classical Mediterranean architecture or the over-ornateness of what Charles had called "Italian gingerbread" *palazzos* and churches, fell instantly in love with the neat simplicity and symmetry of the Georgian style. The Dower House, built in warm red brick, stood three stories high, with two windows at either side of the central doorway and a portico over it. The drive led up to the door in a sweeping semi-circle. The garden pathways were overgrown, but flowers still bloomed in the weed-choked beds and the dark green foliage of massive old trees framed the house like an artist's masterpiece. She hadn't realised till this moment how homesick she had been for England's soft green countryside.

"It's all very wet, Mother," said Harry, shivering. "Does it always rain in England?"

"Not always, dear. Come on – let's find our way inside. Briggs says there's a fire in the kitchen. We shall be able to decide better what to do once we're warm."

While she was speaking, the front door was opened with a loud, creaking sound, and an old woman appeared, as if by magic, from the dark hole that yawned behind it. "Be you Master Charlie's wife?" she asked uncertainly. "They said you were comin', but they didn't say when."

Helen pulled back her veil and the woman exclaimed, "Why, you're nothin' but a girl!" Then her eyes fell upon Harry, standing miserably by his mother's side. "Eh, the poor little lad! Don't stand out here in the cold, Mrs Carnforth. Bring him in!" As they moved forward, she added, "Look at him shiver, then! I've got a kettle on the boil and I can heat up some nice fresh milk in a trice. It's not what you're used to, I dare say, but my kitchen's clean and warm, and you can't beat a glass of hot milk for taking the chill out of a boy."

"She was Charles's nurse!" whispered Mr Napperby. "I'd forgotten she was still alive. She was pensioned off years ago. She must be eighty, if she's a day!"

He took Helen's arm and escorted her into the house, where he paused to say, "Mrs Carnforth, may I introduce Becky Robbins, who was nurse to Captain Charles."

Becky poked him in the ribs as a sign to move on. "Never mind introductions till we've got that boy and his mother warm and dry, Samuel Napperby! You come this way, ma'am. This way, young master. Mind the step!" She hobbled along in front of them and ushered them into the kitchen at the rear, where a crackling wood fire cast reflections on polished copper pans, a plump cat snoozed on the rug and a rocking chair invited one to sit down and toast oneself in front of the fire.

Harry immediately plumped down and began to stroke the cat, for he still missed the little dog that had had to be left behind in Italy.

Briggs took charge of the carriages and, with the drivers' help, saw to the careful placement of the coffin in the front parlour.

Helen left Harry, still sitting on the rug, sipping a glass of hot milk, alternately eating some bread and jam and stroking the cat, which had moved over a little, but had not abandoned its position entirely.

With Becky's help, she directed the men to carry the luggage up to the appropriate bedrooms and then left Mr Napperby to pay off the hearse and the carrier. The other carriage had to wait to take him home to Bedderby, the nearest town, which was, apparently, only five miles away.

It was amazing, Helen thought, how much more cheerful she felt now that she had arrived and seen the house.

Mr Napperby could only marvel at the way Mrs Carnforth remained calm and pleasant in the face of such adversity. He did not realise how hard her life had been before she met Charles, or how resilient this had made her.

Briggs reappeared in the rear door of the hallway, grinning, Mr Napperby thought sourly, like the village idiot. "Yer ladyship, how about I go back to the village with Mr Napperby when he leaves and get some more food from the inn there. They're bound to have something they could sell us. And I could hire a trap, too, to bring me back, I daresay. We should keep it for a day or two, I reckon. We're goin' to need something to get about in and the stables here haven't been used for years."

"I still say we should take rooms at the inn for you," declared Mr Napperby. But though he emphasised his words with a gigantic sneeze, and though Helen absent-mindedly said, "Bless you!", no one was really listening to him. They were discussing the urgent question of food.

Becky appeared in the doorway. "Tell Mrs Willins at the Roe Deer to send for my great-niece Susan to come at once. Lookin' for a place, she is, ma'am, as polite a girl as you'd ever meet, and we'll need more help in the house, for I'm not as spry as I used to be, and that's a fact." Becky was enjoying the excitement and the prospect of company.

"What a good idea!" said Helen warmly. "I think we could do with more than one maid, though, to get this place cleaned up." She glanced round the dusty hallway as she spoke.

"Two maids, a cook, a boy, a groom an' a gardener," declared Becky. "That's what the old lady had as lived here before. But you'll need me as well, to look after the lad." Her eyes gleamed with pleasure at the thought of someone to cosset and care for.

"Nonsense, woman! You've been pensioned off for more years than I can remember. You're too old to nurse anyone!" stated Mr Napperby, annoyed at the way she was pre-empting his role as chief adviser. "And the boy's too old for a nurse."

Becky drew herself up to her full five feet and one inch. "There was no one left," she declared loftily, "*to* look after, seein' as Mrs Gertrude didn't have no children. That's why I was pensioned off." She looked meaningfully at Mr Napperby's plump figure and added, "Nor I haven't let myself run to fat, like some I could mention! I've still got years of work in me! Years."

Helen hurriedly intervened, choking back her laughter at the sight of Mr Napperby's outraged expression. "Yes, Alfred, do go to the village – that's a good idea – and, er, pray give Becky's message to Mrs Willins."

She turned to the lawyer, holding both her hands out to him. "My dear Mr Napperby, I'm so grateful to you for all your help, but I cannot keep you any longer from your family."

"I don't like to leave you like this!" he protested – but weakly. He could get a meal and a glass of mulled ale at the Roe Deer, and be back home within an hour of leaving there.

"I insist."

"Well, if you insist – are you quite sure you'll be all right here?"

"Oh yes, I'm very sure. Becky will look after us."

"Then I'll be off. But I'll call in briefly in the morning, if I may, before I go to see Daniel Carnforth. Just to check that you're all right."

"I shall look forward to that!" Helen escorted him to the door.

"Good riddance!" muttered Becky, in a very audible aside.

Two hours later, Helen was feeling even better. She had plunged, with the help of Becky and later an excited Susan as well, into a veritable orgy of airing bedlinen, dusting and unpacking. They had picnicked in the kitchen on a large chicken pie, sent over by Mrs Willins, followed by fresh crusty bread with honey and an apple pie smothered in thick yellow cream.

Harry, recovering rapidly now that the jolting had stopped

and he had been able to retain some food in his stomach, trotted to and fro, helping where he could. Soon they were all dusty and flushed with exertion, but somehow it was fun. Charles Carnforth had trained his family to enjoy life, if at all possible.

Becky's great-niece, Susan, lost her awe of her new mistress within an hour, and began to think that she had fallen lucky, from what her friend at the Manor told her. And to think she'd been hoping for a summons to go there as a maid! She'd be nothing there, and the old lady was driving everyone mad, by all accounts. But here she'd be the head maid, because she'd got here first, thanks to her great-aunt Becky. Yes, this was going to be much more to her taste, she was sure.

As dusk cloaked the landscape in shadows, there came the sound of a rider cantering up the drive. Briggs set down the chair he was carrying, took off his sacking apron and wiped his hands. "I reckon I'd better answer the door, ma'am."

"Thank you, yes. I'm not at home to anyone, except Mr Napperby."

Briggs was back a couple of minutes later, with a letter. "It was a groom with a letter from Mr Daniel Carnforth, ma'am."

She took the letter and turned it round in her hands, reluctant to face more unpleasantness. "I wonder what he wants?" The handwriting was large and angular, the ink very black. Inside, she read:

> Mr Daniel Carnforth presents his compliments to Mrs Carnforth, and regrets that he was not at home to receive her. He further regrets that, due to a misunderstanding, her husband's body was not taken straight to the library, which had been prepared to receive it, as is the custom. A carriage will be sent tomorrow morning to fetch the coffin, or this evening, if that is more convenient.
>
> The funeral has been arranged for three days hence, and all necessary arrangements have been made to receive mourners at the Manor afterwards. Gentlemen only to attend the ceremony.
>
> D. Carnforth

Helen went white with suppressed fury when she read this curt epistle. She could not even speak for a minute or two.

"You all right, ma'am?" asked the watchful Briggs, who had never seen quite such a look on her face, because he'd never seen anyone try to attack or ill-treat a person she loved.

"Yes, I'm fine." She realised she had crumpled the note in her hands, so smoothed it open to read again, because she could not quite believe what it had said. But the words were still cold and hurtful.

She wished she had not sent Mr Napperby away. How could someone who had never even met her offer her such gratuitous insults, not to mention trying to exclude her from her own husband's funeral?

When she did not speak, Alfred coughed. "The groom has been told to wait for a reply, ma'am."

"Tell him there will be no reply," she said at last. "My lawyer will be waiting on Mr Daniel Carnforth in the morning, and nothing can be done until then."

He didn't like the sound of this.

Without commenting, she passed him the note to read.

He hissed in shock at what Daniel had said. But still, there ought to be an answer, he felt. "Don't you want to write him a note, ma'am? Just a word. To refuse his offer, like."

"Thank you, no." She didn't trust herself to do it with dignity. She was still too angry. Not allowed to attend her own husband's funeral, indeed! Who did that man think he was to tell her that?

Helen was no angrier than Daniel. His mother had informed him that the Dowager Lady Carnforth had called and driven away again almost immediately.

Celia did not quite like to admit that she had refused to see the widow and her son, so she glossed over this point. She also glossed over the fact that the dowager had not been invited to stay at Ashdown, or that she had not even been offered refreshments, emphasising only the woman's refusal to leave the coffin behind. When asked what the dowager was like, she said that she had been unable to tell, as the woman had been heavily veiled. She had taken a quick peep out of her bedroom window and been disappointed to see so little. She had also questioned Jane, but found the housekeeper's answers very unsatisfactory. But the boy was quite young, not more than ten, from the looks of him.

"The lad will need a guardian for a good few years yet," Celia added slyly, knowing that the thought of this imposition still annoyed her son.

Mr Napperby's curt note to Mr Daniel Carnforth, being unfortunately worded, had only served to back up Celia's allegations. It stated baldly:

> Proceeding to Dower House. All contact with Mrs Carnforth to be conducted through the writer, who has the honour to be handling her affairs. Will call on you tomorrow at eleven.
>
> S. Napperby

Daniel could draw no other conclusion than that the woman was deliberately offering him the grossest of insults by spurning his hospitality and refusing to follow custom as regards the funeral. If this was a sample of her manners and breeding, he would have as little to do with her as possible. Only the need to bury his kinsman decently and to keep quiet the disagreements that had already occurred had made him send the groom with a note. As far as he was concerned, the widow could settle into the Dower House and rot there.

Helen's refusal even to reply, passed on bluntly by the groom who had carried the message, made Celia smile in satisfaction and Daniel grow angrier still. Both took to their beds early, Celia to sleep soundly and Daniel to toss and turn. What next? he wondered as a damned loud clock somewhere in the house struck the hour yet again.

Fifteen

The next morning Helen got up filled with determination to manage the funeral herself. She would not be obligated to people who did not even have the decency to treat her politely, whoever they were. She therefore sent Harry, who was his old self again by morning, to look for Briggs and fetch him to her.

Alfred thought she was still looking tired, but didn't say so.

"Will you go into the village and take this note to the parson, Alfred. I've asked him to call on me here at his earliest convenience. We shall need to make arrangements with him for Charles's funeral."

Briggs bowed his head. He was both indignant and disgusted at how his mistress had been treated, but he did not know how best to help her. The gentry didn't like servants interfering in their doings. Mr Napperby would be the best person to see to matters, but Briggs intended to keep his eyes open. Let any of the villagers or the servants from the big house say anything disparaging about Mrs Carnforth in his presence, and he would make sure they never did so again.

Helen sighed. She felt both weary and a little nauseous after the long journey. "After that, would you please ask around and see if you can find us any more help? We need a cook-housekeeper, another maid and a lad to help inside and out. And Alfred . . ."

"Yes, ma'am?"

"I would like to thank you for all you've done. I don't know how I'd have managed without you since Charles died!"

Briggs tried unsuccessfully to hide his pleasure. "It's been my privilege, ma'am – and what the Captain would have wanted, as I well knew."

"You will – stay on with me and Harry?"

He was shocked that she even needed to ask that. "Of course I will, ma'am! I have instructions from the master to look after the boy, teach him to ride and, later on, to shoot. He made his wishes very plain about that."

"Thank you. I can't think of a better person to look after him than you." Helen blinked rapidly to dispel the tears that threatened. Silly, how emotional she'd been lately. She didn't know what had come over her.

The parson was at the Dower House within the hour, all agog to meet the wicked woman who had captivated Charles Carnforth. She must be a very artful creature indeed to have trapped an experienced man like him into marriage, but not, Mr Morpeth hoped, really wicked. He did not think he would quite know how to deal with someone like that in his peaceful little parish.

Helen, afraid of further rebuffs, received him formally in the best parlour, clad in the black her husband had hated so much, but not wearing her veils. She looked young, defenceless and very tired and, when she spoke, it was in a pleasant, low voice.

This is no designing female! thought Mr Morpeth almost immediately, feeling indignant that she should have been so misrepresented.

Why, only the other day Mrs Celia Carnforth had taken him on one side and said confidentially, "Of course, people will not receive a creature like that into their homes! One must maintain standards."

Sheer spite, that's all it could have been, and he, a man of God, had believed it, to his everlasting shame! He felt so indignant at his own gullibility that he preached a rousing sermon the following Sunday on the evils of listening to slanderers and ill wishers. (Unfortunately, Mrs Carnforth quite failed to see the point and just sat there, nodding agreement and studying the bonnets of the other ladies.)

"How may I help you, ma'am?" Mr Morpeth asked gently, touched by the sadness in her eyes. "Your man said it was urgent."

"I wish to arrange my husband's funeral, of course." She would feel much better when Charles was laid to rest.

He could only goggle at that. "But Mrs Carnforth – Mrs *Celia* Carnforth, that is – has already dealt with that!"

"Then Mrs Celia Carnforth has been wasting her time!"

"But – it's customary for the funeral of a Carnforth to take place at Ashdown Park, ma'am!"

"And is it also customary for a widow to be forbidden to attend her own husband's funeral? Or for the new owners of Ashdown to refuse to receive her?" Her voice broke and tears threatened again for a moment.

As she fought to control herself, he suppressed his shock and wondered what had happened the previous day? Had they really refused to receive Charles Carnforth's widow at Ashdown? He could not believe it of Daniel, who seemed a man of good sense. Surely, surely there must have been some mistake?

"My dear Mrs Carnforth, I don't understand all this! Of course they must receive you. And – and how can anyone forbid you to attend? Who would do such a thing?" He spoke gently, realising how upset she was, seeing the damp rag of a handkerchief being alternately twisted and crushed by her slender fingers.

"I was informed that only gentlemen mourners were to attend."

He relaxed a little. Here was one misunderstanding he could lay to rest at once. "Well – usually only the gentlemen follow the hearse and attend the interment, but the ladies of the family wait for them at the house."

"I have not been invited to the house. When I called there yesterday, Mrs Celia Carnforth was indisposed, Mr Daniel Carnforth was out and we were not even offered refreshments, just directed to the Dower House." Her eyes flashed at the memory and when he would have spoken, she raised her hand to stop him. "I tell you this not to seek sympathy, or to make you act in any way disloyal to the new owner of Ashdown, but to show you why I am *obliged* to hold the funeral myself from this house!"

"I am," he fumbled for a tactful word, "shocked – yes, shocked! – by what you say. But I cannot believe Daniel Carnforth is aware of what has happened. I have found him to be a most reasonable gentleman. Quiet, but very just in his dealings." It could only be Celia Carnforth who had made these arrangements, but Mr Morpeth did not say that.

"Mr Carnforth was not at home when we called yesterday, but it was he who sent me the letter specifying that only gentlemen were to attend the funeral." Helen's voice grew fierce. "I loved my husband, Mr Morpeth, as did my son. We have no intention of being excluded from his funeral! We wish to be there when he is l-laid to rest. So – may we discuss the arrangements now?"

He ran a hand through his thin fringe of grey hair, leaving it standing on end round the edges of his bald pate, a sure sign that he was greatly disturbed. If only his wife were here. Sylvia would have handled things so much better than he had done. She always did. He searched for words which would neither upset this poor lady afresh nor imply that he disbelieved her. "I shall be happy to help you in any way I can, Mrs Carnforth, believe me, but may I – would you allow *me* to speak to Mr Daniel Carnforth first? Before we do anything irrevocable?"

Her voice was bitter. "To what purpose?"

"To see if – I am not doubting your word, pray do not think that! But Mrs Celia Carnforth, Daniel's mother, can be a very difficult – yes, difficult is the word, there is no getting round that – a *very* difficult lady, in fact. I am pretty certain that Daniel himself is not aware of – of how you feel, or perhaps, even, the true state of affairs."

"He was the one who wrote the letter!" she said indignantly.

"Yes, but – well, I do not like to malign a lady, but – what did *she* tell him first?" Mr Morpeth shook his head.

"Well . . ." Helen hesitated. She had taken a liking to Mr Morpeth and he did, after all, know the new owner better than she did.

Henry Morpeth decided to be brutally frank. "Ma'am, it would cause a great scandal if you held the funeral from this house! It would put you – and your son – in a very awkward position. May I not, at least, attempt to reconcile the two parties before this misunderstanding goes any further?"

She bowed her head for a moment, but not before he had seen the sparkle of tears on her cheeks. "Well," she conceded, "perhaps you could see him and just find out if there is a misunderstanding. I have no desire to cause scandals, I assure you. My son and I have to live here, after all. But I must and will attend my husband's funeral!"

Mr Morpeth sighed with relief. "Thank you, ma'am. A very wise decision. Very generous, too. I shall ride over to Ashdown at once. This matter must be settled as quickly as possible. But, before I go, may I say a brief prayer over the coffin? I knew Charles too, and liked him."

Now the tears were falling fast. "Yes. It's in the dining-room. Please excuse me. This is all so – so distressing!" Her voice broke on the last word and she left the room hurriedly.

As Mr Morpeth was leaving the house, he met Harry in the hall.

"Good day, sir. Are you looking for my mother?"

"No, young man, I've already seen her. I've been saying a prayer for your stepfather."

"Oh. Are you *il padre* – I mean, the priest?"

"Clergyman, we call it in England. You must be Mrs Carnforth's son. My name is Morpeth. I'm the parson of this village."

"How do you do, sir. I'm Harry Perriman. If you're leaving, I'll come with you to the door." Harry did so and shook the parson's hand as they stood there. "Thank you for coming, sir."

His open countenance, childish dignity and excellent manners only reinforced the good impression his mother had already made upon Mr Morpeth.

At Ashdown Park, Daniel was found to be at home, for once. Mr Morpeth had had visions of having to search for him in the cow byres. He was shown into the estate office and received civilly enough, but his host seemed rather preoccupied. Mr Morpeth was in no mood for soft words and inattention. When his ire was roused, he could be a very lion in defence of what he felt to be right.

"I have just come from the Dower House, Daniel."

"Do you mean you've actually *seen* the woman!" Daniel asked flippantly, still only half attending.

Henry bristled with indignation at this disrespectful way of describing a grieving lady. "What do you mean by that, sir?"

Daniel looked at him in surprise. "I mean, have you seen her face? My mother tells me she goes heavily veiled, like an actress in a farce."

"Of course I've seen her face! She received me inside the house. And she was not wearing a veil."

"Then you're a privileged man! She refused to stop here yesterday, even to take refreshments, so no one else has had the chance to see her. And what is more, she refused point-blank to reply to my message concerning the funeral!" Daniel spoke brusquely, trying to hide his irritation. Given all the things that desperately needed attention on this neglected estate, he had small patience with the fuss that was being made about the funeral of a man he'd never even seen, the man who had neglected things here in the first place. And the affectations of that man's widow roused only his scorn.

Henry was tired of searching for tactful words. "Are you sure Mrs Carnforth was *offered* refreshments, sir?" he asked bluntly, tackling the first point raised. He was pleased to see Daniel stare at him in surprise.

"Of course I am! Are you accusing my mother of not knowing the correct way to treat a visitor?"

"Could we – could we check that fact? You see, Mrs Carnforth says nothing was offered. The housekeeper would know, surely?"

"Is this necessary?" But a dreadful suspicion was beginning to creep into Daniel's mind. Surely, even his mother could not have been – could not have . . .

"Yes, sir, it is necessary!" Henry Morpeth insisted. "If there is some misunderstanding, it is better that it be cleared up at once and that justice be done. And since Mrs Carnforth has kindly given me permission to undertake the role of mediator between the – the various parties, I intend to do just that."

Before Mrs Mossop could be sent for, Mr Napperby was announced. He was very much on his dignity, bristling with indignation at the memory of their reception here the previous day.

"Good morning, sir!" he declared, without waiting to be addressed by his host. "I am glad to see that you *are* available today! Mr Morpeth, your servant."

Seeing Daniel begin to frown at the way in which the lawyer had addressed him, Mr Morpeth stepped hastily into the breach. "I called upon Mrs Carnforth – Mr Charles Carnforth's widow, that is – this morning. What she had to tell me was – shocking. Therefore, Mr Napperby, I have taken it upon myself to come here and try to clear up the misunderstandings that seem to have arisen."

"I have just left her myself. A wonderful woman!" But she had obviously been weeping and this had roused Samuel Napperby's sense of chivalry. "I would hardly call them misunderstandings, however. It was made very plain to her yesterday that she would not be received in this house. I was there! I heard what the housekeeper said with my own ears."

"Housekeeper said!" Daniel took a pace forward. "But surely it was my mother who spoke to her – who . . ."

"We saw only the housekeeper, Jane Mossop. We did not see Mrs Celia Carnforth."

There was a pregnant silence before Daniel said stiffly, "Then I fear that this is how the misunderstanding arose. The housekeeper is new to her job and no doubt confused the messages."

But Mr Napperby was having none of that. He saw no reason why poor Jane Mossop should be blamed for her mistress's bad manners. "I have known Jane Mossop for many years, Daniel, and have always found her a woman of good sense – *not* a person who is prone to confusing messages!"

Daniel flushed a dull red.

"In fact," went on Mr Napperby obstinately, "it is due to Jane Mossop's excellent work as a caretaker that the interior of the Manor has not deteriorated as much as the exterior."

"Oh."

"As to yesterday, let us get things quite clear – Jane had been forced to learn a message off by heart, a very impertinent message. I do not scruple to say that, because it's the simple truth. And she was – I could see that quite clearly – embarrassed at having to deliver it. You were not available, your mother was indisposed, and we were to leave the coffin in the library and told that the Dower House was down the North Drive."

He saw with satisfaction that his words had struck home. "And the last piece of information was quite unnecessary, as Jane well knew, since I have served this estate, man and boy, for more years than I care to remember. I know exactly where the Dower House is situated. Only a stranger to the district would have thought it necessary to tell me that." He was strongly tempted to offer his resignation as a final gesture, but perhaps this would be overhasty.

Henry Morpeth stepped into the breach again. "This is all very distressing – but gentlemen, can we not set aside the apportioning of blame and resolve the more pressing matter of the funeral? It will cause a major scandal if it is not held here at Ashdown. As it would if Mrs Carnforth were kept away from her own husband's funeral."

"Kept away from it!" Daniel stared at him in shock. "Who said she would be kept away from it?"

"Apparently you did."

"I can't—" he tried to think what he had written in the note.

"That was never my intention, I assure you." He was convinced now that his mother had grossly insulted the widow and he felt quite sick at the thought. It was one thing to resent the woman, quite another to treat her in this cavalier fashion. "I shall arrange matters myself from now on. Whatever that woman's character, she *was* his wife, after all!"

"Her character, sir, is that of a lady! In every sense of the word," stated Mr Napperby, bristling anew. "And what is more, I take great exception to your remark. I saw with my own eyes her devotion to your cousin, for I was with her as she nursed him during the final few days. And I think I can safely say that I am not foolish enough to be taken in by false displays of affection!"

Daniel was looking white and shocked to the gills, and so he should, thought Mr Napperby. He did not allow his host time to speak, however, but continued without a pause, determined to have his say in full. "Mrs Carnforth insists on attending the interment – with the boy. And I fully support her wishes."

"It is not customary for a woman to attend. My own mother has no plans to be present at the graveside!"

Mr Napperby's expression was so hostile, so full of ire, that Henry Morpeth rushed in again. "But it would be no problem to allow the widow to attend, would it, sir?"

"No, of course not! Not if she so wishes."

"I can lend her my own carriage and accompany her," offered Mr Napperby, afraid of further snubs. "But I must tell you now that I will countenance no public insults to the lady. This must all be done properly and with due decorum."

Shame made Daniel flush again. "There is no need to say that. She will, of course, ride in the first carriage, with me."

"And afterwards?" demanded Mr Napperby, determined to have every last detail clear.

"Afterwards she will naturally be invited to return here with the other mourners and partake of refreshments."

Mr Napperby inclined his head, his eyes glittering with triumph. "And, as she is a beneficiary, she must also be present with the rest of the family at the reading of the will."

"Of course. And if she wishes to move to the house, we shall be pleased to receive her."

"I think she will be better in her own home, among those who truly care for her."

Silence hung heavily around them for a moment.

"Then I shall take my mother to call upon Mrs Carnforth this very afternoon," Daniel said firmly. What's more, his mother would go with him and be civil, if he had to drag her there by force! How *could* she have behaved like that and landed him in this embarrassing predicament? Had she run mad in her old age?

After that, the funeral arrangements were quickly settled – subject to the widow's agreement, Mr Napperby insisted, with a challenging look in his eyes – and a guest list was drawn up. Mrs Carnforth's elaborate flights of fancy as regards staging the funeral were mentioned by the parson and dismissed out of hand by Daniel, a matter to which she later took great exception. During the discussion, Daniel rose slightly in the two older men's estimation by the common sense he showed about the arrangements and the way he deferred to their greater knowledge of local society.

On the way out, however, Mr Napperby turned round and stared Daniel in the eye as he reiterated, "I have your word, sir, that the widow will be treated with all courtesy?"

"You have my solemn word."

When he had watched the two men leave, Daniel turned round and strode up the stairs to his mother's room, fury sizzling through him.

Daniel and Celia's formal visit to the Dower House did indeed take place that afternoon, but only after a violent argument between mother and son, followed by a fit of hysterics from Celia – though the histrionics availed her nothing.

"You can either," said Daniel implacably, "make the visit with me today or leave immediately for Bath. It's as simple as that."

"You cannot mean that! I am your mother."

"I do, indeed, mean it. Your discourtesy to the widow has shown us in a very bad light and I am deeply ashamed of what has happened. We shall now make every atonement possible to the lady."

"But she is *not* a lady! That is the whole point."

"She is cousin Charles's widow, and as such will be treated with every courtesy, lady or not."

"You cannot expect me to associate with a – a wicked creature like that!"

"You do not know anything about her nature. Mr Napperby assures me she was genuinely devoted to our cousin."

"But—"

"You need do nothing that you do not wish to do, mother. As I said, I shall be happy to place a carriage at your disposal for your return to Bath. Within the hour, shall we say?"

He was all cold dignity, reminding her so much of his father that fresh tears flowed. She sobbed a little, then gave in. She had no intention of missing this funeral, for her dear friends in Bath would want to know all about *that* woman. Besides, it would look bad if she were not there.

The two of them were received at the Dower House by a heavily veiled Helen – who did not wish them to see her reddened eyes – with her son standing protectively by her side. The boy scowled at them the whole time, for he knew that these were the people who had upset and insulted his mother. Briggs had explained it all to him, for no one else would.

A stilted conversation followed. Both ladies were almost monosyllabic in their responses to each other's polite questions, and Daniel, who was not a man famed for his verbal address, found the visit a nightmare. He explained the arrangements, asked if they met with Mrs Carnforth's approval and showed her the guest list drawn up by Mr Napperby and Mr Morpeth.

His mother breathed deeply while arrangements were discussed, and reflected upon ingratitude, which was indeed sharper than a serpent's tooth, or whatever it was the Bible said. She would look that up the instant she got home, see if the good book could offer her any consolation for this embarrassment. And *that* woman looked exactly like a blowsy actress to her, and you'd never convince her otherwise.

After a very correct twenty minutes, the visitors stood up.

As they were leaving, Daniel looked across the room at Harry, wondering if he should say something to the lad, who was, whether he wished it or not, now his ward. However, he encountered a look of such hostility that he just muttered something under his breath and left.

Celia harangued her son all the way home on the folly of giving in to vulgar persons. She went on to decry the ridiculous affectation of women who wore such heavy mourning inside the house – "too theatrical for words" – especially when everyone knew that the woman had only married poor Charles for his money!

"You are not to say that again, Mother!"

"But *everyone* knows it's true."

"True or not, I should be obliged if you would refrain from repeating such a remark in future."

A moment later she was off on another tack. "And one can only wonder what she's hiding under that veil. She's probably pock-marked, or – or raddled from wearing too much paint upon her face."

"Mother!"

She flounced in her seat and hunched her shoulders at him, but said nothing more.

Her son spent the rest of the day out riding.

Formalities, and therefore county society, being satisfied, the funeral was arranged for three days later and the coffin was taken in state to lie in the village church, the compromise agreed upon.

Because she still wept at the slightest thing, Helen continued to wear the heavy veils she would normally have despised. She could not think what was wrong with her lately, but admitted to herself that she was exhausted and promised herself a good, long rest when all the ceremonial was over.

On the sad day, Helen and her son rode to the church in the first carriage with the heir, as was proper. Celia Carnforth, trailing black lace and crepe, stayed at the house.

The boy seems a surly cub, thought Daniel, for again Harry had done nothing but scowl at his new guardian. By the time they arrived at the graveyard, he had to admit that at least Harry was attentive to his mother and spoke like a gentleman's son. No doubt that was due to his stepfather's influence.

Her son's scowls, as Helen well knew, were Harry's defence against the dreadful crime of weeping like a baby for the only father he had ever known. So she didn't reprimand him, just touched his hand from time to time, and put her arm round his shoulders for a minute when they got out of the carriage at the church.

It didn't even occur to Daniel that he had not yet seen the widow's face. He had been up until late the previous night grappling with figures and estimates for the most necessary of the renovations and was more tired than he would admit, so he just sat there during the short journey to the village church and let the well-sprung carriage lull his muscles into a semblance of relaxation. He was very relieved that Mrs Carnforth made no attempt to spoil this short respite by forcing a conversation, and even more relieved that his mother had chosen to stay behind at the big house with the other ladies "as is proper, dearest".

After the ceremony the widow thanked Mr Morpeth for his brief, but moving, eulogy, lingered for a moment by the graveside, head bent, then squared her shoulders and turned resolutely back towards the carriage, her hand on her son's shoulder. Not much longer to endure now, she thought. *I shall get through it.*

On their return to Ashdown Park, Helen hesitated for a moment when offered Daniel's arm to descend from the carriage and walk into the house. Then she decided that, for Harry's sake, she should preserve the civilities and thus accepted the offer. After today, she hoped to see as little of this man as possible.

He led her into the great south drawing-room, where Mrs Carnforth and several other ladies awaited them.

"May I give you a glass of wine, Mrs Carnforth?" he asked, seeing that his mother, now whispering to the lady beside her, had no intention of offering this guest any refreshments or easing her way into the group.

"No. Thank you." It would have choked Helen to try to eat or drink. She was full of grief and very much alone, in spite of the presence of her son, but she couldn't let Charles down now.

She sat quietly in the chair to which Daniel led her, thanked those who came up to offer her their condolences and endured the slow formalities as best she could. Two or three times Harry's hand squeezed hers secretly, which gave her the courage to continue.

By this time, everyone else in the room was curious to see her face, but she made no attempt to lift the veils, or to speak beyond the necessary responses to their greetings and condolences.

After a while the other guests took their leave and Daniel came to offer Helen his arm again. He led her into the library to listen to the reading of the will.

Celia Carnforth walked sulkily behind, furious that such a woman should be given precedence over her, and more than curious to see exactly what provisions her husband's cousin had made for his wife.

". . . to my beloved wife, Helen, I leave all the property and incomes which are not entailed, being . . . and to my stepson, Harry Robert Perriman, five thousand pounds, to be invested carefully and used for his education and later establishment in a suitable occupation . . . the said Harry Robert Perriman to be under the joint guardianship of my dear friend and lawyer, Samuel James Napperby, and my heir, Daniel Carnforth."

Daniel listened to the reading of the will with an impassive face and a bitter heart. *That* woman had stripped his inheritance of all but the minimum covered by the entail. He was left with few reserves to pay for desperately needed improvements at Ashdown Park and an income much reduced after years of neglect by an absentee landlord who had cared less than nothing for the estate.

When the reading was over, he stood up and thanked Mr Napperby for his care of the family's interests. "I hope you will continue to oversee them."

Samuel inclined his head. He had wondered whether to ask Daniel to find another lawyer, and he would have done so had Mrs Carnforth been offered anything but the most civil treatment on this sad day. But all in all, it was best that he keep an eye on things, and on the boy, too.

While her son was speaking to the lawyer, Celia turned to Helen and said with a sweetly acid smile, "Well, you certainly made sure you were comfortably left, did you not, Mrs Carnforth? How much money do you think now remains for my son to restore and run the estate with after *your* husband let it go to pieces?" Whatever her personal failings, Celia had a shrewd brain for finances.

Helen made no attempt to answer this accusation. Was it true that the estate had been stripped of funds? Was Daniel really so short of money? She didn't know, and her head was aching so fiercely that she could not think about it until later. She would ask Mr Napperby for his advice but, at the moment, all she wished to do was to lie down. Besides, nothing she could say would convince this vicious woman that she had not known any of the details of Charles's will before his death, so why bother to try? She had seen the way the group of ladies looked at her after the funeral and it had hurt her badly. That was why she had kept her veils on.

As soon as Daniel had finished speaking to the lawyer, Helen went over to take her leave of him.

"You're welcome to stay for a while."

She shook her head. "I'm feeling a – a little tired." And tearful. And nauseous. She didn't know what had got into her lately. She was usually so energetic, even in times of trouble.

"I'll see you to the door, then, Mrs Carnforth."

"There is no need. You have your other guests to think of."

"I insist! It would be discourteous to do otherwise. And I would not want you to think we had not treated you with every respect due to my cousin Charles's widow." He tried to catch his mother's eye, but she was looking in the other direction.

Helen signalled to her son, who fell in behind her in his usual unobtrusive way. Few children of his age had had such a long training in being seen and not heard, she felt. Now that they were at last settled, she must see that he learned to run and shout, to behave more like a boy should – even to get into trouble at times. In fact, she would make sure he led as happy and normal a life as possible, from now on.

As they were crossing the echoing hallway with its dark panelling, Daniel saw Mrs Carnforth stumble, sway for a moment, as if dizzy, and put one hand to her temple. Quickly he took her arm, ready to catch her if she should faint. His mother, who made great play of her ill-health, had never actually fainted in his presence, but this lady, who had said nothing and asked for no sympathy, looked to be drooping with exhaustion.

"I'm afraid this has all been a great strain for you," he said, his deep voice more gentle than before.

"Yes. I'm sorry to be a nuisance. I'm just – very tired now." She continued to lean heavily on his arm as they moved across the hall, then she straightened up as they reached the main door and tried to compose herself.

Daniel waited there with her until the footman announced that the carriage was ready. He didn't see, but Harry did, that tears were trickling down her cheeks, for she kept her head bent.

As the footman opened the front doors, Helen uttered a choked, "Goodbye, Mr Carnforth," and hurried out to the carriage before he could escort her any further.

Harry, who had not heard what they had said to each other as they crossed the hallway, turned to his host. "I hate you!" he hissed. "You always make my mother cry! I won't *have* you for a guardian! Leave her alone, you bully!"

Daniel, who had been too stunned to say anything, watched him run to the carriage and saw him put his arms round his mother before Briggs closed the door. Mrs Carnforth's shoulders were definitely shaking. She was crying. That would explain why she had hidden behind the veil. Could she be genuinely grief-stricken, then? Mr Napperby seemed to think so, and the lawyer had impressed him as a shrewd fellow.

He sighed and went back to the library and, when the guests had left, escorted his mother firmly to the door, in spite of her protests that she wished to stay, to help her poor, dear son. Then he started going into some details of the estate, which were puzzling him, with Mr Napperby.

If men were allowed to cry in times of trouble, Daniel would have been perilously close to it himself by the time the lawyer had finished explaining exactly how he stood financially. He was left with the bitter knowledge that he would be able to make few, if any, of the improvements he had planned, even those that were desperately needed, like repairs to cottage roofs. He would, in fact, be hard pushed even to maintain the rambling old house that he was rapidly growing to love and whose roof needed urgent attention.

Over dinner that evening, Celia said, "My dearest, my mother's heart aches for you. She has *stolen* your inheritance! Stolen it!"

"Charles Carnforth was at perfect liberty to leave his money as he chose, Mother, as we have already discussed."

"Well, you will just have to put the rents up."

He didn't attempt to argue. She would never understand his concern for the long-term well-being of his land or his care for his tenants, some of whom could barely afford the present rent, and who depended on him for so many things.

A little later Celia started on matters closer to her heart. "We really must find you some proper staff now. I was ashamed of the way that maid served the tea. We are just fortunate that she didn't spill it all over someone. What we need is an experienced butler, and perhaps . . ."

"I don't intend to hire any other servants, Mother, and certainly not a butler. I can manage perfectly well with the staff I already have. I shall be living very simply from now on – indeed, I think I shall close up some of the rooms. I shall not be doing much entertaining, after all. You know I am not fond of parties and such fooleries."

She stared at him in horror. "Not entertain! But dearest, – you are a great landowner now, the owner of Ashdown Park. It is your *duty* to entertain. And I am quite prepared to sacrifice myself to help you until you are married – and we really *must* find you a suitable wife! You cannot delay doing your duty any longer!"

"Mama, I shall be so busy setting the estate to rights that I shall not have time to waste on social exchanges." He took a deep breath. Why did he always find it so difficult to manage her? "I have come to the conclusion that it will be best for you to return to Bath. I'm grateful for your help, but I fear I shall be but poor company from now on."

Spots of colour burned in her cheeks. "Fine thanks you offer me, turning me out of your house!"

"I've just told you – I shall be living very quietly. You would be moped to death here. And – and Mother – I'm afraid I shall have to sell Bellborough. This estate needs so much doing to it. Before I left, Stephen Ferndon approached me and, in short, he made me an offer which I shall now accept."

Surprise and shock held her silent for a moment, then she stood up, pushing her chair back so violently that it fell over. "I see. You are a true Carnforth, are you not, Daniel? *My* family's inheritance counts for nothing with you!"

"You know that I love Bellborough," he said, his quiet voice in great contrast to her shrill tones. "If there were any other way at all to remedy—"

"You do not really care! You Carnforths are all the same! It's all Ashdown, Ashdown, Ashdown! Your father was just as selfish! You haven't even *waited*, haven't even attempted to find other ways to set matters right! A good marriage could—"

"I already have a good offer for Bellborough. And I have no desire whatsoever to marry at the moment." He tried to speak courteously, but he was rapidly running out of patience. Did she think he cared nothing for his old home, for the acres he had loved and cared for ever since his father had died? Did she ever think about anything but her own needs and her puffed-up pride?

Celia almost spat the words at him. "Well, if that's the case, you need not worry about me! I would scorn to stay on where I am not wanted! Scorn it! I have served my purpose and shall not outstay my welcome! A mother is an unimportant thing, easily discarded, after all."

Mouth set in grim lines, he watched her make a tragic exit from the room, handkerchief pressed to her eyes. Heaven preserve him from all women and their melodramas! He did not make the mistake of going after her, or she would probably have found some way to persuade him to let her stay on. He needed to act swiftly, make a clean break with Bellborough and live in as economical fashion as possible for the next few years.

In fact, Celia was not sorry to be leaving Ashdown Park, however much she protested. The woods were just as gloomy as she had always remembered, and the inside of the house was in a shameful state of decay. So old-fashioned! And Daniel had refused even to let her redecorate the drawing-room. He was turning out to be very mean – and penny-pinching was a thing she could not *abide*.

No, if he were to live here as a recluse, she would be much better off in her own little home. And she would have a fine tale to tell all her cronies in Bath about how well *that* woman had feathered her nest . . .

Sixteen

The next day it became obvious that Mrs Carnforth was not at all well. When Susan knocked on the door, she raised her head wearily from the pillows to say, "Come in!" but made no attempt even to sit up.

"Aunt Becky says the boy is all right and has et a good breakfast. She wants to know if you'd like your breakfast in bed?"

"I'd love a cup of tea, but I'm not hungry."

Susan was back ten minutes later with a loaded tray. "Sorry, ma'am, but Aunt Becky said you should eat a good breakfast considering all the things you have to deal with." She squirmed apologetically as she saw the revulsion on her new mistress's face. "I'm sorry about the food. She would send it up."

"It's not your fault. Would you just pour me a cup of tea, please?"

Susan set the tray down on a small table by the window, saw to the cup of tea, bobbed a curtsey and left.

Later, she came back for the tray and found her mistress drowsing, so tiptoed out without asking any of the questions her aunt had charged her with.

Becky took one look at the untouched tray of food that was brought down again and decided to investigate. No good ever came of facing trouble on an empty stomach. She glanced through the window and saw that Harry was all right, talking to Briggs. "Get on with cleanin' them fowls, Susan girl!" she ordered and marched upstairs, knocking on the door.

Helen woke with a start.

"I hear you're not feeling well, ma'am." Becky cast a professional eye over her mistress and found her very pale.

"I'm just – tired. And a little nauseous. The travelling and the – the sad events seem to have upset my stomach." Helen fiddled with the edge of the sheet, then confided in a rush, "Yesterday was a dreadful strain. A morning in bed will soon put me right. I'm rarely ill."

"Are you sure you're not coming down with something, ma'am? Perhaps you have a cold starting?"

"Well, my head does ache – but I'm not at all sniffly."

"And you standing by the graveside yesterday in that cold wind! Asking for trouble, it was!"

"I could not let Charles go to his grave alone! None of those other people cared about him."

Becky's expression softened for a moment. "Aye, well, he was a fine boy, even if I do say so as the one who brought him up, and he grew into a fine gentleman, too. I never thought I'd outlast him, that's for sure!" She realised that this sort of talk would not cheer her mistress up and changed her tone abruptly. "Well, that's all over with now, isn't it? And you still have your son."

"Yes. I do." Helen wiped her eyes. "I'm sorry. I'm not usually so weepy. I – I despise women who cry all over everyone!" She blew her nose vigorously, but the tears continued to flow.

Becky eyed her narrowly. These symptoms – in anyone else, she'd be wondering . . . But Sir Charles had been dead long enough for Helen to know if she were carrying his child, surely? Still, it wouldn't hurt to check up. Some women were very irregular. It was best to be sure what an illness was and what it was not, if you were to nurse someone better.

"Have you had any other symptoms, ma'am?"

"Symptoms? Of what?"

"Of what's wrong with you."

"I told you! I'm just tired and – and the journey has upset my stomach."

"Worse in the mornings, is it, the sickness?"

"Yes, as a matter of fact . . ." Helen stopped in mid-sentence and stared at Becky, then said faintly, "It can't be that! Charles always said he had never fathered a child and . . ." Her voice trailed away, then she stared again at Becky. "But – my courses have stopped, and I'm usually quite regular. I can't remember when – I've been so busy I didn't think about it, but . . ."

"How long?"

Helen did a quick calculation. "It must be over three months. We – made love almost till the end." She could not help smiling. "Oh – oh, I dare not hope!"

"It should be showing a little by now, ma'am. Will you let me look at you? I've delivered half the babies in Ashdown. I'd soon know if you were carrying a child."

Five minutes later, she smiled at her mistress. "Unless I'm very much mistaken, and I never have been before, you're expecting a child."

Helen's white pinched face was suddenly transformed into a glow of happiness. "Oh, to have Charles's child! There's nothing – *nothing* – I can think of in the world that would make me happier!"

Becky's wrinkled hand closed over hers and they sat quietly for a moment or two.

What a nice lass she was! the old nurse thought. At that moment, she decided she would be the one to look after Helen Carnforth – and the baby, too, when it was born. It was for this the Lord had spared her, gifted her with such a long life. "Well, my love, you've got me to look after you and it'll make me happy, too, to see Master Charles's child born. It's terrible sad when a man leaves no one behind to carry on his line, terrible sad."

Helen grasped her hand. "Thank you, Becky. I'm so grateful."

After a few minutes, the old woman stood up and said briskly, for there was no use dwelling on distressing thoughts, "We must send a message to Mr Napperby straight away."

"Mr Napperby? Why? I mean, I shall tell him, of course, but there's no hurry, surely?"

"What if it's a boy?"

It took time for the implications of Becky's question to register, then Helen gasped. "Dear heavens! That would mean – it would mean that . . ."

"That Daniel Carnforth is not the heir. So it's not just a private event, ma'am."

"N-no. But, we could wait a week or two, couldn't we? I'd like to keep it to myself for a while, grow used to the idea. And – I'd like to feel better before I face them."

So weary did she look that Becky nodded. It could do no harm, and the main thing was that her poor mistress should keep the child. "Well, you *are* very tired and, in your condition, it's most important that you rest. We'll give it out that you're suffering from exhaustion until you're ready to face people, my dear – ma'am I should say."

"'My dear' sounds fine to me. Oh, Becky, how wonderful it all is!"

Becky beamed at her. That was how a woman should feel about a child! She had no patience for fine ladies who moaned and complained their way through their pregnancies.

So it was that Harry was left more or less to his own devices for the next couple of days, for even Briggs, who normally spent quite a lot of time with him, was busy acquiring horses and vehicles for his mistress, and making inquiries about a cook-housekeeper in Bedderby.

Although Harry was allowed to go and see his mother, he found her sleepy and disinclined to talk. Becky explained that she was worn out with nursing his stepfather and then coming to England. Harry understood that perfectly well, and tried not to be a nuisance, but he rather wished he could have consulted her about something that was worrying him.

Having had time to think it over, he had become rather ashamed of his outburst at Mr Carnforth after the funeral. He was pretty sure that neither his mother nor his stepfather would have approved of his behaviour. It was not only ungentlemanly to insult a man under his own roof, it was babyish and uncivil as well. The proper thing to do, he decided eventually, was to go and apologise, and the sooner the better.

When, for the second day running, his mother kept to her bed and Briggs disappeared into Bedderby to look at a horse, Harry decided to do something about his rudeness himself. It was all pretty easy, after all. He would walk over to the Manor, which was only just along the North Drive and turn left (he had checked the route out with Susan), and he would tender a civil apology to his guardian.

He sought out Becky and told her that he rather thought he might go for a walk. "Towards the Manor, you know. I'd like to look at my stepfather's old home again. There were too many people there before."

Well, she thought, the boy couldn't come to much harm in their own woods, and it was a lovely day. "Stick to the paths, then, lovie. You don't know the woods yet."

"Oh, I will, Becky, I will!"

But he was tempted away from the path within a couple of

hundred yards by the most splendid tree he'd ever seen. Harry decided to climb it. And while he was up it, he saw another, only a little way beyond, that was even bigger. Not out of sight of the path, or not much. And after that, there was a brook. Before long Harry had his shoes and stockings off and was paddling up the stream. A large elm tree was his final undoing. He got higher up it than he had ever climbed before.

Suddenly there was a creaking, wrenching sound, and the branch on which he was perched broke under him. He clutched vainly at another branch, uttered a high, frightened cry and fell with sickening rapidity to the ground. Luckily there were enough branches on the way down to break his fall and the earth was soft under the tree from the recent rains, but he was still knocked senseless.

When Master Harry didn't return for his midday meal, Becky began to worry, for he had a hearty appetite and was usually ready to eat before the food was. By two o'clock, with Briggs still away, she decided to send Susan over to the big house to inquire if anyone had seen Harry. Perhaps they had given him a meal there.

No one at the big house had seen him and Susan panicked. "He's lost, then!" she wailed, clutching her chest dramatically. "He don't know them old woods, he don't, bein' a foreigner. You could wander about for *days* in there! You could starve to death!"

A voice behind her made her jump with shock and utter a little screech.

"Which foreigner are you talking about?" asked Daniel, who often used the kitchen entrance when he was dirty.

"Ooh, sir! Ooh, you made me fair jump out of my skin!"

"Which foreigner is lost?" he repeated impatiently.

"Master Harry, sir. He went out for a walk this mornin' an' he hasn't been seen since. Comin' over this way, he was, to look at the big house, and he didn't come back for his meal, so my auntie sent me to ask if anyone had seen him. And no one has. He never even got here. Likely they'll find his body one day, a-moulderin' in the woods."

"Don't talk such rubbish, girl! He'll have wandered off to climb a tree." If he had been ten years younger, or less conscious of his new dignity, Daniel would have done the same thing a few times himself. The woods at Ashdown Park had the best climbing trees he'd ever seen.

"Well, he ent come back, sir, and it's past three o'clock now. And that lad wouldn't miss a meal, not for anything. Eats like a young horse, he does."

"What does his mother say?"

"We haven't told her. She's not well. And Aunt Becky says she's had enough upsets, so we're to wait till we know something."

"She's ill?" His voice was sharp.

"Just suffering from exhaustion, like. Fair done up she was after the funeral, poor thing."

"Where's Briggs? He seems a sensible fellow. And he knows the boy. What does he think about it?"

"Briggs? Gone off to the other side of Bedderby, he has, to look at an old horse. Won't be back till after dark, I reckon, and it'll be too late then." Susan was determined to look on the black side.

Daniel sighed. He could see nothing for it but to send some men out to look for the boy. And he supposed he'd better go himself as well. He *was* the lad's guardian, after all.

An hour's search of the woods close to the North Avenue brought no results. Nor had Harry returned home. Daniel began to feel anxious. He set off back from the Dower House, his men behind him, and decided to follow his hunch about climbing trees, stopping every few paces to stare into the woods. Sure enough, at a bend in the avenue, he looked to the left and saw a magnificent beech tree, the sort to tempt any lad. He went over to examine it and found scrape marks on the trunk, as if it had been recently climbed.

"Spread out!" he told the men with him. "I'd say he made those marks."

"Ah, boys will allus climb trees," agreed one of them easily.

"An' boys will allus hurt themselves," said one of his fellows, who was more pessimistic about what life could bring. "That poor woman's just lost her husband. Be a downright shame if she lost the boy too. My niece Susan said she fair dotes on him. Nor she isn't like all them silly tales we heard. Real nice, she is. A pleasure to work for, our Susan says."

Daniel told them curtly to stop gossiping and start looking

around, but their words lingered in his mind. The boy had shouted at him after the funeral only because he thought Daniel had made his mother cry again, and that childish accusation had hit home. The Carnforths had treated her pretty shabbily. Though he'd not been treated well, either. But he didn't like to think of her crying, with no one but a boy to comfort her.

Only yesterday, Napperby had admitted that even he hadn't realised quite how run down the estate was, since he'd only ever dealt with the agent on his quarterly visits, and naturally the agent had always tried to put the best face on things. The accounts might be in order, but the buildings weren't. "Mrs Carnforth will be very sorry that the way Charles has left things will have such a deleterious effect on the running of the estate."

"You're not to tell her."

"But perhaps she could—"

"I don't want anyone's help – or their pity. The estate is my responsibility now." Daniel had written to his old neighbour immediately after his mother had left and had agreed to sell Bellborough. "Anyway, the sale of my old home will give me the money I need," he said with determined, if false cheerfulness. "After all, I don't need two houses, do I?"

Mr Napperby was not convinced by the tone, but when he stole a glance sideways, he saw the pain in Daniel's eyes and made no comment. What could you say? Sometimes, necessity was a harsh master.

Frowning at the memory of that conversation, Daniel stood by the tree and looked about him. What would have tempted a lad to go further into the woods? Another fine tree drew his attention, then the stream. Just the sort of place he had loved as a boy! Would Harry have gone upstream or down? Up, he decided. It was always more fun to wade against the current. He set off along the bank. Aha! A small branch had been broken off there not long ago, probably to poke into holes and swish in the water. He smiled reminiscently. He had done the same thing himself many a time.

He rounded a bend in the stream and came upon the most magnificent climbing tree he had ever seen in his life. An ancient elm! What tales that could tell! He walked slowly round it, then exclaimed in dismay. At its foot on the other side, half hidden by a dip in the ground, lay a small figure with shining golden hair and very muddied clothes. Daniel knelt down and ran his hands over the small body.

With relief, he found that Harry was still alive. But he had a nasty bump on his forehead and a swollen ankle. With deft hands that had set more than one broken limb on an animal, Daniel felt the ankle. No, it didn't seem to be broken. Thank goodness! But the boy was still unconscious, and that might be more serious.

There was something very vulnerable about that still figure, he found. He brushed the damp curls from Harry's bruised forehead and discovered that it felt hot. Some nice cool water would not come amiss to bathe the wound. The boy must have been lying in the sun, for he was quite flushed.

He raised his voice to call for help, but no one came. The men must have gone the other way.

For lack of any other receptacle, Daniel sacrificed his hat and went to fill it with water at the stream. After he had bathed Harry's face with his handkerchief and then laid it on the boy's forehead like a cold compress, he was rewarded by a sigh and signs of returning consciousness in his patient.

"Oh, sir, my head hurts!"

"Lie still until you recover."

But Harry couldn't lie still, though he was not yet fully conscious.

"I'm so glad to see you, sir. I've so much to ask you! I've missed you dreadfully!" he babbled, thinking for a moment that the figure bending over him was his stepfather. "They've made my mother cry so, and she's not well. Why did you leave us?"

"Shh, lad. Don't try to speak. You've hurt your head."

When Daniel spoke, Harry blinked up at him and realised his mistake, for the voice was nothing like that of Charles Carnforth, nor was the face. Tears came into his eyes. "Oh! I – I thought you were my stepfather, sir," he said. Tears started to roll down his cheeks.

A large hand covered his small grubby one. Daniel found himself very touched by the lad's grief. "You must miss him very much."

Harry rubbed his other hand across his eyes, leaving another smear of dirt. "Yes. I – I'm sorry. I don't usually cry. But he was – he was such a *splendid* person. I'm getting more used to it now, and I don't let my mother see me crying, of course."

"Of course not!"

"It's just – you look quite a bit like him, only younger, of course. And with the sun behind your head like that . . ." He tried to struggle up into a sitting position, but yelped and fell back as he put some weight on his ankle. He turned even paler and gulped. "I feel sick."

Daniel held him while he vomited, then moved him away from the mess and fetched more water to rinse his mouth. Anyone who had seen Daniel Carnforth tending a sick beast could have told you that he had a way with distressed creatures that was nothing short of miraculous. He now found that he also had a way with sick boys. When Harry thought he could stand to be moved without vomiting again, Daniel picked him up and started to carry him home. For some strange reason they didn't meet any of the other searchers on their way back. They did, however, establish a tentative rapport.

"I'm very grateful to you for finding me, sir. I wouldn't want my mother to worry about me. She has enough to upset her. And – and I'm sorry to be such a nuisance to you."

Daniel gave one of his quiet smiles, the sort his mother never saw. "Show me a boy who doesn't get into scrapes! I know I used to!"

"Did you really?"

"Oh yes!" He described a couple of them, one involving a dog, and had the pleasure of seeing the boy smile.

"I had a dog once, too," Harry confided. "It – it made a bit of trouble in the hotel. The manager shouted at me. But my stepfather said I could keep it, so I did." An unhappy look came into his face. "But I had to leave it behind in Italy. Mr Napperby said my mother had enough to worry about on the journey and I could see that he was right. I miss Nico, though."

"The dog would have hated the travelling, especially on a boat. And it might easily have got killed or lost on the way."

"Yes, I suppose so. Besides, I had my mother to look after. My stepfather said that after he was dead I was to help her as much as I could. He said I'd be a great comfort to her."

"Did he – talk about dying?" Daniel knew very little about Charles Carnforth and none of it good, though the servants seemed to have liked him well enough.

"Oh, yes. We always tried to face up to problems. He said it was the best thing to do. It was hard to stay cheerful when he was dying, though. He got so thin. But he didn't like us to cry or be sad."

What a strain that must have been! And what a contrast to the way Daniel's own mother behaved! "You got on well with Charles, then, did you? I never met him."

"Didn't you? Oh, yes, he was the *best* of fellows! We all had such fun together. He made my mother laugh a lot. I don't remember my own father very well, but I do remember him making my mother cry. And I always had to be very quiet when he was at home, or he would hit her."

Daniel tried not to show his shock. And was surprised at how angry the thought of anyone hitting a lady could make him.

Harry continued his tale. "And after my real father died, she had to work so hard to keep us. She gave English lessons, you know, and she sewed. She was always sewing, even in the evenings. I used to carry the wood in for her and empty the slops, or fetch the bread. I was too little to do much then."

Daniel was conscious of a feeling of pity for this child, who had faced so much in his short lifetime. He also felt envious, for at least Harry had had a loving father figure for a couple of years. Daniel had never had that privilege. "You were lucky to have had such a stepfather. My father was a bit like your real father. Only he didn't hit my mother." But he had ignored her and spoken to her scornfully, as if she were quite worthless, and that had hurt her greatly. Perhaps that was why she had become so fussy and attention seeking after his death.

The Dower House came into sight just then and Harry wriggled in his rescuer's arms. "Do you think I could get down and limp along, sir? I don't want my mother to get a shock if she sees me being carried."

"I think I'd better continue to carry you. You shouldn't put any weight on that ankle for a day or two."

Harry sighed and lay back. Truth to tell, he still felt rather weak. "Very well, sir. Oh, and I was coming to apologise to you, and I haven't. I'm very sorry I shouted at you after the funeral. It was ungentlemanly."

"You were right in what you said, though. We hadn't been kind to your mother. But I didn't understand – didn't mean to upset her. I'll try not to do it any more."

"That's all right, then."

Before they reached the door, Helen came running out to meet them. "Harry! Darling, what happened? Are you all right?"

"Oh, yes. I'm sorry, Mother, but I fell out of a tree. Mr Carnforth found me and brought me back. I've sprained my ankle, but he says it'll soon get better."

It was a good thing all her attention was on her son, because Daniel could not help staring. Without her veils, he realised, in stunned astonishment, that Helen Carnforth stood revealed as a beauty. Not a showy sort of woman, as he had expected, but truly beautiful nonetheless. When she bent over the boy, her glorious hair was only inches from his nose. Her skin looked creamy and soft to the touch, and he had a sudden inexplicable urge to run a finger over it and bury his face in her hair, which utterly amazed him. He was not one to run after women.

Having made sure that her son was all right, Helen raised a glowing face to his rescuer, which made Daniel feel – strange. She didn't seem to notice anything, thank goodness, and just went on to thank him unreservedly for his help. "Won't you come inside the house, Mr Carnforth? Harry must be heavy. Have you carried him far?" She had quite forgotten the animosity between them, in her joy at having her son back safe and sound, for of course Becky had not been able to keep the secret for long.

Once indoors, Harry was deposited on a couch and Becky was summoned to inspect the damage to one whom she now regarded as *her* nurseling. She and Mr Daniel had a brief consultation about the ankle, which was then bound up.

"If you'll carry him upstairs, sir?" Becky asked, but it was an order rather than a request.

"Of course."

The sufferer was carried, protesting, to his bed, to be delivered completely into Becky's hands. Not until she had given him a thorough wash and seen him consume a light meal did she leave his side, by which time he was falling asleep.

Shyly, Helen asked Daniel if he would take tea with her, and he accepted. Like her son, she had been struck by his resemblance to Charles when she first met him and it made her feel strange. But the resemblance lasted only until he began to speak. Unlike her late husband, Daniel Carnforth seemed to be a man of few words, even perhaps, she realised now, rather shy. The silences between them were not awkward, however, just peaceful, for both were tired, he from his exertions, she from her condition.

"Yes. Tea would be nice."

"And something to eat?"

"I'd appreciate that."

She rang for Susan and ordered tea and sandwiches from the cook whom Alfred had found for them in Bedderby by a fortunate chance, and who had started at the Dower House that very day.

Susan bustled out again with a cheerful, "Won't be long, ma'am."

Daniel leaned back in his chair, feeling very tired now. "I'm sorry to impose on you, but I'm afraid I missed my lunch entirely and I'm rather hungry."

"It's no trouble. Was that Harry's fault?"

He nodded. "But don't get angry at him. He's only a boy. He didn't mean to get lost."

"It's about time he did start getting into mischief," she admitted. "He's been so *good* since – since—"

"Yes. He was telling me how he tries to help you."

"He does help me. Greatly." Her eyes misted up again.

He pretended to brush some dirt off his sleeve to give her time to recover.

Susan rescued them by clattering back in with the tea tray, forgetting to knock, but smiling so proudly as she set it before her mistress that Helen hadn't the heart to correct her behaviour.

Helen poured out some tea and saw her guest supplied with sandwiches, taking one to nibble on, so that he wouldn't feel uncomfortable. "I'm sorry," she said, after a while, with her quiet smile. "I'm being very remiss as a hostess, just sitting here like this without speaking."

"I was enjoying the quietness. Life has been a little hectic lately – and my mother is not a tranquil person to live with. I was glad when she left for Bath." He smiled with such visible relief that she smiled too. How could this quiet sensible man be that silly woman's son?

"Let me pour you another cup of tea. And have another piece of Becky's fruitcake, do!"

"Thank you. I must confess to a hearty appetite."

"You Carnforths are large men. Charles was the same." A shadow crossed her face at the memory of her husband.

Daniel concentrated on stirring his tea and choosing a piece of cake. You could not be with her for long and not realise how genuine her grief was. His cousin had been a lucky man. He felt deeply ashamed of his previous suspicions and hostility towards her and, he realised with surprise, she made him feel rather protective. Not because she sought anyone's help, but rather because she was so brave about things.

"Would you and your son care to take tea with me at the Manor one day?" he asked, after a few moments. "You might like to see round the house where your husband was born. And there's a portrait of him as a boy. He looks full of mischief."

"Oh, I'd like that very much. He remained full of mischief right until the end. Do you know, he was laughing at something at the very moment when he died! I was so glad about that. It was the way he would have chosen to go." She described the incident with Giuliana and the kitten, unaware of how closely her companion was watching the play of emotion on her lovely face.

"He seems to have been a remarkable man."

"Oh, he was."

Daniel was astounded to find himself feeling jealous of his cousin. He was more astounded when he found himself thinking about the beautiful widow rather more often than he should be doing. And enjoying her company when she came to tea. And inviting her to come again. And even enjoying the company of his ward.

For the next week or two, Helen let life drift past. The rainy August gave way to an Indian summer. She found herself disinclined to do much, and spent a lot of time sitting in the garden under a tree. She started a piece of embroidery, but did not get very far with it. Instead, she soaked up the sun, allowed her skin to become an unfashionable golden colour and slept a lot.

It was like the period she had once spent at the convent, a much-needed rest after a very trying time. She kept meaning to write to her friend Roxanne and the Hendrys to tell them she was back in England, but she didn't. She also kept putting off revealing her condition to anyone and Becky was so busy bossing the new servants about, including the new cook-housekeeper, who was nominally in charge, that she, too, forgot how time was passing.

Now that peace had been established between them, Daniel found himself popping in to see his new relatives quite often, every day or two, in fact, and he never refused an invitation to take tea with them. There was the excuse of discussing the boy's future, or he had heard of a pony that might be just the thing for Harry to ride, or even just the truth that he had been passing the house, though he didn't add that he had come that way quite deliberately.

The pony was inspected by Briggs, approved and bought. Then Harry was given a puppy. A bitch at the Manor had recently had a litter. The pups were ready to leave their mother now. "Would Mrs Carnforth allow her son to come and inspect them, even, perhaps, choose one for himself?" Harry was ecstatic.

Another tea party was held at the Manor and, after long and serious consideration, a puppy was chosen.

It was Becky who suddenly realised how much time had passed and she watched all this with a little frown. Mrs Carnforth had still not made her condition known, and, if Becky were any judge of the matter, and she prided herself on having a sharp eye for such things, Daniel was fast falling in love with his cousin's widow. And that, as things stood, was not exactly the best thing that could happen. Let alone the fact that it was hard for a man to watch the woman he loved grow heavy with another man's child, it was also too soon yet for Helen, who still wept for Charles at night.

Moreover, there were nasty rumours still circulating about the type of woman Mrs Carnforth was. Becky had given a few people the rough side of her tongue when she heard them gossiping, but she knew the malicious rumours had spread too far for her to stop them. Only time would remedy the damage, as the neighbouring society got to know Mrs Carnforth and saw her worth.

Well, Becky decided one day, there'd be no hiding the child soon, so she'd best speak up. That poor young woman was just drifting along in a fool's paradise at the moment.

"Isn't it time you called in a doctor and spoke to Mr Napperby, ma'am?" she said bluntly that same night, after she had seen Master Harry to bed.

Helen's face clouded. "I wish I need not! I don't want to – to spoil everything."

"You won't be able to hide it for much longer. You're putting weight on quickly now. You'll have to tell people. You'll have to get some new clothes made, too."

A sigh was the only answer.

Becky looked at her mistress sympathetically, but was not going to let matters drift along any more. "Shall I send for the doctor, then?"

"Yes. I suppose so. But – not tomorrow. Let me have one more day in peace. He can come the day after. Besides, I want to tell Harry myself first."

So she and Harry went for a gentle stroll in the woods. She explained about the baby and he listened gravely, as he always did to important things. When she had finished her tale, however, his gravity deserted him, and he turned several somersaults round the room.

"A brother! I'm going to have a baby brother!"

"It might be a sister. You can't choose, you know."

"Well, even that's better than nothing." Something occurred to him and he stopped dead. "Oh, the poor baby! It won't even know its own father!"

He always understood things so well. "Yes. It's," her voice thickened with tears for a moment, "very sad. But you'll be able to tell it – him, her – about Charles, won't you? You'll be a very special big brother, just like you're a very special son."

His face brightened. "Yes. I'll do that. And it can play with my puppy, too." A very great concession, that. Chiggy was his pride and joy. "Have you told Mr Carnforth about the baby, Mother? Will he be its guardian, too, like he's mine?"

"No. I haven't told him. It must stay a secret for a while. We have to tell Mr Napperby first."

"We couldn't tell Daniel now, anyway. He's gone to Bellborough for a few days. We'll have to wait till he gets back."

The doctor came and, after the most cursory examination, pronounced Mrs Carnforth to be in a delicate condition and expecting a child in February. No, of course he would not tell anyone until Mr Napperby had been informed. He quite grasped the complications a posthumous heir might create!

Mr Napperby was summoned. He was shocked rigid by the news, but tried to appear pleased, for her sake, because she was glowing with happiness about her condition. "My dear Mrs Carnforth – allow me to offer you my congratulations. But – but why did you not tell me before? You must have known for a while." He was wondering how he could ask, as ask he must, if it were truly Charles's child.

"I've only known since the day after the funeral. It was Becky who realised. I had been so – so busy that I had not noticed. Foolish of me, you will say!"

"But – even that is a month ago. Why did you not tell me then?"

She blushed. "I was tired of being an object of curiosity. I felt that I needed a rest before I faced people again."

"I have to ask this – it is, of course, Charles Carnforth's child?"

She looked at him indignantly. "Of course it is. How could you even think—"

"I don't doubt you, my dear. I just – must be certain." He shook his head. It was a great pity that she had waited and he would not be able to hide from her the damage she had done. "I am, of course, happy for you, but my dear Mrs Carnforth, I must tell you that keeping such news secret was greatly unfair to Mr Daniel Carnforth. If if is a boy, he will be . . ."

"Disinherited. I understand."

"Yes, but there is worse than that, I'm afraid."

She became very still. "Worse?"

"I'm afraid, because the estate is so run down and – it must be said – because he is so short of money to amend matters, he has just sold Bellborough, his other estate."

She went white. "I – didn't realise he was thinking of that. He never said a word to me, not a word, or I would have told him about the child immediately!"

"He isn't the sort of man to make a parade of his feelings, I've found. It was quite a wrench for him to sell Bellborough. He only told me about it recently. I am not acting for him in this. In fact, that's why he has gone to Bellborough this week."

Her hands went up to her cheeks in a gesture of distress. "Oh, what have I done? Is it too late to stop him? Surely we can do something?"

He sighed. "The final documents were to be signed yesterday. I shall, of course, send a messenger after him, just in case we can stop him, but I don't hold out much hope. The documents were only a formality. Everything had been arranged for a while and the new owner, a former neighbour, has already taken up residence there."

She buried her face in her hands and began to weep softly.

"Mrs Carnforth? My dear lady, please! Don't distress yourself. Here, drink this!" A glass of brandy was held to her lips and she sipped a little. Its warmth was vaguely soothing and the faintness receded.

Mr Napperby was glad to see a little colour return to her face. "Sit quietly for a moment or two, my dear. You've had a shock!"

Mutely she obeyed and lay back in the chair with her eyes closed. After a while she opened them and looked at him. "I hope the child is a girl! I didn't care before, but now, I shall pray with all my heart that it's a girl! Oh, Mr Napperby, I shall never forgive myself if he loses both his homes!"

And Daniel would never forgive her, either! Had she made a friend only to lose him? Was she never to keep the people she lov— liked?"

Seventeen

Telling Daniel Carnforth that he was not, perhaps, the heir to Ashdown Park, was one of the most difficult things Samuel Napperby had ever had to do. He could not help being aware of the deep love that the new owner had developed for the family estate, even in this short time, and he also knew that Daniel was an excellent landlord – something Ashdown had lacked for many years. He had already done several kindnesses to those of his dependants in need and had made a good impression on people usually slow to accept newcomers.

Mr Napperby decided to wait until Daniel returned before he told him about the baby. He simply sent a message to Bellborough by a groom who had instructions to make the best time possible on the journey and to spare no expense. The message asked Daniel not to sign the contract for sale, if at all possible but, if he had already signed it, to return as quickly as possible to Ashdown, as something urgent had cropped up.

But the groom brought a letter back to say that the message had arrived too late and that Bellborough now belonged to someone else. Daniel added that he had already planned to return later that day and would be happy to see Mr Napperby early the following morning, if there was some problem.

After hours of worrying how to break the news, Mr Napperby could find no easy way and, in the end, when he had refused every offer of refreshment and was sitting with his host in the library, he said simply, "I have to inform you, sir, that Mrs Carnforth finds herself to be expecting a child by her late husband."

Like Helen, Daniel turned white as the implications of her condition struck him and he could not for a moment speak. Unlike her, though, after the first shock, he became very angry indeed. Rarely did he ever give way to his emotions like this, for, apart from the time he spent with his mother, he was not a man quick to anger. But now, he felt, life had dealt him too cruel a blow.

"Damn her, why could she not have said so before? My mother was right! That woman is wicked, wicked!" he shouted. "She *must* have known how things stood here when Charles died. She must have! Or soon after, anyway. Indeed, I'm amazed that a man who was in his condition could find the energy to father a child."

"Mrs Carnforth did not realise her condition until after the funeral. I believe it was Becky who pointed it out to her. And then, well, she was very weary and somewhat reluctant to face the world."

"Reluctant, indeed! That was a full month ago! And how can we be sure that it is Charles's child? A dying man doesn't usually father a child! And my cousin never had any before that I've heard. In fact, it was commonly believed in the family that he couldn't, since his first wife never quickened, nor did any of his mistresses – and we knew of quite a few, believe me, for he didn't trouble to hide things."

Mr Napperby drew himself up to his full height. "I hope you are not implying that Mrs Carnforth would behave in an unprincipled manner!"

It was amazing how coldly dignified a short fat man could become. Daniel closed his eyes and took several deep breaths. He refused to think about Helen. Refused. "When is it due?" His voice was harsh; his face looked suddenly older.

"The baby is expected in early February. And, having seen Charles and his wife together, I myself have no doubt, no doubt at all, that it is his! She would never have betrayed him."

"So I shall lose Ashdown as well as Bellborough!" It was a cry of anguish. Daniel heard how he had lost control, stopped and tried to pull himself together. "And I shan't even know my fate for months, until," his voice was still unsteady and thick with emotion, "until the damned brat is born!"

"I'm sorry for your disappointment. And Mrs Carnforth sends her apologies, her very sincere apologies."

"Oh, hell and damnation!" Daniel muttered, as if he hadn't heard that last remark. "To lose the estate that had been in my mother's family for over a hundred years – you will never know how much it cost me to part with it! – and then to lose Ashdown Park as well." He groaned, "It's too much to bear!

I tell you quite frankly, I shall pray every day that the baby is a girl."

Mr Napperby nodded sympathetically.

"Does she know that I've already sold Bellborough for the sake of Ashdown Park?"

"Yes. I know you wished it to be kept secret, but I felt I had to tell her."

"How she must have laughed!"

Mr Napperby so far forgot himself that he thumped down hard on the table. "She did not laugh! You wrong her greatly, sir, even to think it. She was very distressed indeed!"

Daniel laughed. At least, it was meant to be a laugh, but it came out more like a sob. "That makes it all right, then, I suppose. Shed a few easy tears and say you're sorry! And what am I expected to do in the meantime – until matters are settled one way or the other? I've nowhere else to live now, you know!"

"Mrs Carnforth told me to tell you expressly that she does not wish anything to change. She's very happy living at the Dower House and for you to continue living here. Believe me, she does not wish to cause you any trouble."

Daniel swung round and went to stare out of the window. "Not cause me any trouble! That's a joke! A farce! What more trouble can she cause me? She's already done her worst." An image of Ashdown Park made his anger rise again. "Oh, damn the woman!" he muttered savagely, pressing his hands against the coolness of the window panes. "Damn all women, but damn her most of all!"

And he had been thinking – he didn't know exactly what he had been thinking. He only knew – she'd been on his mind too much lately. Though that was going to change now. He wouldn't give her another thought. She didn't deserve any attention from him.

Mr Napperby's voice was very gentle. "Mr Carnforth, please! Let us—"

Daniel could stand no more. Like an injured animal, he had to be alone to lick his wounds. He flung himself out of the room, pausing briefly at the door to order, "Come and discuss it with me another time," before striding across the hall, pushing aside one of the maids who got in his way and slamming the outer door behind him.

He rode through the park at a bruising pace, his mind afire

with anger and despair. For once the beautiful woodland was no refuge from the world, but a heart-rending reminder of what he stood to lose. As he passed the end of the North Drive, he saw Harry on his new pony, accompanied by Briggs. The boy waved and turned the animal towards him, his face eager. Daniel felt as if he were choking with anger. He could not bear, he absolutely could not bear, to speak to anyone, least of all her or her son.

"Get out of my way!" he yelled as his ward started to trot in his direction.

Harry's mouth fell open in shock.

Behind him, Alfred made an exasperated clicking sound.

"And," Daniel's chest heaved with the agony of it all, "tell your damned mother not to come near me from now on, or I won't be responsible for what I say or do!"

Harry jerked to a halt, sawing on the reins in a way that would normally have brought Briggs's wrath down upon his head. Lips quivering, Harry watched Daniel gallop away, then he turned to the man he spent most of his time with nowadays for help. "Why did he shout at me like that, Briggs? What have I done wrong? And why was he so rude about Mother?"

An equally stunned Briggs moved his horse beside him and reached across to pat his shoulder. "It's not you he's angry at, lad. It's – it's circumstances. He'll have found out about the baby, I reckon."

And then Briggs had to explain, as Helen had not been able to bring herself to do so, the problems the baby might cause for Daniel. "So you see, it's not you he's angry with, it's – well – circumstances."

"Well, whatever the circumstances, he has no right to say things like that about my mother!" Harry's voice trembled for a moment, for his guardian's rejection of him had hurt as well, but he managed to control himself enough to declare, "And he'd better not make her cry again, for I won't have it!"

Negotiations about interim arrangements were conducted through Mr Napperby, and the details of the waiting period were gradually settled.

Mrs Carnforth would be grateful if Mr Daniel Carnforth would continue to oversee the estate. She had no desire whatsoever to move into the Manor herself.

Mr Carnforth presented his compliments to Mrs Carnforth and informed her that he would accede to her request and supervise matters until the baby was born. After which, if it proved to be a boy, she should make arrangements to bring in an estate manager at once. In the meantime, Mr Napperby would no doubt see that the income from the estate, such as it was, was paid to her.

Mrs Carnforth declined to accept any of the income from the estate.

So did Mr Carnforth.

Only with the utmost tact did Mr Napperby manage to persuade Daniel to accept some of the money coming in for spending on estate matters, though all major improvements had now been suspended. However, Daniel refused point-blank to touch a penny for his own expenses, whether they were incurred in the running of the estate or not.

And woe betide any servant, estate worker or villager who mentioned Mrs Carnforth in his hearing.

The landlord of the Roe Deer said to his regulars after one such encounter, "It's turned dangy difficult to know what to say to any of the family lately. *He* do only bite your head off, and *she* d'look ready to burst into tears."

"Aye, and as for Master Harry, that's two fights he've got into this week. Don't care how big anyone else is, he don't. If they say anythin' about his mother that he don't like, he just lights into 'em!"

"Well, you got to admire the boy for that."

After all the arrangements had been made, the only communication between the two principals was, for a time, through stiffly worded notes on matters of pure estate business, for Daniel would change nothing without her written permission.

Both of them turned into near recluses for a while. And if truth be told, each of them was missing the other's company. They had discovered very similar tastes in books and music, as well as a common love for the countryside. Helen had found Daniel a very peaceful companion, after two flamboyant and demanding husbands, and Daniel had found her a restful woman, with a refreshing sincerity about life, as unlike his mother and the silly girls to whom she had introduced him as could be.

Several times Daniel saw Helen or her son in the distance and turned his horse to avoid them. It was weeks before his anger subsided yet the pain of the possible loss remained as sharp as ever. Even with these brief glimpses, he could not help noticing that the baby was beginning to show and that she now took only gentle walks in the vicinity of the Dower House. He also noticed the signs of battle on his ward's face, a face which usually bore a sulky or unhappy expression these days.

The county families, after the first shock wave caused by the news had died down, spent the waiting period speculating about the probable sex of the child. That the Carnforths usually had more sons than daughters was a well-known fact. Bets were laid. Rumours spread. Gossip was rife.

Some said that the way a woman carried a child was a clue to its sex, but no one could get near enough to see whether Mrs Carnforth was carrying high or low, because the few people who ventured to call on her were turned away by a dragon of an old woman.

"My mistress thanks you for calling," Becky always said with implacable politeness, "but she don't feel up to receiving visitors today." She never waited for an answer, but simply closed the door in their faces after that statement, whoever they were, the only exceptions being the Morpeths, who were always welcome visitors, and Samuel Napperby.

There were even some deliciously scandalous rumours circulating that this was not Charles Carnforth's child. No one knew where that idea first came from, but it persisted to a remarkable degree.

That piece of gossip came, of course, from Bath. Celia was almost as upset as her son by the news of the baby. When she first heard from Daniel, she wrote him an impassioned letter demanding that he investigate "*that woman*'s past".

When he declined absolutely, she wrote several more letters, imploring him to "defend yourself against usurpers" or begging him "not to let a scheming female get the better of you".

He refused out of hand his mother's offer to come and stay with him, and when she went as far as to tell him the date of her expected arrival, he sent a very sharp message back to say that if she tried to set foot in Ashdown Park, he would leave it at once.

Until he was confirmed as owner, he did not feel he had the right to invite guests to stay there.

It was several weeks before Celia gave up trying to persuade him to take action, but a complete lack of response to her letters – he had started burning them after one cursory scan of the pages – in the end caused her to desist in her appeals.

But it did not stop her taking action of her own. By some means or other, she got hold of Helen's maiden name. And when her son made it clear that he would do nothing to defend himself, Celia set out to do it for him. She decided to trace Helen's family and see what *they* had to say about their errant daughter!

At first she had no luck, but then she came upon a very promising lead.

She wrote to tell Daniel that she had discovered something of importance concerning "*that woman*", and would like to spend a weekend at Ashdown to discuss it with him. But he wrote back saying he had not changed his mind and did not wish to see anyone at the present, not even her.

"If that's not the grossest ingratitude," Celia stormed to her maid, "then I don't know what is! He's just like his father! Worse, even. I don't know how I ever came to marry a Carnforth. But I lived to rue it, oh I certainly did. Still, I know my duty and shall not be deterred from pursuing matters."

Later on, she forgave her son and wrote inviting him to spend Christmas with her in Bath. That offer, too, was curtly declined. He had duties to perform at the Manor, he said.

Really, Celia told her friends, what did one *do* with a son like that? But she was a mother, with a mother's love for her child, however ungracious he was, and she *would* help him, in spite of himself! She would continue the hunt for any remaining Merlings who might be able to shed more light on the dowager's character, and she had no doubt what she would find.

After a while Helen began to feel much better, certainly well enough to resume attendance at church on Sundays, and (more difficult) to put up with the stares of the congregation. The worst of the people she had to face were two elderly spinsters who lived at the same side of the village as herself. The Misses Hadderby were inveterate gossips, of the sort who gushed and fawned all over their victims and then tore characters to shreds behind people's backs. It was impossible to avoid them completely in so small a community.

Helen also knew from the servants, for it never occurred to Susan not to speak her mind to her mistress, that many of the villagers thought it "a great shame" that Mr Carnforth might lose his inheritance. From the way Susan spoke of him, he had made himself loved very quickly! Strange, that, with so taciturn a man!

But then, Helen's thoughts drifted off to the days when she had begun to consider Daniel a friend: he could be very kind, had been so good to Harry, had lent her books, had given his ward the little dog which was now Harry's most constant companion. He was a man of some reserve, but he had a lovely smile and – what was she doing thinking about him like that? He was behaving in a despicable manner to her.

But he must be so hurt about Ashdown.

Helen cradled her belly. "You must be a girl," she whispered to the child stirring gently inside her. "Oh, please be a girl. He loves Ashdown so."

She discussed matters with Becky sometimes, for the old nurse was full of wisdom, even if it was not offered in flattering phrases. Becky said Mr Daniel had done a lot of good around the place, in a quiet sort of way. "I were fond of Charlie, don't get me wrong, but he wasn't a good landlord. He was a roistering Carnforth, my boy was. Right from the day he was born. And Daniel's just the opposite. He's a farming Carnforth."

And even Becky, devoted as she was to the dowager and her son, hoped secretly for a girl.

Fortunately Mr Morpeth was that rare thing: a good preacher who didn't run on for ever. Helen enjoyed listening to his sermons and it was a relief to get out of the house for a little while. She had become very moped, she decided, staying at home and brooding on her troubles. After all, she had done nothing wrong. Well, not intentionally, anyway.

Helen was still missing Daniel's (she found it impossible to think of him as Mr Carnforth, somehow) visits very much. She knew, too, that Harry had been greatly hurt by his guardian's defection, though she had explained several times that it was her fault, for she was the one who had hurt Daniel greatly, and that he was not really angry at Harry.

He had not entirely forgotten his duty to his ward, however. He waited for Mrs Carnforth to do something about her son's education and, when she didn't, he took matters into his own hands. In late October, another curt note arrived at the Dower House.

> Mr Daniel Carnforth begs to inform Mrs Carnforth that Mr Morpeth tutors a small group of local boys in the mornings and that he is willing for Harry to join them. With her permission, Mr Carnforth will arrange this.

A note was sent back the same day.

> Mrs Carnforth thanks Mr Carnforth for the information and will arrange the matter of her son's education herself.

Daniel swore and headed for his writing desk in the library. Ten minutes later, the long-suffering groom who carried their correspondence to and fro heaved a sigh, saddled up again and rode off through the rain.

> Mr Daniel Carnforth begs to inform Mrs Carnforth that he has already spoken to Mr Morpeth, so she need not trouble herself with making the arrangements. Mr Carnforth feels it his duty not only to ensure a sound education for his ward, but also a very necessary contact with other boys of his own age and station in life.

Helen could not but acknowledge that Daniel was right and she very much appreciated his reminding her of Harry's needs. She had been giving her son lessons in the afternoons, but she knew he would be better off with a proper tutor.

Forgetting her dignity, she wrote at once to thank Mr Carnforth for his thoughtfulness in remedying her own neglect and asked Alfred to take this second note across to the Manor.

The realisation that Mrs Carnforth could be remiss (and acknowledge it) about her own son somehow comforted Daniel and took the edge off his bitterness. He had recently abstained from attending church, because the sight of Helen, in her widow's weeds, with her thickened figure, infuriated him, he knew not why. Now he decided that he had been taking the coward's way in avoiding her so studiously. Early in November he turned up at the church.

To his horror, the verger led him straight towards the Carnforth family pew, which was already occupied by Helen and Harry. Why had he not remembered that they would be expected to share the same pew? He stood stock-still for a moment, half turned to seek another seat, caught the brightly curious gaze of two elderly ladies sitting across the aisle, and realised with a sinking heart that if he walked away, he would cause even more gossip and speculation.

Damn them all! he thought, bowing very stiffly to the Misses Hadderby, and to several other people he knew, and taking his expected place with a grim nod at Helen.

Harry scowled at him quite openly and moved as far away as he could, but after a poke in the side from his mother, he lowered his gaze to his prayer book and scowled at that instead.

Helen, who had blushed furiously as Daniel walked down the aisle, responded to his slight inclination of the head and muttered greeting with an equally brief nod and an equally indistinguishable murmur.

The three of them then concentrated on their prayer books, but it is doubtful whether a single word was read.

As the service progressed, a ray of sunlight haloed Helen's head and made a russet beauty of her hair. She had now stopped wearing the heavy veils and was wearing an elegant bonnet instead, but soft waves lay on her white forehead, drawing attention to her beautiful eyes. She was quite unconscious of the picture she presented, but her companion was only too aware of it and could not keep his eyes off her.

She looked, Daniel decided with a frown, much too pale still. He must find out if she was keeping well, eating properly. After all, he was head of the family pro tem, even if he could not guarantee to continue at Ashdown. But perhaps it was her mourning that made her look so pale. Black definitely did not suit her. No wonder Charles Carnforth had not wanted her to wear it.

(Mr Napperby had judged it expedient to inform Daniel of his predecessor's request to his wife not to wear black, for, with the rumours that were circulating, he did not want anyone to think that she did not truly mourn her husband.)

Daniel found it as impossible to attend to the sermon as to the prayers, and the choir's singing might have been the mating calls of corncrakes, for all he knew. Again and again, his eyes came back to her face, to linger, to devour almost. The gentle beauty of her soul shone through as clearly as her physical beauty.

Something within him began to soften. He admitted to himself at last that she could not have played her husband false. Not this woman. She could never play anyone false. And – he had missed her. The anger was still there, for he might lose his land, but something else had crept in as well. And it puzzled him as to what that something was, for he could not quite fathom his own feelings about her.

Eighteen

When the church service was over and Daniel stood up to leave, he realised that common civility obliged him to wait, offer Mrs Carnforth his arm and escort her from the church. As he hesitated, feeling a reluctance to do so, and yet at the same time an eagerness to spend more time with her, twittering voices behind him reminded him of the two most interested spectators of his actions and that settled the matter.

Wooden-faced, he left the pew, stood waiting in the aisle as Helen gathered her things, then offered her his arm as she came out. "Mrs Carnforth? May I escort you to your carriage?"

"Thank you, Mr Carnforth." Blushing, realising that everyone was staring at them, she took his arm. A warmth seemed to radiate from him. It was almost as if her hand were tingling as it lay on his sleeve. She looked down at it, glanced up at him, blushed again, and began to move along the aisle next to him.

Harry marched along behind them, hands thrust deep in his pockets and a sullen expression on his face.

Briggs, who acted as coachman as well as general factotum, stood back and allowed Daniel to hand Helen into her carriage. It had been found by Briggs in the stables of the Dower House and he had cleaned it up carefully. Daniel frowned to see how old the vehicle was, then gave way to the temptation to ask, "Are you keeping well? You look better."

"Yes. Yes, thank you, Mr Carnforth. And – and you? Are you – well?"

"As well as can be expected in the circumstances!"

Tears filled her eyes. "I'm sorry! I'm so very sorry."

A small body threw itself at him and two fists began to pummel him. "You beast! You've made Mother cry again!"

"Harry!" exclaimed Helen, shocked.

A quick look round showed Daniel that this incident was being watched by a very interested audience of people who had gathered in front of the church to chat. Wasting no time, he picked the boy up and threw him into the carriage. "If your son doesn't mend his manners, he's the one I'll be making cry!" he threw at Helen.

She grabbed her son's arm and pulled him to her side.

He saw the two elderly ladies begin to move towards them. "Damnation!" There seemed nothing for it but to get into the carriage. He slammed the door shut and shouted to Briggs to move off quickly, before the gossip mongers could make a feast of it all.

"How dare you tell Alfred what to do?" Helen's tears were forgotten. "And who invited you to ride with us, anyway?"

"I did! Those two old biddies are the worst gossips in the county. Your son had already given them a fine show. *You* may want tales of a quarrel between us spread from here to London, but I don't!"

"Oh!"

He turned to Harry. "And you, young man, had better learn to control yourself in public. Next time you behave like a street urchin, I shall allow myself the pleasure of dusting your backside for you, I promise you!"

Harry's bottom lip stuck out mutinously. "I don't care what you do to me! I won't have you making my mother cry!"

"She's not crying!"

"Well, she was just now! You're always making her cry. She's cried a lot since she's come here."

Embarrassed by this revelation, Helen tried to intervene. "Please, Harry!"

He would usually do as she wished, but this time he glared back at her, then glared at Daniel as well for good measure and, although he said no more, the looks he threw at his guardian from then on were blackly resentful.

Was she really weeping a lot? Daniel wondered, stealing a glance sideways. Her expression was certainly very sad. He began to feel like a bully. "It's – um – been a fine autumn, has it not?" he managed, in an effort to bridge the distance between them.

"Yes. Very fine," Helen said faintly, realising that he was making an effort to be amiable and she tried to respond in kind. "The woods still look very pretty."

"I was speaking to Mr Morpeth the other day. He told me Harry is doing well at his lessons and making friends with the other boys – when he isn't fighting with them."

Her face lit up with that luminous smile which always twisted his heart, for some reason, and she gave her son a proud nod. "Yes. I'm pleased about the lessons, though not as pleased about the fighting." She looked sternly at Harry. "And he won't even tell me why he's fighting like this."

Daniel could guess, but he wasn't going to tell her, either. He exchanged glances of complicity with Harry and the atmosphere in the carriage lightened a little.

Both adults searched their minds desperately, but neither could think of another remark, so they developed a great interest in the scenery and stared out of their respective windows.

At the Dower House, Daniel bowed to Helen and said mendaciously, "It's been a pleasure to see you both again. I shall now enjoy a brisk walk home."

Before she could think of a suitable reply, he had set off walking rapidly along North Avenue towards the Manor, his own coachman not having had the wit to follow her carriage to the Dower House.

Helen watched him go, and wondered whether to call out to him to invite him to stay to tea, or to offer to let Briggs drive him home.

"I think he'd prefer to walk, ma'am," Alfred said quietly before she could speak. "Give him time to come round."

She turned, with a sigh, to go inside. As they sat down in the parlour, she looked at Harry as sternly as she could manage. "You were very rude to Mr Carnforth," she scolded gently. "Please don't behave like that again."

"Well, he has been making you cry."

"It's not him, it's the – the situation in which I find myself."

Harry's lower lip stuck out. It was Daniel who had made her cry and nothing would convince him otherwise. But at least his guardian had not betrayed the reason for the fighting. You didn't tell women about such things, Alfred had told Harry. You just saw to it that no one said unkind things about your mother in your presence.

The following Sunday, after tossing and turning for hours, Daniel decided he might as well attend church again. It was a mistake.

Mrs Carnforth and her son were not there, the sermon was uncommonly tedious and the two old ladies cornered him after the service.

"I do so hope poor, dear Mrs Carnforth is not indisposed today," Miss Annabel said coyly.

"Have you, perhaps, heard anything of how she is?" Miss Rosemary cooed. "Or does the boy's hostility prevent you from calling upon his mother?"

Before an astonished Daniel could respond, Miss Annabel took the conversational lead again. "We could not help noticing his attack upon you last week. Such an unruly boy."

"He's a fine young fellow. A lad any father would be proud of. And last week was a slight misunderstanding, that's all. Harry's only fault, if fault it is – and I for one consider it a virtue – is the impulsive way he rushes to his mother's defence."

"We're so glad to hear that," they murmured in unison, exchanging delighted glances at this information. "Perhaps, if you find out how Mrs Carnforth is today, you would let us know? One wouldn't wish to be remiss in any little attention."

"But that dragon of a nurse stubbornly refuses to admit callers," Miss Annabel wound up. "We have tried to visit Mrs Carnforth several times now and been denied entrance."

"Becky has become very fond of her mistress," he said through gritted teeth. "Very protective. As have all her servants. And as for refusing *all* callers, that's nonsense. She just – she gets tired sometimes. I shall be calling upon Mrs Carnforth on my way back to inquire about her health, as I often do, and shall give her your regards." Then he realised from their expressions that this might not have been the most tactful thing to say and that his visit would doubtless give rise to more gossip. Damnation!

"So thoughtful of you!" they twittered. "She will be glad of your support at this trying time. A woman on her own."

Hiding his anger at their damned prying questions, he saw them to their carriage, bowed, then stalked across to his own vehicle. "Drive to the Dower House," he ordered his coachman loudly, so that everyone would hear, and flung himself inside.

Once there, he knocked vigorously on the front door, anxious to get this call over, so that gossip should have nothing more to feed upon.

Susan answered it.

"I've called to – to see if your mistress is all right," he announced.

Helen, who happened to be crossing the hall at that very moment, turned to greet him with a smile and was surprised how her pulse started to race at the sight of his tall figure.

As he caught sight of her, looking so fresh and pretty, Daniel could not help smiling. "Oh, there you are! You weren't in church and," his voice softened, "I was worried that you might not be – well."

She came forward to offer her hand. "Won't you please come in for a moment, Mr Carnforth? It's a terrible day! So cold. I'm afraid I was feeling lazy."

He hesitated, but her hand was warm in his and a gust of icy wind swirled down the hallway just then, reminding him that he was keeping her standing in a draught.

"Please stay for a moment or two," she repeated.

He shrugged, gave his hat and coat to the maid and followed Helen into the parlour. How well he remembered it from his previous visits! Nowhere at Ashdown was half as cosy. He stared at his hostess. She had on a new, fuller gown in a rich blue and a lacy trifle of a cap, with her hair massed in a chignon. He had never seen her look so lovely. Even her thickening body did not detract from her beauty.

"You look well in blue," he said through a mouth gone suddenly dry.

She stiffened. "But you do not approve of my wearing it, when I am still in mourning."

"I said no such thing! Do not be putting words into my mouth! Mr Napperby explained the circumstances to me, your husband's wishes." He saw the distressed expression on her face and realised how sharply he had spoken. "I'm sorry. I didn't mean to sound – I am not, um, noted for my tact."

He sounded ungracious and he knew it. He wished he had not come. No, of course he didn't. It had been his duty to come, if only to allay gossip. Now that he was here, he wished he had not stayed away for so long. Oh, hell, he didn't know what he wished any more! He just knew that he was glad to see her looking so well, so lovely, so – healthy.

She thought it best to change the subject. "Will you take tea with me before you leave?"

"No, thank you." It would seem too intimate.

She looked as if he had slapped her in the face. He couldn't bear to see that hurt look. "Oh, very well," he growled, even more ungraciously. He saw her swallow hard, open and shut her mouth, as if she'd nearly said something, then change her mind. Since she was still looking upset, he added hastily. "I'd be happy to take a cup of tea with you. It's a – a very chilly day. I just – I didn't want to trouble you."

She smiled at him. "It's no trouble. Indeed, I shall be glad of some company." She rang for Susan and ordered a tea tray.

"Yes, ma'am. An' I dare say you'd like some of cook's fruit cake, too, wouldn't you? Freshly made, it is. Master Harry's et four slices of it already, so you'd best take some while you can."

When Susan had gone, silence fell, both of them trying desperately to think of something to say which would not make the situation worse.

Stealing a glance at him, Helen suddenly realised how like Harry he was behaving. Just so did her son scowl and pretend indifference when he knew he was behaving churlishly. The thought gave her courage to continue.

"I have wanted to speak to you properly – quietly, Mr Carnforth, about our situation. Wanted it for a while."

"There's no need."

"I think there is. I want to apologise to you myself, not do it through Mr Napperby. I know that I have been greatly at fault and that my – my *cowardice* has put you in a most difficult position. And – and I deeply regret it. I shall never forgive myself if—" She broke off, blushing again, and gazed down at her lap, twisting a shred of a lace handkerchief around her fingers.

His eyes devoured her. And in that moment he realised how very much he loved her, and knew that he desperately wanted to take the heavy burdens from her shoulders and coax the sadness from her face. And he could not. He had not the right. Not yet, anyway. She was not only recently widowed, but she was carrying another man's child. That thought hurt him like a physical pain in the chest.

He saw that she had stopped speaking and was waiting for an answer, her beautiful brown eyes fixed anxiously on his face.

"You were not to know – that I intended to sell Bellborough, I mean," he managed. "I asked Mr Napperby to tell no one."

"I should have spoken sooner, though, told people. I didn't even realise my condition at first, I truly didn't. You see – it all happened so quickly. Charles hid his illness from me for some months. When I found out, well, there was not much time left."

"You need not—"

But she was determined to make him understand, determined to show no cowardice this time in explaining it all to him. "Suddenly, I had Charles to nurse. And he insisted that we face facts and make preparations. That took – all my strength. To keep up an appearance of normality and – and even cheerfulness, well, it was very difficult at times."

How would he feel if she were dying and he had to nurse her, try to smile and live normally? A pang shot through him at the mere idea. "It must have been – quite harrowing for you."

She drew in a quivering breath. "Yes. We were such good friends, you see, Charles and I."

He looked at her in puzzlement. That did not sound like a woman who had been madly in love with her husband. And yet she clearly grieved for him.

She not only wished Daniel to understand, she needed to talk to someone about it. "It was not – not a marriage – not for love. Well, he had fallen in love with me, but I did not think I could ever love anyone again in that way after Robert, my first husband. I was – very unhappy with him, you see. But Charles taught me to laugh, and – and I came to be very fond of him. Very fond indeed." But had still not fallen in love with him. She had thought about it often since his death. He had been her friend, her dear friend, but not her lover in the true sense of the word. "He once said there were many shades of love. I came to understand that."

The shred of lace was damp and useless. He took out his own handkerchief and knelt before her to wipe her eyes. "Ah, Helen . . ." he began.

"You've made her cry *again*!" With the advantage of surprise, Harry managed to knock Daniel to the floor.

"Harry!"

Daniel threw off the small body, trapped the waving fists and dragged Master Perriman to his feet. A swift shake made the boy stop struggling and go rigid, his blue eyes staring at his captor resentfully. Daniel shook him again, enough to bring home the message that this behaviour must stop, but not enough to hurt, then let go of his hands.

Harry took a step backwards and stared from one to the other, lower lip jutting ominously.

Daniel glanced sideways and saw how upset Helen still was. He could not for the life of him leave her then, so distressed and with only a boy to comfort her. He put an arm round Helen's rigid shoulder and said gently to her son, "This time it wasn't me who made her cry, Harry. She was telling me about your stepfather, how he died."

"Oh."

"You've behaved very badly, Harry," said Helen severely.

"But he was only acting in defence of his mother," Daniel pleaded. "And I *have* been uncivil to you lately, but I promise you both that I'll try not to act like that in the future."

She felt his look like a warm touch, felt something shift inside her and relax. As happiness trickled through her, she looked at him and smiled slightly.

His answering smile was a caress. As was hers.

Harry gulped, sniffed and wiped his smeary face on the back of his sleeve as he watched the two of them, not understanding the currents flowing between them, but nevertheless sensing that something was happening.

Still with his hand on the back of Helen's chair, Daniel turned towards him and, for a moment, the man and boy stood there looking at one other, Harry searching the face of his guardian and Daniel half smiling in encouragement, then the boy stuck his hand out. "I'm sorry, sir."

Daniel stepped forward and shook the hand gravely. "Apology accepted. As I hope you will accept mine for my recent incivility to your mother." But his eyes were on Helen as he spoke, and it was the memory of her warm smile as she watched the two of them that he carried away with him that day.

Her face began to fill his dreams again. He could never quite remember what happened in those dreams, but they left him feeling – content. Hopeful. If only – no, he could do nothing until she'd had the baby. And anyway, he might have nothing to offer her.

* * *

After that, cordial relations were re-established between the two households, though there was sometimes a faint sense of constraint between Daniel and Helen that had not been there before, an awareness of each other that tingled through them whenever they were in the same room. At other times there was a closeness that was unspoken, but impossible to ignore, even when they were only strolling round her garden together on the milder afternoons.

This was not, Helen knew, how Charles had affected her. This feeling was altogether more – more exciting, more compelling. In the darkness of one stormy night, she at last admitted openly to herself what it was. She was deeply in love with Daniel Carnforth!

The child stirred within her and her smile faded, but she put her hands protectively round the mound of her belly. I love you, too, little one, she thought, but that's a different type of love again. A wry expression flitted across her face. What a time to fall in love! Could she never do anything sensibly? And of course, she and Daniel could do nothing about their feelings until the baby was born.

From being content to wait for nature to take her time, Helen suddenly became impatient to have the child, to know whether it was a boy or a girl, to know whether she would have to struggle to make Daniel admit his love for her or whether he would turn ridiculously noble and try to leave her. She didn't think she could bear that. Not now. For he was, she was quite sure, the love of her life. Robert had been an infatuation and she had been such a foolish ignorant girl then. Charles had been a dear friend, but only a dear friend. But Daniel, ah, he was a fire in her blood now.

If it weren't for her condition, she thought she might even have spoken to him about her feelings first, since he was so diffident. But the baby was there between them, so tangible a proof of another man's love. No, on all accounts, they would have to wait to sort things out.

But that did not prevent her from looking at him with open affection and she knew, she just knew, that he realised how she felt and was feeling the same.

From then onwards, try as he might, Daniel could not be completely at ease with the woman he loved, the only woman he had ever loved. Like Helen, he no longer tried to deny his own feelings. And yet he did wonder sometimes why he loved her so much. He asked himself that question many times. It was, he decided, her tranquillity that appealed most to him, the atmosphere of peace and warmth that she created around her, given half a chance. But he found her beautiful, too, especially when she was not wearing black. So beautiful that he wanted to touch her, hold her, and, if he could not do that, at least be with her.

He also admired her character, for she genuinely cared for those around her and the poor of the village were benefiting from that. Now that she was feeling better, she was making her presence known, helping those in need in many small but practical ways.

And he loved to see her with her son. Daniel couldn't remember his own mother ever spending much time with him when he was young, or walking along with her hand on his shoulder, giving all her attention to what he had to say, as Helen did to Harry. His mother had no sense of humour, either, never saw the point of a joke, even when it was explained to her. Helen was always ready to laugh at something. She had a lively wit, too. It was yet another thing he liked about her. And she had such a soft chuckle, more a gurgle, really, when she was amused about something. He found himself listening for that sound.

As Christmas approached, Daniel made many excuses for spending more time in Helen's company, since they were in some sense joint patrons of the local festivities. Mr Morpeth mentioned how, in the old days, the Carnforths had been responsible for decorating the church (there should still be a crib somewhere at the big house) and how they had distributed presents to the poor of the parish. Finding Mr Morpeth's stories inspiring, Daniel and Helen decided to undertake those tasks again.

As it was a bad winter generally, they also felt that they should work together to alleviate the distress, for Daniel was out and about in the district and would hear if anyone were ill or in need. Several sheep were slaughtered just before Christmas to provide presents, as food was far and away the most welcome gift to those who were really poor, for whom meat was a real luxury.

Helen also suggested that men short of work during the winter should be employed to clear the woods of some of the dead branches and thus provide both fuel and employment for themselves.

A disagreement was narrowly averted when Helen offered to pay their wages, but she withdrew her offer when she saw how alarmingly formal Mr Carnforth had become at her suggestion. It was agreed instead that she should provide lengths of warm flannel for the womenfolk and toys for the children and that he would pay the woodcutters.

"It quite reminds me of the days when I was a seamstress in a theatre," she said reminiscently, once that little problem had been sorted out. "Bolts of cloth. Interminable seams." She realised that Daniel knew very little of her past and raised her chin defiantly. She had long wanted to set him straight about her antecedents. "You perhaps ought to know, Mr Carnforth, that I was extremely foolish to marry my first husband."

He had guessed that, but he nodded, for he wanted to know all about her and felt honoured by her confidences.

She took a deep breath and added, so that he should know the worst from her own lips, "I had to get married because I was expecting Harry and – and I realised later that Lord Northby and my father had to force Robert to marry me, for he would not have done so by choice. My parents disowned me immediately after the wedding and – well, I never saw them again, though my brother is still alive."

She sighed as she remembered some of those times. "After a while, since my husband was not – er – able to support us, I found ways to earn a living for myself and my son, mostly with my needle." She saw the expression on Daniel's face and misinterpreted it. "I am not ashamed of having worked honestly, Mr Carnforth." She lifted her chin defiantly.

"My dear Helen, I was not *blaming* you." He was merely shocked that any man should not wish to provide for a woman like her. And in fact, he'd heard something of the first husband from Harry, whose naive confidences sometimes revealed more than his mother would have wished.

Daniel saw that she was still looking at him uncertainly and added, "No one need ever be ashamed of honest work, Helen." He had a sudden savage wish that Harry's father were still alive, so that he could knock the scoundrel's teeth down his throat.

"You should know, too," Helen went on, determined that Daniel should be under no false illusions about her or her son, "that Harry's father was an actor. And not a very good one, either! He – he later became quite addicted to gambling, which caused a lot of problems for us."

Daniel discovered that his hands were clenched into two fists. "My father might have been a gentleman, but he was also a drunkard," he offered in exchange, "and I hated him with a passion." He had never confessed that to anyone before. "He treated my mother abominably and mostly he ignored me. He didn't beat us, but the tongue can be a vicious weapon, too, and he did not hesitate to use that against us. Which is perhaps why I have been rather – some would say – tolerant of my mother's foolish ways."

A flurry of rain against the window distracted Helen's attention for a moment and Daniel eyed her almost hungrily. Today she was in a deep rose colour, with a shawl draped discretely over her stomach. Why did ladies think it was unseemly to show their pregnant figures? If it were his child she were carrying, he'd be proud of it!

Bitterness twisted his guts. Ah, to have the right to look after her! He ached sometimes to cradle her in his arms and kiss those soft cheeks! He concentrated on his breathing, for it suddenly felt as if there were not enough air in the room. Fool, he told himself! You cannot make passionate advances to a woman big with another man's child! And you don't even know whether she would welcome your attentions!

He smiled at the thought. No, he was not being conceited, but he rather thought she would welcome his love. When she looked at him, there was a warmth in her eyes that he could not mistake. And she kept calling him Daniel when she wasn't thinking. How wonderful his first name sounded on her lips!

Then his smile faded. But if that child were a son, he would be in no position to propose marriage, for then he would not even have a home to offer her. He had to keep reminding himself of that. He hoped – hoped quite desperately – that the baby would be a girl. Was there ever such a tangle?

He could not resist continuing the conversation, wanting to find out more about the woman he loved. "Might I ask you about your family, Helen? You are obviously of gentle birth."

"Am I? It never feels like it. But thank you for that compliment, at least." Her voice had grown a little strained. "My father was born a gentleman, I suppose. He was a clergyman and also," she took a deep, shaky breath, for she rarely spoke of him, "a harsh, bigoted man, which is, I suppose, why he did not get on in the church. It was a very poor living, so all we had was our gentility. That's where I learned about poverty, and what the poor really needed. Even before my first husband began to gamble."

He forgot his resolve to keep his distance and stretched out one hand towards her. "My dear, I'm so sorry."

She took the hand, then blushed as she realised what she had done, and dropped it gently. "My father is dead now, Daniel, my mother too, and they say we should not speak ill of the dead. But I still bear the scars of his belt buckle from the beating he gave me when he found I was carrying a child." She hadn't meant to tell him about that terrible day and looked down at her hands, now clasped tightly in her lap. "I didn't – didn't even understand how children were made, let alone wish to commit a sin. What an ignorant young fool I was!"

"Ah, Helen—"

"Don't pity me, Daniel! It all happened a long time ago. I would just – I would rather you knew the truth about me than listen to the rumours about . . . the wicked woman who entrapped Charles."

"You know of that silly gossip, then?"

"Oh, yes." Becky had told her, said it was better to be prepared. And she had overheard things in church as well. Whispers could carry more easily than people realised in a high-vaulted building.

He picked up her hand and clasped it in his. And the gesture was so warmly comforting that this time she let her hand lie there for a time.

But neither talked openly of their love for one another nor did they discuss the future. Neither dared put the depth of such feelings into words. Not yet. Not until after Charles Carnforth's baby was born.

Nineteen

It did not go unnoticed in the village that Mr Daniel Carnforth and Mrs Charles Carnforth were becoming very friendly. More than friendly, some said, for they seemed remarkably at ease with each other, for two people who were not actually blood relatives.

"Well, *she* has had plenty of practice at getting on with men, hasn't she?" the spiteful said. "Two husbands dead and buried already and she is what? About twenty-seven or so?"

On the whole, most people thought a match between the two would be quite a good thing, since it would tie up the estate and the money nicely. But everyone, without exception, disapproved of the haste of what appeared to be a courtship, especially with her in *that* condition!

Helen would have laughed at them. She had never been as happy in her entire life, even during the time she had spent with Charles. He had been a very good friend, and she still missed him. But Daniel was her beloved, and she was madly, passionately in love with him. If she didn't see him, the day seemed less bright somehow. And she knew, she really did, that he was in love with her, too. You could not mistake that look in a man's eyes.

She was in no hurry to do anything about that love, but was enjoying the leisurely courtship, enjoying the sight of him, feeling glad that he and Harry were getting to know and like one another. Dear Harry. If he understood what was going on, he was keeping quiet about it – though probably he didn't understand. He was not of an age to care about things like love and marriage. His passions were focused mainly on his dog and pony. And on his mother, of whom he was still very protective.

The Misses Hadderby observed developments with great interest. "Did you *see* the way they smiled at each other in church this morning, my dear?" Miss Annabel would say.

"I most certainly did. So common to show one's feelings like that, don't you think?"

And, "I hear, sister, that they have been out walking in the woods again today. With the boy, of course," the elder Miss Hadderby would offer.

"Well, at least she does take the boy along, I will give her that much. She is not totally lost to decorum."

"That makes three times this week that Carnforth has called on her now, does it not? My goodness, where will all this lead?"

In the meantime, at least once a week the two old ladies dined out on the fact that they lived close enough to see nearly everything that was happening, since any carriage going to the Dower House had to pass their gates. And what they could not see, for *he* sometimes walked or rode over from the big house, their maid found out from her friend, Susan.

The gossip spread and spread, continually being renewed and added to, the ripples widening until the rumours had reached as far afield as Bath.

The idea that her son might be contemplating marriage with *that* woman shocked Celia so much that she even forgot to have hysterics when she found out. Instead, she mystified her staff by taking to her bed, where she lay thinking things over.

"It cannot be," she whispered again and again. "It just cannot be. She shall not ruin my son." Tearlessly, selflessly, she resolved to save Daniel, even from himself, and most definitely from the temptress. And she set about doing it most determinedly. A mother's love, she told herself – enjoying the drama of the phrase, even when there was no one else present to hear it – would brook no resistance.

Since she had very wide connections, she had now gathered considerable information, putting the pieces of gossip together like one of those dissected maps that children sometimes played with to teach them about geography. It was time to strike, to put an end to this intolerable situation.

The gossip about Mrs Carnforth also penetrated the stronghold of Northby Castle in the next county. Lord Northby found it highly distasteful to have a relative so much talked about and became very huffy if the matter was mentioned in his presence.

Two husbands dead and being courted by a third even before the second one's child was born!

"That is too much," he told his wife. "Something must be done about it! Whether the young woman is foolish or scheming, she must be brought to behave more decorously."

"Yes, dear." Personally, Her Ladyship cared nothing about her husband's relatives. Her own love was saved and spent lavishly on her two sons. But if Basil was in one of his fusses, there was nothing she could do but acquiesce in his plans and leave him to deal with it.

"That's what comes of living abroad! Those foreigners have damned loose morals!" His Lordship had never left his native soil, and hoped he would never be called upon to do so, but he knew how superior England was to all those rackety foreign places.

"Yes, dear."

He walked up and down the drawing-room, slurping his port and spilling some on the pale carpet, which made his wife frown in annoyance. "Well," he stopped to replenish his glass, leaving a sticky trail of wine across the side table, "my duty is plain. There is no one else who can act, so I must do something."

"Is that really necessary, dear?" She watched in alarm as he jerked round and the port slopped to and fro in his glass. "She is, after all, only a connection, not a close relative."

"Necessary? Of course it's necessary? Haven't you been listening to me? Do you want our name bandied around the county, dammit?"

"She's called Carnforth now. Surely no one will know she's related to us? Not if we don't tell them."

"I don't care what she's called. She's a cousin of sorts and her parents are both dead. I see my duty clear as head of the family."

She persuaded him to wait, see if the gossip would die down. But it didn't.

A week or two later he declared loudly over breakfast. "I have waited long enough. Now that Christmas is over, I intend to drive over to see her, remonstrate with her."

Her Ladyship sighed. When Basil got that stubborn look on his face, you could do nothing with him. "Whatever you think best, dear."

"I'd like you to come with me. A woman's touch, don't you know."

"Yes, dear. But not today." And she would find some excuse not to go every time he raised the matter. She had no desire to meet this young woman, no desire at all. The father had been a dreadful man, the brother was a mealy mouthed fool. The daughter had clearly rebelled against her strict upbringing, not that you could blame her for that, given the circumstances, but she was bound to be even worse than gossip had painted her.

Once she had taken her decision to save her son from *that woman*, and even from himself, if necessary, Celia became more practical and made some specific plans. Now – while that woman was heavy with child and therefore at her most unattractive – was the time to face her with her unsavoury past. Celia had to force her son to see the error of his ways before he did anything irrevocable. The mere thought of her poor dear Daniel being entrapped into an unsuitable marriage with Charles Carnforth's widow was giving his mother the most dreadful nightmares, not to mention headaches and megrims.

It took her a while, however, to persuade Mr Edward Merling, who seemed to be the sole surviving member of *that woman*'s immediate family, that it was his duty to speak out, but Celia did it. Oh, yes, in the end she made the man see just now essential it was for him to take action!

And now that she was quite ready to make her move, she arranged to hire a carriage, not wishing to borrow one of her son's and thus inform him in advance that she was coming to see him, risking him carrying out his threat of absenting himself if she tried to go to Ashdown. Surprise was a necessity.

In his shock at hearing the truth – for she intended to reveal all, sparing nothing – Daniel would understand at last that a Carnforth born and bred could not ally himself with the widow of a common actor, a woman who had, moreover, been cast off – and rightly so! – by her own family for gross immorality.

Happy in her cosy world, busy helping others and impatient now for the birth of her second child, Helen had no idea that the gossip was so widespread, or that she was still being painted in such very dark colours, until Harry came home one day with a black eye, a split lip and his clothes all torn.

She caught him sneaking up the stairs. "Harry! What's happened?"

"Oh, nothing, Mother. Just a – a disagreement."

"Come down at once." She led the way into the parlour. "This has gone on long enough. I insist on knowing why you've been fighting."

He stared down at his feet, avoiding her eyes.

Fear settled in her belly like a heavy stone. "It's not – not about me again, is it?" Surely not? Surely that nonsense had all died down by now?

"It was just a chap I know. We disagreed about – about something we read in Horace."

But he could not meet her eyes. He was definitely lying. Helen stared at her son. "I shall not let you go till you tell me what you were fighting about. I mean that."

"Mother, it's nothing. Really."

"I shall sit here all night, if necessary, until you tell me." She folded her arms.

Harry's resolution, at first firm, began to falter. He was not used to defying his mother. But he couldn't tell her what people were saying, he just couldn't.

The minutes dragged past. Half an hour of cold silence from his mother was as much as he could bear. He gave a sob and flung himself down with his head in her lap, begging her not to make him tell.

She stroked his hair. "Harry, I must know. How can I help you, if I don't know what's wrong? This is not the first time it's happened, after all!"

"Please, Mother! It's better not to talk about it."

"I think it must have something to do with me, then. Is that what it is, Harry?"

Silence. But a sob betrayed him.

She sighed and stroked his head. Why wouldn't people leave them alone? "Darling – what are they saying about me now? Let's face up to it, as dear Charles would have told us to do."

He looked at her miserably. "They, they're making jokes about you and – and rhymes."

She stiffened. "Go on. What exactly are they saying?"

"They – they're talking about who your third husband will be. They say you've had him picked out for a while and that," he gulped, "and that you'll have the knot tied as soon as the baby is born. And they say things about the baby, too – who its father is. Some people are even betting on *when* you'll re-marry. But I smacked Frank on the nose, so *he* won't say anything about you again. He bled all over his shirt," Harry added, with relish.

"Thank you for hitting him, darling. It serves him right! Who – who do they say I'm going to marry?"

He wriggled uncomfortably and her hand tightened on his shoulder. "Who, Harry?"

"Mr Carnforth."

Until that moment, Helen had not faced up to all the social implications of her feelings for Daniel. She had been drifting along, as pregnant women sometimes do, oblivious to the world around her, secure in her own little cocoon of warm happiness. Oh, she knew that the baby had caused some talk, but she thought that if she lived quietly and decently, it would soon pass – was actually passing already.

Now, she realised abruptly that this had not happened and that her reputation, however unfairly earned, was likely to damage several lives. Her son's. And Daniel's, too. She could not bear the thought of people ostracising Daniel because of her. But it was even harder to face a separation from him. He had become so much a part of her life in the past month or two. There was nothing she'd like more than to marry him and spend the rest of her life with him and, although he hadn't actually asked her, she knew he would do after the child was born. And she had intended to say yes. She didn't love him in a gentle, fond way, as she had Charles; she loved Daniel deeply and desperately.

Too much to ruin him!

How dared people make that love the subject of bets! She stared unseeingly into the fire. It was no use. She had to face facts. Nothing would more surely damage Daniel in the eyes of the world than to marry the widow of a common actor, a woman with a bad reputation.

With Charles, it had been different. His life had been nearly over and he no longer lived in England. But Daniel was younger. His life lay before him. And if he would not think of himself, then she must. She swallowed hard, to prevent herself from bursting into tears.

"Mother! Mother, are you all right?" Harry's voice was gentle beside her. He was looking at her, with such concern in his poor battered face. Another one who was suffering because of her.

"Are you all right?" he repeated. "You don't look all right. You look unhappy again. I didn't mean to make you unhappy. Why did you make me tell you?"

"What? Oh, yes dear. I'm sorry. I was just – just thinking what to do. I – we – have to face things." However unpalatable. "So leave me to think, and go and get some supper now. We'll talk about this again tomorrow."

He left, but did so reluctantly. And ate so little supper that Becky gave him a sound scolding, then wormed out of him what was wrong.

When he had left, Helen pulled her shawl around her and sat on by the fire. It didn't take much thought to make her tentative decision a firm one. She must act in such a way as to persuade Daniel that she did not love him and could never love him. Or perhaps she could convince him that she did not want to re-marry?

And – however much it hurt – she must make him see that the best service he could do for her and her son was to find himself a nice young wife, one of unimpeachable respectability. Only then would these dreadful rumours about her die down. Only then, could she and her two children live in peace. She put one hand protectively on her belly. Two children to think of now. *Oh, please, little one, be a daughter!*

It took her the rest of the evening to compose a letter to Daniel, and then she had to write it out again, because of the tear smudges on the first copy. She must, she decided bleakly, get everything settled as quickly as possible, for Harry's sake. And for her own. A clean break was kinder. And if a letter was not enough, if he insisted on seeing her, then she must not weaken. She loved him far too much to let him marry her.

> Mrs Carnforth presents her compliments to Mr Carnforth and begs that he will abstain in future from calling upon her. In view of the rumours currently circulating around the neighbourhood, and bearing in mind her son's future, and that of her unborn child, she believes it best to give the gossips no further fuel for their speculations about her plans for the future.

> Those plans are, and must remain, to devote herself solely to her children. They do not include any possibility of remarriage.

Only then did she go to bed. But she found it very hard to sleep for long and spent most of the night tossing and turning. She would have got up if she didn't fear that Becky, also a light sleeper, might hear her and come to scold her. Goodness, the baby was as active as her mind tonight, and all she could do was doze uneasily until she realised suddenly that the house was full of the sound of servants starting the day and that her bedroom was filled with the cold grey light of a dreary winter morning. She was relieved to see the sky lighten. Things never seemed as bad in the clearer light of day.

When Becky popped her head in to see if she was awake, Helen forced a smile and agreed to a breakfast tray in bed.

"You'm near your time now," Becky said abruptly, coming over to pat her hand, not deceived by this assumed cheerfulness. "So stop that worriting! You need to think of yourself now, yourself and the baby. Never mind the rest of 'em."

"Yes." But try as she might, Helen could only think of Daniel. "I wonder if you could ask Briggs to deliver this letter for me?" she said with, she thought, a fair assumption of cheerfulness. "As soon as he can, please."

Becky took the missive, put it in her pocket, frowned at her mistress and then left to get that breakfast tray. Something had upset Helen Carnforth. It was more than Harry's fight of the previous day. It was something very serious indeed.

"She don't deserve it," Becky grumbled. "Times like this, a woman deserves cosseting. Poor lamb. I better keep my eye on her."

When she gave the letter to Briggs, he frowned. "What does she need to write to him for? He was over here only yesterday morning."

"That's what I thought. So you ask to see him when you take this over, Alfred Briggs, and tell him from me he's not to do anything to upset her. She's near her time now, I'd stake my life on it. So tell him straight out. Whatever it is, he's to stop it upsetting her until the baby's born."

Then she went back into the house, grumbling about the effects of cold weather on old bones, and the way folk wouldn't let other folk live in peace. "She don't deserve any more trouble. She surely don't," she told Susan, then snapped her great-niece's head off for responding to that remark and daring to make a comment on her betters.

Susan rolled her eyes at the cook and got on with her work in silence.

Upstairs, Helen crumbled one of the slices of toast, threw the pieces out of the window for the birds to dispose of, then sat gazing out for a long time, unaware that both her attackers and her defenders were marshalling their forces that very day.

Twenty

Briggs went off to deliver the letter, fretting about his mistress and what Becky had said. Harry, sternly forbidden to get into any more fights, whatever the provocation, went off to his morning lessons at the parsonage, but had difficulty concentrating on his work. And when one of the other lads made some joking comment, he turned and said, "Shut up!" so fiercely that the lad's mouth fell open.

When she got up, later than usual, Helen decided to spring clean the dining-room and rearrange the furniture, to take her mind off the aching misery her decision to break with Daniel had caused her.

Becky looked at her a little strangely when she announced her plans, but did nothing to stop her, only made her promise to get help before she moved anything heavy.

When, at two o'clock on a cold grey afternoon, Lord Northby's carriage drew up, Helen was busy pulling all the silver out of the massive sideboard. She knew nothing about the unexpected arrival until Susan rushed into the room and gasped, "It's a visitor, ma'am. Lord Northby, he says he's called. We've put him in the parlour. Becky says to come quick!"

Helen stood up so quickly that it gave her a stitch in her side. She stood still until it had passed, then pulled off her apron, tidied her hair in the mirror, pulled a face at how swollen her belly looked and went to greet her guest. What on earth did Lord Northby want? She had written, out of courtesy, to inform him of her return to England, but had expected that to be the end of it. She had not even written to Roxanne yet, because she didn't want to face her friend until matters were settled.

Basil Northby heaved himself to his feet as she came into the parlour. He remembered a diffident young girl, quite pretty, in a subdued sort of way. Now he was confronted by a stunningly beautiful woman in an advanced state of pregnancy and could only stand and gape at her for a moment.

"Good afternoon, Lord Northby. How kind of you to call on me! Do, please, sit down."

He resumed his seat, refused an offer of refreshments and tried to approach the matter delicately. "So – you are a widow now, Helen my dear? For the second time, I believe?"

"Yes." She hated to be reminded of that. It made her feel so old.

"Twice married, eh?" he repeated.

She stiffened. "Yes. Twice." Was it possible that he too had heard the gossip? Could it have spread so far afield? She felt quite sick at the thought.

Lord Northby cleared his throat. When she refused to come with him, his wife had said it'd be difficult and she was right. "And – er – how is your son?"

"He's well, thank you." Helen waited, offering him no help. Let him speak first, reveal why exactly he'd come. She had done nothing to be ashamed of and would accept no criticism, whatever others had said about her.

Before he could continue, there was the sound of another carriage drawing up.

He stood up and went to stare out of the window. "Expecting someone, are you?"

"No." She joined him, but too late to see who it was. Not Daniel, that was sure, for this was a hired carriage by the looks of it. Who could be visiting her? She wished they would all leave her alone. There! Standing up quickly had pulled her side again. She rubbed at the stitch absentmindedly, and braced herself mentally to receive more callers.

A moment later, Helen and Lord Northby exchanged surprised glances as an altercation broke out in the hallway.

Becky had not liked the tone in which Celia had demanded to see her mistress. Becky was not having her lady upset, not with the birth due any moment, by the looks of it, and with Mrs Helen acting so strangely. When Celia pushed her way into the hall, Becky pushed right back.

"'Tis no time to be callin'. You can leave your card," she said, failing to push the caller out of the front door again, but still barring the way to the parlour. She had never liked Mrs

Celia Carnforth, whose main pleasure seemed to be stirring up mischief. "Go back to Bath and pay your dangy visits there!"

"Well!" Celia glared at Becky. "I shall do no such thing. How dare you speak to me like that, woman! Get out of my way at once."

"My mistress is busy. 'Tis you who should get out of *our* way."

Helen, who had just sat down again, for she was feeling strangely weak today, threw an apologetic look at Lord Northby and struggled to her feet again. Before she could move towards the door, it flew open and Celia Carnforth burst in, followed by a plump, pasty-faced gentleman in clerical garb, with Becky hovering disapprovingly behind them.

"I told her you were busy, ma'am, but she *would* push her way in. I don't call that good manners, I don't indeed."

"Aha! There you are!" exclaimed Celia, fixing Helen with a cold stare of triumph. "I knew you were in!"

Helen sighed. No avoiding this meeting now. "You may go, Becky."

Becky eyed her mistress narrowly and shook her head. "Send *her* away. 'Tis no time to be callin', but she wouldn't be told."

"Becky, please!"

The nurse left the room, but stayed in the hallway, unashamedly eavesdropping. She would be needed before too long, she could tell that.

"Unhappy woman, all is discovered!" Celia announced, in a throbbing, dramatic voice.

For a moment, Helen could only goggle at her. Had Daniel's mother taken complete leave of her senses? She did not know whether to laugh or to grow angry at this stirring entrance, so reminiscent of the New Moon Theatre.

Lord Northby's mouth also dropped open in astonishment. He began to wonder whether the woman who had just arrived was deranged and decided that he would have to be ready to protect Helen if the woman attacked her. What was the world coming to when a gentleman could not make a call without the house being invaded by lunatics?

"Has my son, my poor deluded boy, arrived yet?" demanded Celia, clutching her scraggy bosom and looking round as if she expected to find Daniel lying dead beneath the table.

"No." Helen was beginning to recover her powers of speech and to feel angry. "And I'd like to know what you mean by . . ."

"He will not be long. He will not refuse a mother's plea. And when he comes, I shall reveal everything to him! You cannot escape your past! I shall not *let* you harm him."

"Woman's mad as a hatter!" stated Lord Northby, who had been observing Celia closely. He turned to the clergyman who had accompanied her. "Shouldn't be allowed out and about. Why did you let her come here? Dammit, you should have stopped her."

"I – really I . . ."

"A mother dares all for her child!" announced Celia, moving to strike another dramatic pose closer to the fire, for it was a cold day.

Helen suddenly experienced a strong desire to laugh and it was a moment before she could control it enough to speak. Just as she was opening her mouth to ask what Celia meant by this intrusion, Daniel strode into the room, having entered the house from the rear.

His eyes met Helen's across the room and the amused glances the two of them exchanged were so shockingly intimate that Celia could only gape at them for a moment. Then she pulled herself together, drew a deep breath and prepared to launch her attack at once.

"Good afternoon, Mother," said Daniel, but his eyes were still on Helen and he had a half smile on his lips. "I got your message and came at once. Good afternoon, Mrs Carnforth. I hope I find you well. Pray introduce me to your other visitors." His tone was affable in the extreme, as if this were an ordinary social visit, and it threw his mother out of her stride again.

Helen bit her lip and shook with repressed laughter as Daniel's eyes twinkled at her across the room. She couldn't help smiling back. They might have been alone in the room for a moment or two, for no one else spoke.

Celia threw her son a hostile glance. Was he taking her warning so lightly? Was he daring to laugh at his own mother? Well, he should learn! He should indeed.

"This is Lord Northby, a connection of mine," said Helen, keeping her voice steady only with the greatest difficulty. "Lord Northby, Mr Daniel Carnforth."

The two men approached one another and shook hands. Lord Northby studied Daniel for a moment, then nodded, as if he approved of what he saw.

Daniel did not notice. He had eyes only for Helen.

"And," she continued, still having trouble suppressing her desire to laugh, "I – I'm afraid I don't know this other gentleman's name. He came with your mother." Though he looked familiar, somehow.

"This," declared Celia addressing only her son, "is *that woman*'s brother!"

"Edward!" Helen stared at his doughy face, so unlike her father's lean features. "Good heavens! And I didn't even recognise you!"

"*You* have not changed!" he replied, shaking his head and eyeing her with disapproval. "I would have recognised you anywhere."

"Mother, you must not continue this . . ." began Daniel, but broke off in bewilderment as Celia darted forward to place herself protectively between him and Helen.

"I am here to save you from the machinations of this evil adventuress!" she announced in a shrill voice.

"Said she was mad!" repeated Lord Northby, satisfied that his analysis of the situation was correct. "No manners, either. *Not* the way to talk about your hostess! If she's your mother, Carnforth, you'd better do something about her."

"I intend to." Daniel had lost all desire to laugh when his mother insulted the woman he loved. He seized Celia's arm and pulled her to one side, his grip like iron. As he glanced for a moment at Helen, his eyes were warm and tender and he had no need to say what he was feeling, for it showed clearly on his face.

He turned reluctantly back to his mother, wishing for the hundredth time that she would leave him to get on with his life in his own way. He decided that only bluntness could serve, and if that didn't work, he'd carry her out bodily if he had to. "I don't need saving from anything or anyone, thank you, Mother. I love Helen and intend to make her my wife as soon as possible after the baby is born."

The look in his eyes made Helen's heart beat faster, but she shook her head at him. "No. Oh, Daniel, you mustn't! My reputation—"

Forgetting the roomful of people, he let go of his mother and moved across to take Helen's hand. "You could never make me believe that you meant what you said in that nonsensical letter, my dear." He raised her hand to his lips, not as a romantic gesture, which he would have scorned, but because it seemed the natural – the only – thing to do. "Nothing you do can shake my love for you. And my mother will tell you how stubborn I can be."

She couldn't help raising her hand to touch his face. "Oh, Daniel! You must not."

"Say that you don't love me, and I'll leave you alone."

Helen blushed furiously as he caught hold of her other hand and pulled her towards him. They might have been alone in the room.

Celia gasped in outrage, but could not for a moment pull herself together enough to launch another attack.

Lord Northby watched the exchange between Helen and Daniel with great interest. So it wasn't her trying to rush Carnforth to the altar, after all, but the other way round. That put a slightly different face on the matter, though it was still too soon. But it'd be a good match and he had no objection to it. In fact, he'd wish her well. About time she was properly settled and by the looks of him, Carnforth was a sensible chap, though Lord Northby didn't like the looks of that mother of his. Mad as a hatter, she was!

Helen tried desperately to be sensible. "You can't marry a woman with my reputation," she insisted, though it cost her a lot to say such a thing. "You'll be grateful to me one day for refusing you."

"Will I? You still haven't said you don't love me."

Celia tugged at his coat. "Shameful!" she exclaimed. "You have taken leave of your senses, Daniel Carnforth! *Daniel.* Are you listening to your own mother?"

He wasn't even aware that she had spoken.

Helen took a deep breath and raised her eyes to his. "I – I don't . . . Oh, Daniel, I can't say it! You know that I love you. But you also know it will not do for me to marry you!"

"Let me be the judge of that, if you please. I care nothing for idle gossip."

"You ought to care a bit," Lord Northby joined in the conversation unexpectedly. "People are already talking about you both.

Saying some dashed insulting things. That's why I came over to see my cousin here. Mud clings, you know!"

Daniel shrugged. "Sir, I don't care in the slightest what people say or how much mud is flung." He turned back to Helen and smiled at her again, his voice softening. "My dearest, most precious love, you will marry me, if I have to drag you to the altar in chains!" He reached out for her hands again.

Celia made a final desperate effort and jostled her way to stand between them once more. "Unhand my son, you – you brazen hussy!"

Helen put her hand to her mouth to hide a smile and the laughter welled up again. It might have been full summer with the sun shining in at every window, so full of light did the world suddenly seem.

When Daniel struck a pose and declared, "I shall never let her go, Mother!" a chuckle escaped Helen.

This inspired Celia to leave her son unguarded again, dart over to the shrinking Edward Merling, who was edging towards the door, and demand that he step forward and *tell all.* When he did nothing, she poked him in the ribs and hissed, "Go on! Tell them."

Daniel drew Helen into his arms and waited. "She's very hard to stop once she gets going," he murmured apologetically. "I usually let her run on for a bit. But if this farce is upsetting you, my dear . . . ?"

Helen gave up the attempt to convince him that he should be sensible and allowed herself the luxury of leaning against him. He gave her shoulders a squeeze.

Edward, dragged into the centre of the stage much against his will, cast another panic-stricken look at the door. He was a man who preferred a quiet life. He could see that his sister still had no shame and he wished desperately that he had not allowed this hysterical woman to drag him along on such a wild goose chase. Why, Helen was smiling at that Carnforth fellow and positively nestling against him! In her condition! And – another terrible thought struck him – she was not even in mourning! This heinous crime was the final straw which inspired him to speak out. "Very well then."

Celia beamed at him. "Go on!"

He drew a deep breath and addressed Daniel. "It is my sad

duty to inform you, sir, that my sister – for I cannot deny the relationship, much as I would like to – has no sense of morality. Her husband," he tried to lower his voice confidentially, but as it was rather a high-pitched one, his shocking revelation came out more like a squeak, "her *first* husband, that is, was a common actor!" He shuddered at the mere thought. "And she had carnal knowledge of him *before* they entered into wedlock. Lord Northby will be able to confirm that the fellow had to be forced to marry her."

"I expect he was quite good looking, if he was anything like his son," said Daniel calmly.

"He was!" Lord Northby gave a sudden crack of laughter at the expression of outrage on Celia's face and tried unsuccessfully to turn it into a cough. Damn if he didn't like this Carnforth fellow! "And Helen was only seventeen and as green as they come," he added, out of a scrupulous sense of fairness. "I was at the wedding, paid for it myself, in fact. Fellow didn't have a penny of his own. As for my cousin here, well, she didn't even know she was with child until *they* guessed and confronted her with it. They'd kept her very ignorant."

"My poor love," Daniel said warmly in Helen's ear.

"Silly, naïve child," she whispered back.

"And her father beat her senseless, too," Lord Northby added. "With his belt, the coward."

The smile left Daniel's face. "If he were still alive, I'd make him pay for that."

"People didn't think much of that sort of behaviour from a man of God, I can tell you. Not in the dark ages now, are we? Never had much to do with the fellow after that. Couldn't stomach his hypocrisy. He was a brute."

Daniel bent to brush Helen's cheek lightly with a kiss, but his expression was grim still. He found the thought of someone beating Helen senseless almost too painful to bear. His arms tightened around her. Well, no one would ever beat her, or even treat her unkindly again. He would make sure of that personally.

Celia, who had been listening in rapture, for such revelations delighted her, cried, "Oh, shameless!" wringing her hands. Then she squinted short-sightedly across the room and realised how close the two of them were standing. "Let go of him at once, you wanton Jezebel!" she shrieked.

"Felt sorry for the poor little thing, actually," interrupted His Lordship, scowling at Celia. "Could hardly stand as she walked into church."

"Please!" Helen begged, feeling embarrassed by this public parading of her shame.

"Trembling like a leaf, she was, too," Lord Northby continued, determined to get the full truth aired now. "Not that I approved of the actor fellow! Weak chin. Bright blue coat, too! Shockingly vulgar colour. Knew he wasn't a gentleman the minute I set eyes on him. Daresay he led her a merry dance."

Celia clamped her fingers around her son's wrist. "Daniel, now that you know her shameful past, surely you must realise how unsuitable she is?"

He looked at her and said very solemnly. "I love her and I intend to marry her, Mother. Make up your mind to that."

"But you *know* how she preyed on your cousin Charles, got him to leave her all his money! She took advantage of an old man! She is a – a man-trap!"

"She is indeed, and I am well and truly trapped by her." He shook off his mother's hand and his grip tightened round Helen's shoulders. Now that he knew she loved him, he didn't care what anyone else said. It would not even change his mind if the baby were a boy. He felt gloriously happy. For so long he had wanted to speak to her, declare his love, ask if she loved him as much as he loved her. But he had tried to do the proper thing and wait until after the baby was born. Now that he knew Helen loved him, however, even his foolish mother had no power to hurt him.

He turned to Lord Northby. "Sir, I intend to marry Mrs Carnforth as soon as possible after the child is born. With your support, I think we can scotch some of the worst rumours. But I'll marry her with or without it."

"You're damned sure of yourself, Carnforth!"

"I am, sir. Now that I know she loves me."

Basil Northby, a sentimental man under that rough exterior, allowed himself to smile encouragingly at them. This fellow wasn't like that damned actor. This one was a gentleman, even though he did let his sense of humour get the better of him at times. "Do my best to help," he promised gruffly. "Deuced awkward situation, though."

"It is. And I must admit that I'd still prefer the baby to be a girl – I can't lie to you about that, my darling – but I *am* going to marry you, whatever the outcome, so you had better get used to the idea!"

"Oh, Daniel! Daniel, my love!" She didn't know whether to weep for joy, or to laugh.

Celia chose this moment to stage a theatrical faint, which fooled only Mr Merling, who ran across to her and began to bleat, "Oh, I say! Someone help her!"

A pain shot through Helen and she gasped, clutching Daniel's arm. No one but he noticed, however, for Harry came into the house at that moment, whistling merrily, and people's attention was drawn from Celia's recumbent, twitching body to the bright-eyed lad. He stood in the doorway of the parlour, blinking in surprise at the number of people he saw there. However, as soon as he noticed that Mr Carnforth's arms were around his mother, he ignored the strangers, remembering a previous occasion when he had found his mother being cuddled by a gentleman.

"I say, sir! Are you going to marry my mother like your cousin Charles did?"

"Should you mind?"

"Oh, no, sir, I'd like it above all things. I'd like to have another stepfather. And you're the next best thing to Charles. As long as I can bring my pony and my dog with me to the Manor."

"Of course!"

"What a lark!" Because of the visitors, Harry refrained from turning a somersault in his mother's parlour, but he did clap his hands together and shout, "Hurrah!" at the top of his voice.

Daniel turned back to Helen. "Can you really deny your son a lark like that and a second-best stepfather to boot?"

She stiffened. "Oh!"

He began to guide her towards the doorway, for she had clutched her stomach again and was looking pale. His years as a farmer made him guess at once what was happening. "Well, can you deny Harry that treat?" he asked, to take her mind off the pains.

She began to breathe more easily. "No, Daniel, I can't."

He turned her round to face him, his hands on either side of her face. "And you won't let anyone make you change your mind while you're away from me? For they'll try, you know."

Behind them, Celia, still lying unattended on the floor, began to wail loudly and drum her feet, but no one paid any attention to her. Basil Northby was watching Helen and Daniel, a fond smile on his face. Who could fail to be moved by such love?

Edward Merling began edging towards the door, ready to make his escape to the carriage outside as soon as he could. He grimaced in disgust as he heard what his sister was saying. She had no shame whatsoever. If he never saw her again, he'd be very happy.

"No, Daniel," Helen said softly. "I won't let anyone persuade me not to marry you. I can see that you're a very stubborn man and that it's impossible for me to escape from you. But I must leave you for a little while now. You'll stay until it's over, won't you?"

"Of course." He swept her into his arms and kissed her quickly. "Ah, there you are, Becky. I think your mistress needs you."

"I've got everything ready. I knew what was in the wind as soon as she started cleaning out them dratted cupboards."

Helen could not resist turning back to clasp his hand again and whisper urgently, "Daniel, I haven't said it properly before, but – I do love you."

"My darling Helen, I shall love you for ever and shall make it my mission in life to keep you happy from now on." He pressed a final kiss on to her hand and watched her climb slowly up the stairs, leaning heavily upon Becky.

Miss Victoria Emily Carnforth was born exactly three hours later, after an easy labour, and Harry was the only person to be disappointed that the baby was a girl. But he nobly hid that disappointment from his mother because he did not want to make her cry again when she seemed so happy about everything. In fact, everyone in the house seemed rather happy today.

"What a lark!" he told his dog. "Mother's going to marry Daniel. We're going to live at the big house soon. And I've got a little sister. What could be better than that?" And this time, he did do a somersault or two, before rushing off to find Alfred and make sure he was going to come to the Manor with them, too.